ALSO BY ELIZABETH McKENZIE

Stop That Girl

MacGregor Tells the World

Random House Trade Paperbacks

New York

MacGregor Tells the World

the World

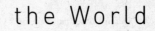

A NOVEL

Elizabeth McKenzie

A Random House Trade Paperback Original

Published in the United States by Random House Trade Paperbacks, an imprint of The Random House Publishing Group, a division of Random House, Inc., New York.

RANDOM HOUSE TRADE PAPERBACKS and colophon are trademarks of Random House, Inc.

ISBN 978-1-4000-6225-6

LIBRARY OF CONGRESS CATALOGING-IN-PUBLICATION DATA

MacGregor tells the world: a novel / Elizabeth McKenzie.
p. cm.
ISBN 978-1-4000-6225-6
1. Young men—Fiction. 2. Family secrets—Fiction.
3. San Francisco (Calif.)—Fiction.
PS3613.C556M33 2007
813'.6—dc22 2006049736

Printed in the United States of America

www.atrandom.com

987654321

Book design by Dana Leigh Blanchette

For SVW,
now and then

PART ONE

C.W.

I am the son of a man and
a woman, from what
they tell me.

—Comte de Lautréamont,
Les Chants de Maldoror

Above all, the quest.

MacGregor West—Mac, or simply West, or even Ho-ho, or some-times just Soldat duBois—had been walking past a certain Pacific Heights mansion in the city of San Francisco over the course of several weeks. He'd been recently delivered a shoe box full of his mother's loose ends, and a stack of empty envelopes in it had borne this return address—as much to go on as anything he'd ever possessed. It had brought him to the outside of a place that looked more like a civic building than a residence. But he could not get up the nerve to apply his knuckles to the door.

June. The hemisphere was heating up, all over but here. Fog rising in floes off the bay. Housekeepers and nannies, gardeners and florists, all wrapping up their work for the day. Quaint bumps in the sidewalk, approved bumps, because nothing was out of place around here. An older couple strolled by, walking pugs in handsome sweaters.

"Evening," Mac said. "Good evening," they replied. Around here, the animals dressed better than he did.

How many serfs had it taken to quarry and haul this granite here, to build this looming edifice? Tonight balloons tied to the front posts smacked lightly against one another in the mist, and the windows flickered with childish silhouettes. Not the time to knock and ask about a matter concerning only him.

Even so, his talent for loitering was rewarded. The front door flew open, and he froze beside the trunk of a street-side mock orange tree to see who emerged.

Not a who—a what. A bed on wheels. The sort that folds in half like a sandwich and rolls squeaking out of the closet when a guest appears. This one was being yanked onto the front landing by a handful of adolescent girls. And with a full-size person wedged within the frame, thrashing and trapped—the unexpected sight seemed like an omen. Two bare soles protruded from one side, a set of shoulders and a downward-facing head from the other. One mischievous girl peered up and down the street. Others were busy securing the bed with string. Then, to Mac's surprise, they all dashed back into the house. Firmly shutting the door. Leaving the bed alone outside.

He heard a muffled "Help!" His mouth felt dry. Should he butt in? Spoil the game? "Help," the voice cried again, and he ambled over to offer a hand.

"This as serious as it looks?" he asked.

Her face was upside down, hidden by a spread of auburn hair as full as a hula skirt. "Very!" she said. "My narm is numb."

"That's the worst." He began to struggle with the iron latches on the sides of the folding bed. The brackets were jammed, strangled with yarn. "How did this happen?"

"Oh, it's burning now! What's wrong—can't you get it?"

In the bright porch light, Mac fumbled with the knots while the crummy old frame jittered on its casters. His suave rescue attempt was fizzling away. What a pitiful sensation it was when his arm brushed the bottom of her stone cold feet. Pitiful because it was the most contact he'd had with a woman in a long while. Pitiful because the feet were cute, and though they belonged to a total stranger whose face he had yet to see, it crossed his mind to warm them with kisses. And perhaps most pitiful because he associated frigid feet with his mother, cuddling him as a child, taking advantage of his thermally desirable young trunk. Then it so happened that he worked the flesh of his index finger too near the main hinge. "Wait, now, don't move," he said hoarsely.

She moved. "Nnnnn!"

The folded bed keeled over, impact jarring the clasps. Mac's finger came loose, allowing him to pull it apart and let the girl roll free. She stood and tossed back her hair and showed him her face.

"God, sorry!" she said. How often do you remember the exact moment you first see a face? Especially when the vision's wed with pain. And he'd struggle ever after describing her. She was close to his age, he'd venture. Her green eyes were large and comically round, her forehead broad, her chin small, like the bottom of a heart. She had a pretty mouth, which looked like it would dole out secrets and fun. She had crease marks on her neck where the bed had squeezed her. And balls of lint strewn through her hair.

"Oh no," she said. "That happened here?"

His finger was blossoming with color; he shrugged. "How's the narm?"

"Better by the second. Can I get you some ice?"

No—to accept ice would reduce him to a bully-pummeled crybaby at the hem of the school nurse. "It's fine. Forget it."

"It's not fine. They thought they were being so funny." She shook out her limbs, kicked her frigid feet into circulation, looked behind Mac to the street.

"So, where's our stuff?"

"What stuff?" He noticed, looking back, that the mock orange tree he'd been lurking beneath was dotted with worn, weathered shoes, swinging merrily in the breeze.

"You're not bringing the pizza?"

"You think I'm a pizza guy?"

"Well, aren't you?"

"Funny you mention it, I used to be one." Sensing her confusion, he added, "I'm kind of between things."

Whispers floated down from overhead; he glanced up at the open casement from which the girls bulged like a cluster of toadstools.

"You're not delivering our dinner."

"Right. You see—"

"He's not our pizza guy!" she yelled at them.

"Get back in the bed," someone called back.

At that moment the van arrived. A huge, crusty wheel of dough painted on its side. Teo's. The best in North Beach.

"Sorry for the mistake. You look very familiar. Have we met?"

"Never," he said. "I'm MacGregor West."

"Carolyn Ware," she said. "What an unusual way to meet someone. Thanks again for helping me." She hesitated with touching discomfort, then tripped down to the van, where the real delivery guy was stacking pizzas and salads and soft drinks, and the girls burst forth from the house, heels thundering like hooves. One of them wore a Giants cap over a head of licorice black hair, an old wooden clothespin clipped to the bill.

"We had a whole experiment set up," the girl with the cap told him.

"What was the point?"

"To see if there's such a thing as love at first sight. We're postulating that there is."

"Postulating? About him?"

She nodded.

Mac glanced jealously at the intended, in a muscle shirt with a vomiting skull on it. "Maybe it was not meant to be."

She was studying him with acorn-colored eyes. "It's my birthday," she announced. "I'm twelve. My mother thought I was turning fourteen; she always gets it wrong."

Surrounded now by a throng of girlish forms, Carolyn Ware held aloft a stack of white boxes and turned back up the walk; because he had not moved away from her house, Mac could see her trying to make a decision on what to do about him. He wondered if he should blurt it all out straightaway. "See, I'm looking for my—" But she was occupied, it wasn't right. "Need a hand?"

"You've done enough. Do you live around here?"

"I go running in the Presidio."

This seemed to satisfy her. The girls were heading back inside. "It's the coldest summer ever!" she said.

Then inspiration came in a flash; he cradled his throbbing finger, and she noticed.

"Hey, want some pizza at least? I don't usually invite people in—"

"No, you wait outside for them in a bed, like bait."

"Right. And you got hurt by the hook."

"All right. Payment. I accept."

She moved through the doorway, and Mac followed and found himself standing in an entryway as tall and austere as a monk's tower. A grand stairway climbed to a landing on the next floor, while on one wall rose an elaborate mural, of the type one might find in a medieval church. Sheep, grazing on a hillside, an angel watching over the flock from a cobalt sky. His sneakers squeaked on the floor, and he felt a deep chill rising from the black marble, as if he were skating the surface of an enormous tomb.

"Come on back here," she called. He passed through a high,

wide archway, from which he could see into—what, the living room? It contained a fair collection of modern sculptures, ancient statues, busts mounted on plinths of stone; the air smelled musty and closed. As he continued through the house, he passed a dining room with a long table and many chairs, and caught a glimpse out the window. It was a fogged-in view of the Marina, Alcatraz, the Marin Headlands, the mouth of the bay, and of course, the Golden Gate Bridge.

"In here," Carolyn called. He followed her voice out through another door, across a hallway, and into the kitchen. The girls ran past him, practically knocking him over with their parcels and bags.

"I want pepperoni!" someone yelled.

The kitchen had high ceilings and old fixtures, and looked as if not a thing had been disturbed in fifty years. "You can have one of everything," Carolyn was reassuring the gluttons. "Molly, get the napkins."

"We all went riding today," said Molly, the birthday girl. "My horse is an Arabian called Omar; he's ten years old."

"I blew in his nose, and he tried to knock me over," said another.

"Horses make friends by blowing in each other's noses, but Omar doesn't know any other horses," said Molly. She stacked her plate while the clothespin bobbed on her bill, and Carolyn was directing them to the long table in the dining room and providing beverages to each girl, and once she finished there was still so much chatter and sound she suggested, "Let's get out of here," and Mac followed her into another immense room, with books on shelves floor to ceiling and a covey of worn leather armchairs by a handsome stone hearth, across from windows with that same faultless prospect of the bay.

"So, this is your actual . . . living space?"

"I grew up in this house. So did my father."

Mac was thrilled. "So your family's been here for years and years."

"My grandparents built it in the twenties."

"Great. I mean, that's useful. For me. See—"

She was over at a sideboard cluttered with bottles and decanters. "Let's have something to drink. What can I get you?"

"How about a beer? I'll wrap my hand around it, which will feel good."

There was evidently an icebox in the cabinetry below, and she presented him with a frosty green bottle, the color of her eyes.

"Thanks. Where does your sister go riding?"

"Old friend with land and a stable. She keeps Omar there."

Another silence. He felt out of his league.

"Is that a fresco in the front hall?"

She seemed pleased he'd noticed. "My dad was traveling around Italy a long time ago, and he saw it in a crumbling chapel in some little town, so he bought it and had it shipped over in sections. You think we shouldn't have it?"

"No, it's beautiful. I feel like I've seen it—maybe in a dream."

"It's one of the great debates here. The populists want us to break it into millions of pieces, one for every household."

He disliked her for saying "us." *I* was always okay, but someone else's *us* made him feel as forlorn as a baby in a dumpster. Yet he realized at that moment how much he wanted to like her. She flopped sideways across one of the armchairs, her feet swatting the air.

Mac didn't own much, but he had his own art of acquisition: once he could remember something clearly, he counted it as his.

"You're staring at me!" she said.

"I thought it would be rude not to," he said, bolting his beer. The twinkling bridge was peeking out of the fog. "Your view could be better. Shouldn't you be able to see at least one factory?"

"I used to perch my telescope in the window and spy on people. That house that sticks out, down the hill? Three brothers live there. They're all bankers, but each one works at a different bank. At night they come home, take off their suits, and run around shouting at each other in their underwear."

"Where else are they going to run around in their underwear and shout?"

"Is it a basic human need? I actually envy them for some reason."

"I used to envy people who just had underwear."

She laughed; maybe that meant she liked him. With that, the girls burst in, smelling of pizza dough and oregano. "We're going to try on clothes now," Molly announced.

"Wash your hands and don't forget the hats," said Carolyn.

The hooves thundered away into a distance that could be achieved only in a huge house. "So tell me what you were doing tonight before you ran into us," she asked.

Mac took a huge bite of pizza. He hoped grease wasn't running down his chin. He chewed and chewed and realized he had about five seconds to decide what he'd admit to. "Not much."

"Let's start with the basics. I guess no one was waiting for you for dinner."

"No."

"I eat alone all the time," she said.

His life under examination was full of dents and holes. "There's a taco truck in Redwood City I go to a lot."

"All the way down there?"

"I've been living with my cousin about a year. *Down there.*"

"Who's your cousin?"

"Fran Bixby. Know her?" he said sardonically.

She seemed to consider the name. "I don't think so."

Mac said, "I could probably stay there forever, but I don't want to be the kind of person you find ten years from now in some moldy, shag-carpeted back bedroom, buried by stacks of newspapers and dead cats, if you know what I mean." A spasm of laughter ripped out of him. He was morbidly attracted to news items about such types.

"Oh, you have a cat?"

"No. Don't have a dead one, either."

"You have no kind of cat. Okay. And, you were driving home to eat at a taco truck."

"Maybe."

"Then what?"

"That might have been the high point of the evening."

"These tacos—they're delicious?"

"Pretty delicious. And you get free radishes, too."

She raised her eyebrows. "Free radishes."

He was exposed for sure. "Come down and check it out some-time. You're obviously in a rut."

"It's true, a free radish can be better than something everyone's making a fuss over." She picked at a seam on the arm of the chair. "I've noticed when something's billed as of special importance, there's often a gulf in how you feel about it. You feel self-conscious in your appreciation. For instance, I never feel good when someone says something nice to me. I have a very strange handicap. If some-one says something nice, my brain selectively filters it out."

"Seriously?"

"I never hear it. It's like at that moment there's a blast of static and I end up having to ask the person to say it again."

"That could definitely kill the moment."

"It does. If someone were to say"—and she began to speak in a bloated male voice, like a lounge singer's—" 'Baby, you mean the world to me,' then I'd be like, *What? Huh?*' And by then the mo-ment's passed, and can never be re-created."

"That's really sad. It's like you're sabotaging yourself."

She said, "But maybe it's for the best."

"Why?"

"Because I'm completely immune to sweet talk."

She seemed to be a very strange person, and Mac liked her more by the minute. "If what you say is true, it should be written up in a medical journal."

"Your hand will be written up if you don't keep it cool. Want another one?"

She had a funny way of walking, he noticed. Kind of like a kid pretending to be a train. "Sure. Did you know your sister was trying to fix you up with the pizza guy?"

"He's not my type, anyway."

"She seems to think you could use some help."

"Well, pretty clearly, I can." Her voice rose and fell with feeling. "So how come you were walking by, right when I needed you?"

He was so on task, he failed to notice the tender quality of her voice just then. "Right. Time to get down to business. It'll probably sound lame, but I'm on a mission. See, it started with this—" He pulled the stack of empty envelopes, bound by a loose rubber band, from his breast pocket.

She straightened her back. "What's that?"

"Here," Mac said. "See—"

"Those are from here?" She reached and took the small bundle from him, studied the front, where his mother's name and address had been inked: Cecille West, Somerville, Mass., and turned the pile over and saw her own address embossed on the back: Pacific Avenue, San Francisco.

"This is my father's stationery," she said.

"Then this is a breakthrough."

"But I thought you were just walking by!"

"What's the matter?"

"So you're just another jerk-off coming by to meet my dad?"

"No!" Mac protested blindly. "Who's— What jerk-offs? I don't know anything about your father."

She began to pace and squeeze a pillow against her chest. She went and poured herself a drink, knocked it back. "Who's Cecille West?"

"You know the name?" Just asking, he felt a cold snake in his gut.
"No."

Of course not. It seemed to him his mother was at once the most universal and the most obscure person ever to have existed. He wondered, as he did sometimes, if she could still be alive somewhere, amnesiac, going through her days with her braying French and the uneasy sensation that she'd left something essential far behind.

"Cecille West was my mother."

"My father's name is Charles Ware," she said.

"The writer? Your father is *Charles Ware*?" Mac let out a groan.

"You do know."

"Well, yeah—I read *Tangier* when I was a kid. But that has nothing to do with—"

Or did it? His mind was all over the information, and it seemed potent, and suddenly he was scared stiff.

"What's this about?" she demanded.

"You're— This sucks! I'm not going to blurt it out if you're upset."

She stopped pacing. "I am so sick of people—especially smart, good-looking guys—stopping by here, wanting nothing more in their putrid, empty lives than to meet him."

"Hey, listen, I didn't know it when I came." His voice faltered. "My mother took a little trip when I was nine, and I came out to visit my aunt and cousin, and I was pacing around making little key chains waiting for her to come back, but that turned out to be impossible, because—ha ha ha!—she never came back. That's my story. My aunt gave me a box of her junk a few weeks ago, and I've been checking out the stuff inside because—hell, because I don't have anything else to do. How's that?"

Now would come the variety of response he despised—false pity, a maudlin sigh. But not from this person. She was still wrapped up in her own reaction and said, "If you think they were exchanging steamy love letters, forget about it."

"Gladly."

"You should have said something about why you were here. Right away."

"This is right away."

"No. Before you even came in. I feel misled—"

Mac said, "Okay, big mistake." Somewhere, deep down, he was choking out, *Don't you care about what I just told you?* But in realizing this, he felt humiliated. "Sorry to put you out. Thanks for the *ice.*" He started out past the dark aperture of the gallery.

"But wait!" she called. "You don't understand—"

He headed to the entryway and reached for the door. Beside it, rumpled and abandoned, was the fold-up bed, the mattress squashed and akimbo within. A sad and empty feeling washed over him. "Nope. Guess not. See you." And with that, he let himself out, pulling the door tight behind him.

His feet cut like pickaxes down the sidewalk littered with cast-off seedpods from the trees. He crossed to Lyon, found his matches and cigarettes in the gravelly pocket of his coat. He noticed an ancient burn hole on the sleeve. The garment probably looked Edwardian from the wear he'd given it. Down went the hot air to each lobe of his lungs. *Think not, think not. To have is to lose. To lose is to die. Again and again.* He had mottos for every occasion. Most of them stank, like his life. He smoked the cigarette nearly down to the filter in a few long pulls.

He was twenty-two years old. The duck, among animals, aroused in him the most sympathy (an aircraft and boat that walked). He was six foot two and rangy, and his feet were size thirteen; his dark hair grew shaggy and fast. When his socks weren't right, he felt restless and cursed. When miserable, he festered with images of people drowning, of oil spills spreading in the seas, of serial killers squatting under railway trestles, and of the disappearance of wild, galloping herds off the face of the earth. He worried that some form of recklessness or depravity lay sleeping like a wolf in every cell of his body. His mother had all but told him so. He'd had nightmares of all kinds since he was a kid. When he woke in the night, he grabbed books, felt the spines yield, latched on like an orphan at a borrowed and bristly teat. (His own image, the result of some careful self-scrutiny.) By now he'd drunk up a small library. He's gone through a series of fascinations, with figures such as Julius Caesar and U. S. Grant and Rasputin, to name only a few. He had plenty of "inner" resources, few outer ones for balance. Sometimes it seemed his one goal in life was to love extravagantly; but against that impulse he struggled with all his might. In dreams his mother appeared to tell him things. He had an internal conversation with her that always began "See, what I was thinking was that—" and then he'd draw an unholy blank.

He heard the steps rushing up, in advance of the voice.

"Wait, wait," she called.

He turned and beheld her, Carolyn Ware, in a red cape trimmed with fur. Flying from her body like bat wings.

"Now what?"

"I need to get milk for the girls," she said.

"How good of you."

"And I want to talk to you more," she said, ducking a wave of his smoke.

"I'm leaving your neighborhood."

"Why in such a hurry?"

He threw his cigarette into the storm drain. "Too many animals in sweaters."

"My fault again," she said.

"Why?"

She said, "Well, I—I gave those dogs—those."

He said, "You gave dogs sweaters? Damn."

She tried to keep his pace. Down from the hilltop, past Union to Lombard, back with the bright lights and motels and liquor stores.

He entered the first such store they came upon. The man behind the counter had a sharp nose with a ridge of short, coarse hairs growing up the bridge. They grew straight into his eyebrows, which were thick and arched, and gave the man a look of perpetual surprise. He said, "How can I help you?" *Though I barely eke out a profit in this miserable little shop, I'm always cheerful and willing to come to the aid of my customers, no matter how callous they are to the chains of my toil.*

He's right, Mac thought. He had this little game he'd played, ever since he first experienced trauma. *I take it for granted he's open and sacrificing his life, sitting here.*

The man telegraphed to him next: *I see that you are one who defies the trends in order to set his own course, in order to justify that deep rift in your soul which makes you feel apart from others. With this beautiful woman, perhaps you can heal yourself. But you'll need a little help. Spirits can drown a man's sorrows, but they are also the starting point for half the human race!*

"Give me a half-pint of George Dickel," Mac concurred. Carolyn purchased milk. Out on the sidewalk, their hair and jowls were whipped by cars racing to cross the bridge, and the fog was thinning over the broad, full face of the moon, and the briny smell of the Marina was mixing with all his instincts to flee. He gulped bourbon instead.

"So tell me more," she said. "About your mother."

"You were listening?"

She didn't say a thing but grabbed the bottle from him and took a swig, too. "What happened—if you want to talk about it."

"Nobody knows, nobody cares," Mac said.

"What about your father?"

"How would I know?"

"You don't know him? You're estranged?"

"You could say that. Estranged from birth."

"Oh," she said.

"Fathers are overrated," Mac proposed.

She took another gulp, and her cheeks turned red. "They are. So you never found out what happened to your mother?"

Mac said, "We know some of it. She drowned in the Seine, in Paris."

"How horrible!" .

"I shouldn't have mentioned it. Puts people on edge."

"Yes, a bit."

"I can't rest with it. Plus—" Should he tell her about the voice in his head, and what it had said about the cache of envelopes in the box? *"Avenge me, and these will help you do so."* Probably not.

"So—what are you trying to find out, exactly?"

"I'm rebuilding," Mac said, with some conviction. "Do you happen to know the story of the Colossus of Rhodes?"

"Remind me."

"Okay, you probably know it's one of the Seven Wonders of the Ancient World, right? A bronze statue of Apollo, and more or less the world's first skyscraper, a hundred and ten feet tall, for the purpose of welcoming ships into the harbor at Rhodes. Imagine a monolith like that at a time when, granted, a lot of great things were going on but people were otherwise chomping on dormice and thrashing their slaves. About fifty years after it went up, there was an earthquake, and the Colossus fell over and cracked apart. Superstition ruled the day, so no one dared put it back together—they figured the gods were jealous and angry. But to the credit of the Colossus, for years after, even the pieces on the ground brought in the crowds like nothing else. The fingers especially were considered awesome. Poets waxed on, honeymooners carved their names, run-of-the-mill gawkers chipped out chunks for souvenirs. Then followed eight hundred years of studied ruin, until some enterprising Syrian brought in nine hundred camels and hauled it away for scrap."

She nodded. "Your mother is one of the wonders of the world to you. And you want to put it—her—back together."

"I think you've got it."

"This is a noble thing. You'll need to talk to my father," she concluded.

"Might get me somewhere, who knows?"

"He's on a trip. When he gets home, why don't you come back?"

"All right, thanks. I'm sorry if this touches on a sore spot."

"I'm sorry I overreacted. It sounds like this is something different. Now I'd better get this back," she added, shaking her carton of two-percent. "Want a piece of cake? It's devil's food with chocolate frosting—I made it this afternoon."

Mac loved chocolate cake more than any foodstuff, so he could not refuse. He used to buy such cakes at bakeries and eat them whole at a sitting. He wouldn't mention that. Carolyn stumbled once on a bump in the sidewalk, and he lent his arm, and the look on her face when they touched made his gut flutter.

At last they reached her most unhomey of homes. "Thanks for offering cake, but I think I'd better split," he said. He was trying to douse his eagerness. As glossy and polished as a porcelain sculpture, a perfect lemon tree grew in front. Mac pulled a lemon off and began to peel it.

"Ooh—plain?" she said. "How sour."

She watched him tear off the first segment, slide it into his mouth. He knew he was doing it to seem interesting and eccentric, though he loved lemons and ate them when alone, too. This one was deceptive: plump and waxy outside, desiccated within. He wanted to spit it out.

"Wait, come see our yard before you go," she said.

"Okay."

He followed her down the side of the house, through a fence covered with tangled honeysuckle. There was a thick, sweet smell hanging in the mist. An old, tended garden in California, Mac had discovered, could be as close to Eden as he ever hoped to see.

In the foggy spray, she stumbled ahead through the brambles. And then turned, as though she were truly his Eve and had a new world to offer him. Beneath a canopy of tall, elegant cypresses was a circle of old citrus trees, laden with large, wrinkled fruit. On stony paths weaving through the trees, gnarled jade plants leaned topheavy out of terra-cotta urns. And pots crowded with absurd cacti, a circus of prickly, twisted dwarfs, ringed a pool thick with silent carp. Crumbling stone faces, like a group portrait from Hades, hung on the back wall of the house; ivy choked them all. Ivy strung everything together; it grew over decaying statuettes of goblins and geese, a fragile roaring lion, and a tall California bear.

"Here's my world," she said. The milk went down in the grass. "You should see it in the day. Really crazy and strange. What would I do without it?"

Over her head a moth danced, as if she were a slow-burning flame. "Maybe you'll find something else crazy and strange," Mac said.

There was no doubt what would happen next. They moved toward each other in the dim light that bounces down from a ceiling of weather, and he realized how much thicker the air feels at night. Their first kiss was seasoned with drops of moisture from the sky. "I can't believe this. You're very beautiful." Then, loud and clear, he said, "Hear that? *You're very beautiful.*"

Indeed, she showed no recognition of his words, as if she were as hardened as those old statues, crumbling all around them in the grass.

2

Between long kisses, feet deep in the weeds, knees pressing between knees, holding bunches of her hair in his hands, he said, "I didn't expect this."

"What's your name again?" They laughed. Inside, the girls were shrieking and rampaging, and a light suddenly went on that lit up all the yard.

"Carolyn!" a girl called.

"Help," she said.

"Everyone wants you," he said, kissing her temples, which were endearing in a way temples had never been before.

"Can't I have a little fun?" The edge in her voice surprised him.

"I'd like to help."

"And now the milk's warm."

"It'll make them fall asleep," he said.

"What?"

"Warm milk," he said.

"But after cake, we rented *Psycho*," she said.

"Ooh—the stuffed mother. Maybe I should stick around."

"Carolyn!" screamed the sister from the door.

"Okay, maybe not." He laughed.

She went from sheepish to burdened in the blink of an eye. "I mean—what about tomorrow?"

"Tomorrow is great."

"Here?" she said. "Say around three?"

"We want cake!" yelled the girls.

"I'll be here," he said. He kissed her again and ran out of there, tripping on his own legs.

He joined the anonymous clog of cars and trucks pushing through the streets of the city, barely trusted his driving. He smiled and then frowned and then smiled. He let out a demonic yodel. Had he really been holding in his arms that adorable and beautiful woman? She was a princess! No—not just a princess, since they are often pasty and angular from generations of inbreeding. Her legs were slender and tapered like roots, the roots of the mandrake; and if he were to go mad from unearthing them, he'd be no worse off than ever. Could it really be happening? The daughter of Charles Ware? And had he forged a link between his mother and the known world?

In the morning he was back in the city, but on Mission Street. Ablaze in every fiber of his being, muscles flooded with sap. A slightly uncomfortable, shifting incline in his groin. Laughter expelled like a cough. Nowhere to park, but he left his pocked orange Cavalier halfway into a bus stop because he was feeling lucky. This was the first part of the city he had gotten to know, and he felt comfortable here. For a while, through his cousin Fran's connections, he'd had a part-time job at a small neighborhood library; one slow afternoon he found a roly-poly kid hunched over in the restroom, staring intently at the wall.

"Whatcha looking at?" he said.

"Come over here."

The old blue tiles were rimmed with wizened caulk. A soldierly line of ants marched along them to the sink, but they appeared to be materializing from thin air. "Look right there," the boy said. Mac squatted beside him. From a tiny spot between the tiles, he saw the caulk begin to darken, then bulge. All at once the black head of an ant poked through the surface of the thin membrane and, with a quick struggle, the ant hauled the rest of its body out of the minuscule crevice. There was something almost shocking about it. For minutes they watched as ant after ant pushed through and joined the line.

"They're so, so . . ." The boy searched for the word.

"Desperate it's repulsive?" Mac supplied.

"Something."

"Maybe I'm just projecting. Were you thinking something else?"

"I don't know. So desperate it's repulsive. Yeah, pretty much."

Mac felt as if he'd put a dark thought in the boy's head. He had a protective feeling for him from then on, and in the weeks that followed, he took note of the boy's arrival in the afternoon and would have a book picked out and ready for him, and when the boy turned up the next time, he'd have questions, and they'd crouch beside the shelving truck and go through the text. Filipo had come up with his mother from El Salvador only three years before, but his English was excellent; Mac was so caught up in his pupil's progress, he failed to listen to the head librarian's warnings and was called into her office one day and let go.

"But he's super smart! He's going places," said Mac indignantly.

"Three times I've told you that's not your job. I'm sure your intentions are good."

"You really want to fire me from a library because I'm helping a kid who loves to read?"

"You're supposed to be shelving and dusting!"

"Shelving and dusting? Get your priorities straight and fire me," Mac said.

"I just did."

Fran had pulled some strings to get Mac in there. She was mad.

"Couldn't you just shelve and dust and tutor the boy later?"

"You've missed the point, as is your wont."

"You have to learn how to fit in, Mac."

"That's not fitting in, that's being a mindless drone."

"You have to be a drone before you can be anything else. Just swallow your pride and stick with something for a change!"

"Haven't we had this conversation before?"

"We'll be having it on our deathbeds."

"Our skeletons will probably be having it," he said. "Our dust will, and someone at the library will be dusting us while we're having it."

*W*ind coursed down Mission Street, a canal of nasty air. Newspapers and food wrappers scuttled along, catching around ankles and legs. The sidewalk was crowded with women bundled in down jackets over tank tops and shorts, their faces bearing the strain of the heavy sacks they carried; with baggy-panted, red-nosed old men; with strollers pushed by young mothers wearing their harsh, bright barrettes against the wind.

Many signs were hand-painted—PANADERÍA, JUGOS Y LÍQUIDOS, SNAKES, OPTIMO CIGARS, KEYS MADE, CHECKS CASHED, NOTARY, MI PUEBLO, and Mac's favorite: BAYVIEW MENTAL HEALTH—in fading letters on a second-floor window over a liquor store. Loading ramps clattered from the rear ends of trucks, dollies thundered down with their loads. And here and there were quick deals handled right on the street: a pickup full of green bananas, twenty-two cents a pound;

a man with a box full of real stuffed miniature alligators; a crone selling roses from a swampy bucket. He dodged a peanut fight between two girls arguing over a hopscotch game on the sidewalk.

Mac went into a small Mexican market and bought a pineapple drink, like piña colada without the rum. Then he buzzed the cage door barring the stairs and climbed up to Filipo's. From the top, he could see the gray industrial underbelly of San Francisco, angular and metallic, surrounding the various arteries that fed the city through the fog. He craned his neck in the direction of Pacific Heights. Out of sight.

Filipo's mother, Elena Ayala, opened the door. A rush of steam beaded on his face.

"Mr. Mac! For you!" Before he was even inside, she handed him a pink wad of dough—a sweet from a different world of taste buds. He tried to appreciate them, but more than once he had set his treat on the windowsill and later, when no one was looking, pushed it out. "Thanks, Elena," he told her. He almost told her about meeting Carolyn, but it seemed premature, so he chomped down on the dough ball instead. "Filipo up yet?"

"He waits for you." She swept him through her front room, crowded with the industrious sewing and ironing crew she managed. One woman stood at an ironing board, briskly eliminating wrinkles; at her feet was a large pile of newly washed or mended garments. And there were three women sitting in a line on the floor, their backs against the wall, pulling thread through alterations and rips and hems. They worked at an amazing pace. Their hands were blue and bony, and the veins bulged all over them, and he never failed to see that one or another had to stop and rub her hands and shake the effort from her joints. Water trickled down the windows, condensed by the cold air outside. The room smelled of starch and electricity and parrot: the jungle bird paced in his cage on an old console TV.

Mac went to the room in back. Filipo and his mother slept to-gether in it, Filipo on a single mattress in the corner, his mother on the couch. Knees drawn up to his chin, the boy with the bowl hair-cut was perched by the window. Mac noticed he was starting to out-grow his baby fat.

"Hey."

"That guy still keeping track of you?"

"He was out this morning with binoculars!"

The narrow gray courtyard was decked with rows of sagging con-crete balconies; most residents were afraid to use them for anything but trash. Steel rebar jutting from the crumbling edges were brittle with gull droppings and rust.

"Maybe he's just watching the birds."

"Yeah, the bird is my mom. Last night he knocked on the door with that."

Sitting on the floor was what looked like the butt end of an old telephone pole, carved into the shape of a donkey head. For eyes it had two woebegone slits. A red line of paint wrapping around the rough, splintery end made a gloomy-looking muzzle.

"He made it?" Mac said.

"The great artist."

"Anyone who tries to make something is automatically cool," Mac proclaimed, sympathetic to anyone with love in his heart. He wondered what memorable curio he could give Carolyn. "How'd your mom like it?"

"She started laughing."

"Be careful, she might be falling for him."

"What did you have for dinner last night?" Filipo always asked this hungry question, and Mac admitted that he'd scarfed on Fran's leftover steak.

"Well done or rare?" Filipo pursued.

"Kind of burnt."

"Potato?"

"Yes. A baked potato, with sour cream and chives."

"You eat the skin?"

"No. It was covered with foil, and it was soggy."

"Oh, too bad. The skin is really good. That's where all the vitamins are."

This said, Filipo was ready to talk about the book.

He lovingly picked up his copy of *Great Expectations*. To Mac's surprise and satisfaction, Filipo had taken to Dickens with a vengeance and was identifying with Pip, and not simply because Pip's real name is Philip. The first book of childhood duress they'd read together was *Oliver Twist,* which had been an early favorite of Mac's, and Filipo had been captivated by the boy's attempt to procure larger portions; now *Great Expectations* had his favorite food scenes: "Pip's sister, Mrs. Joe, she makes him eat drumsticks—with the feathers on! That would be bad. Got to get the feathers off a bird before you eat it. . . . Gravy, that's what saves him. . . . You ever eat tongue, Mac? Pip loves tongue. Tongues don't have bones. No feathers, either. . . . Cold fowl, is that chicken or just any bird? . . . You think Miss Havisham's cake's full of maggots?"

Today something else was eating at him. "What makes Pip like Estella?" he asked, clutching his book. "She's a creep, man. I hate her guts! I wouldn't put up with that. So what if she's pretty!"

"Filipo, know any pretty girls?"

"One, but she growls at me."

"That's actually a good sign."

A clatter and a groan in the courtyard caused them to turn their attention outside. A man appeared in the glass doorway across the way. He was built like a porpoise, head disappearing into his body, buttons pulling apart, his teeth scattered loosely in his mouth like pegs. "There he is," Filipo whispered. "El Monstruo!"

"Jesus!" Mac said. "That's the guy?"

"He's gonna step out there someday and the whole thing's gonna fall and I'll laugh."

"Just because he's lonely, malformed, needs dental work, and is a Peeping Tom doesn't mean he's evil," Mac said.

"How'd you like it if he wanted to be friends with *your* mother?"

A fair number of rejects had orbited the woman known as Mac's mother; once, when they ran out of toilet paper, one such man used a T-shirt of Mac's from the hamper. A day that would live in infamy! Mac was proud to remember that his mother told the man to get lost because of it.

Elena brought them mugs of cinnamon cocoa, and Filipo slurped it hot. He called after her in a whiny, exaggerated fashion, "Please, sir, can I have some more?"

"He always wants more!" cried Elena.

"Ah, the fruit of our labors," Mac said. And Filipo picked up his notebook and wrote: FRUIT OF OUR LABORS.

The boy read aloud the chapter in which Pip first meets Miss Havisham and Estella, but Mac was unusually distracted. He was remembering Carolyn's shoulders, and the smell of her hair, and the way she'd looked at him when they kissed.

"Are you listening?" Filipo said.

"Of course," Mac said. "Let me see that." He took the book and examined it a moment. Filipo had circled words he didn't know, such as *farinaceous, penitential,* and *hunch.* And he would look them up, and write each one ten times in his notebook. Mac appreciated such diligence. Collect words, he advised willing youths who'd pay heed—they're everywhere and they're free.

"So here was Charles Dickens, possibly the most productive human being ever to live on this planet. By the time he wrote this novel, he and his wife had ten grown kids. And he'd written fifteen other novels already, and a lot of them were over nine hundred pages! He was also putting out his own magazines and acting in plays. You'd think with a father like that the children would have a great role model, right? But no. They went into debt and floundered around. Total losers."

"So we're lucky we don't have dads?" Filipo said.

"Could be. Anyway, ready for your assignment? Here—between chapters eight and nine. After Pip leaves Miss Havisham's, after Estella treats him like a dog. Before he goes home to Joe and Mrs. Joe. Imagine that Dickens wrote another chapter but that there was a fire at the printer's and the only copy was lost."

Filipo said, "What's missing?"

"Imagine something happening with Pip before he went home. That's your assignment. To write up the missing section."

Filipo said, "Me?"

"Sure. Why not you?"

"Before he went home."

"Imagine what happened, and let it unfold, simple as a movie."

"Okay."

"Good," Mac said. "Go for it." He looked at his watch while the boy took up his pen and began.

Maybe Mac was about to write the missing chapter of his own life. For until yesterday, seeing Filipo once a week was one of the best things Mac had had going—besides eating tacos, drinking bourbon until he passed out, and turning the pages of a book his cousin's husband, Tim, had in the bathroom called *Women of the Sud-Tyrol*. His mind was always elsewhere, looking for a nice, warm place to curl up. And here was where his thoughts went just then, so fast he couldn't stop them—*simple as a movie*. To Tres Osos, California, where he'd gone to live with his aunt and uncle and cousin after his mother abandoned him. This guy named Cesar had shown up in ninth grade in a jacket with patches of Chairman Mao and Karl Marx sewn on the sleeves, with his long black hair and pocked skin. And when Mac introduced himself, behind the trees on the Tres Osos Junior High athletic field, where Cesar was sitting on a rock, smoking, Cesar had said, "You know why I'm so ugly? Very bad karma. Karma's contagious, a creeping disease. We start talking, we get to know each other, your karma turn black, and all you hear is the weeping of the world."

It was without a doubt the best deal Mac had been offered in a long time. Otherwise, there was a group of guys who hung out in their cars after school, driving backward as fast as they could around the parking lot. Or the other group, which chewed tobacco and shot birds with pellet guns. When he was younger, Mac had thought he knew who he was; until he found Cesar it seemed as if that self had evaporated into the hot, dry air.

Cesar's family moved in over the hardware store in Tres Osos. Mac spent all his time there, though Cesar claimed his parents were typical frumpy immigrants aspiring to the bourgeoisie. To train them from their impulses, he forced them to listen to Buddhist chants on a pint-size record player. He and Mac listened, too, stoned out of their minds on pot they bought in bags as big as the grass catchers on lawn mowers. Usually they were busy discussing, and writing what they hoped was "literature." Cesar said they needed pen names, and while he picked The Scorpion, Mac chose Soldat duBois. In one fast burst, Mac and Cesar read Apollinaire and Éluard and Baudelaire and Desnos and Rimbaud, as well as all the Beat poets who had benefited from the French guys.

They read *Tangier* together, too. Carolyn was right—he barely wanted to admit how right—that her father and the people in his world had been of interest to Mac. He could still remember ridiculing passages, for the book was known to be based on Charles Ware's friendship with the publisher William Galeotto, and was on the reading list for young men questioning their identities, and for young men questioning their affection for other young men. (Mac and Cesar were reasonably certain they weren't questioning anything of the sort.)

How different things could be now! The summer before their senior year, riding the motorcycle he went everywhere on, Mac's best friend found himself unable to avoid the temptation of speed on a country road after midnight with the smell of cattle floating over the warm hills. He went airborne for half a second here or there as the uneven ground gave way, as crickets chirped along the road in chorus, as he tested his reflexes when ground squirrels scurried before him, as an old pickup coming home over the next rise, a local, mindless shit-for-brains, loaded with his father's masonry equipment, tore too fast around a negligible curve and, fearing for the integrity of the masonry equipment, which included an old, battered hand mixer and some crusty trowels, straightened out the truck in the wrong lane and veered into the path of a cycloptic beam of light, thus sending Cesar into an airborne spin, landing him upside down on a rock, which snapped his neck and killed him on the spot.

Despite the differences, Filipo reminded Mac of his lost friend, and Mac had told him so from the get-go. Searching for substitutes was the one true way of the world.

"Okay, I did it," the boy said. He looked up from his work sheet, ready to hold the floor.

"Let me hear it."

Filipo cleared his throat. " 'A cold, howling blast of wind stung my face under the penitential clouds. I trembled at the sight, for fear of what being caught in such a storm would mean to me and all others who had no coats or umbrellas. I pushed onward, my face cold, my lips in a rigid line like a Popsicle stick. I tried to halt my shaking appendages and force the tears from my sockets. Then the storm began.

" 'I bravely knocked on the nearest door. The door slowly swung open on its rusty hinges. Facing me was an old man in his late forties. His gray eyes showed relief in seeing me, but also there was a great sadness that showed he had a hunch.

" 'A woman's body, grossly misshapen, lay dead on the earthen floor. Her face was contorted, and a soiled knife was buried deep within her chest. I stifled a bellow and withdrew. Upon returning to the door, I found the man struggling to speak to me.

" 'I saw the farinaceous loaf and the meat on his table. In a rage unknown to me, I grabbed them and thrust myself out the door. Into the light of the street I ran, home to my punishment. I chewed the bread and meat. I laughed, I realized, I cried.' "

He finished and looked up at Mac.

"My God," Mac said. "You're a good writer. Who is this person?"

"He lives across the road from Miss Havisham."

"Why is there a grossly misshapen woman on the floor?"

"Because," said Filipo, "things like that happen."

"Yes, they do. But—" Mac stopped himself. "Interesting. Imaginative!"

"Now what?"

"I'm not all here," Mac admitted. "I met a woman."

"What's that mean?"

"Don't be alarmed. I'm just explaining why—"

"Are you going to stop coming?"

"No! I'm feeling happy, that's all."

"Could you read the next chapter to me? I like hearing it, because then I can listen to every word and see them like you told me, hanging in a tree like fruit, ready to pick."

How could Mac refuse?

"All right, sure. Sit back and listen. And when you learn to drive, don't go too fast, okay, and look out all around you?"

"I want to have a good life," said Filipo.

*L*ater Mac was on Union Street, with its leather shops, down shops, Scandinavian toy shops, and antiques, and all the elegantly bundled perusers of those dolled-up boutiques. June, and everyone was wearing woolens. Mac found himself caught in a crowd of Siamese twins—that was how couples looked to him sometimes, absurdly attached. But what a cure for loneliness! He had seen interviews with Siamese twins, and they couldn't get enough of each other. Think of it! Had his mother and aunt been Siamese, they could have had a fine old time all together.

He wanted to find flowers for Carolyn Ware. Finally he found some pale rosebuds in a pot, a doll's bouquet, and retraced his steps into her neighborhood. It was about ten after three, and soon Mac was approaching the heavy façade of her residence.

No one answered. But sticking out from under the doormat was a scrap of paper with his name on it. He scooped it up. BE RIGHT BACK. HAD TO TAKE MOLLY TO A FRIEND'S. —C.

"Are you leaving something for my husband?"

Mac turned and beheld a woman coming up the steps; a well-dressed, attractive woman with short, silvery hair, pearls on her earlobes, and a nice color to her skin. Her throat was tight and lean. "Are you a friend of Charles's?" she asked. Her voice moved like cold pitch.

"Mrs. Ware? I'm a friend of your daughter's," he said. "Mac West."

"Some people call me Adela, Mac."

Mac looked at Carolyn's mother—her eyes were oddly watery. The irises were swimming. "She left me a note," he said.

"Who?"

"Carolyn."

She studied him curiously. "I didn't know Carolyn had any friends," she replied. She opened her bag and pulled out a monogrammed handkerchief, then dabbed her eyes. "I am very proud of my daughters." She smiled. She might have had a beautiful smile, but her mouth looked distorted to him, like that of a horse with a painful bit.

A car door closed on the street, and a wiry older woman moved up the walkway, swinging what looked like a small sack of take-out cartons.

"I can come back a little later," Mac said.

Adela Ware's swimming eyes watched him. "Will you stay with us for dinner? Isabel's staying—" She fumbled with her keys in the lock.

"Dinner?" said Mac. "Thank you, let's see what Carolyn says."

"No one will have dinner when Charles is away," Adela Ware said flatly. "There was a time when people came to see me as well."

"He's here to see Carolyn," the older woman said, climbing the steps. She squeezed Adela's arm and rubbed it gently. "I'm Dr. Porter," she said to Mac.

Adela said, "My father loaded railcars near the slaughterhouses, you see. I was five when he went into an alcoholic coma and died. Mother raised us girls alone."

"That's pretty harsh," Mac said uncomfortably.

Adela pushed open the door, and he followed them in. He spotted remnants from the party the night before. Shreds of a popped balloon on the floor. Chocolate cake crumbs. Balls of wrapping paper and ribbon. The fold-up bed rested there still.

"We lived in a messy neighborhood close enough to the slaughterhouses to hear, on still nights, the groaning of the cattle starving before the kill," she said.

"Then you've come a long way," said Mac.

"Mother supported us making pickles, if you can imagine. Thirteen grocers she supplied with their pickles and relishes. She'd met my father at a party; he was a handsome Irishman who told wonderful stories, and she'd been a fool. Now that he was unable to decimate her life with his drinking, she was doing better. Pickling cucumbers, peppers, corn, watermelon, onions, beets, and peaches, with fifty-pound bags of salt stacked in our basement, and a hundred clay pots filled with fruits, vegetables, and vinegar. I always imagined I was leaving the house smelling of brine."

They drifted into the kitchen, and the woman named Dr. Porter said, "Sit down, I'm warming some soup."

"I love real minestrone soup," Adela Ware said. She sat on a high stool next to the chopping block as Isabel fussed with the bag and a bowl from the cupboard. "I'd hate to tell you what I used to eat," she said. "Horrible, horrible things."

"Like what?" Mac said, interested in such stories.

The microwave bell dinged, and Isabel removed the soup and placed it in front of Adela Ware on the chopping block. To his surprise, she actually tied a towel around Carolyn's mother's neck.

"Tell him what I used to eat," Adela said, blowing on a hot spoonful.

"I don't know what you ate," Isabel Porter said.

"You see," Carolyn's mother said, "by pickling and preserving, Mother wanted to preserve a place for us in the world. She opened accounts for our schooling and paid for lessons—she herself had taken music lessons as a girl in Hamburg—and my sister and I both played piano and danced and sang. She even managed to enroll us at St. Ursula's. Somehow we were very popular! By the time my sister was nineteen, she had been proposed to by Marcher Wyndham Reilly—do you know the name? His father owned the third-largest rendering plant in Chicago. The reception took place at the family's home in Winnetka—a thirty-room house on the lake. And I remember saying to Mother that Marcher's brain had been rendered of dead meat, and that I'd marry someone who could think, no matter if he hadn't a penny. Oh, it's cold!"

"Stop talking and drink up," Isabel said. Then she said, "Mr. West, I'm not sure at all when she's coming."

"It won't be long," he said. "I can wait out here."

"She's not an easy one to pin down," Isabel said. "I'd be surprised if she came back when you expected her."

"Don't tell him that," Adela Ware said.

"I'm only saying that perhaps your wait will be somewhat fruitless."

Mac said, "She left me a note. It's fine."

"I wouldn't wait myself," Isabel said.

Feeling annoyed, Mac said, "Maybe I'll take a walk after all."

Isabel said, "Let me take those flowers."

He recoiled.

It was then he heard some fidgeting at the front door.

"There," he said defiantly. "See?"

He recognized the choo-choo shuffle of Carolyn's walk. When he turned and saw her entering the kitchen, he was pleased by the chastened look on her face.

"Sorry I'm late."

" 'S okay," he said, and he handed her the little rose pot.

"Oh, these are so pretty! Thank you."

"Carolyn?" her mother said. "Offer him something. We have ice cream, I think."

"It's icy and tastes like a motor," Carolyn said. "Like some?"

"Maybe later," said Mac.

"I told this young man you weren't coming," Isabel Porter said, and shook her head.

"That wasn't very nice," Carolyn said.

"I couldn't be sure, dear girl."

Carolyn gave the old bag a kiss, then her mother, and said "Come on!" to Mac.

"Soup? Ice cream?" the mother called again.

"Thanks, Mother," said Carolyn.

She took him down a wide hall with a number of rooms off of it.

She darted into one, came out with an armload of clean, unfolded laundry, and suddenly she was on the run. A narrow, cheerless stairwell ascended through the dark hindquarters of the house. "This way!"

Her slim ankles disappeared at the top. Up he went, landing in a musty corridor, hexagonally shaped, with large black doors appointing every other side of it.

"Over here," floated her voice.

Following her into her room that first time, he registered only space—it was as long as a ballroom.

"Whoa."

Carolyn heaved the clothes onto her bed.

"God!" she said, and shut the door behind him.

"Is everything okay down there?" Mac gasped.

"Okay as ever."

"Your mother all right?"

"Quite all right," Carolyn said. "I mean, she has asthma and takes a lot of steroid stuff, and then something else to relax." Her hair fell before her face, and she was speaking as if through a mask. "You know, she's actually a remarkable person. She has all kinds of hidden talents."

"Is that her caretaker?"

"Isabel? No."

"Who the hell is she?"

"Our family doctor. She's taken care of Dad since he was a boy."

"Lucky guy."

"Don't say anything bad about her! She's a great, great person."

"Oh. Not too experienced with the greats."

She began snapping wrinkly T-shirts in the air like whips.

Well, then. Everything seemed awkward suddenly. Was he going to break the spell in just a day? Mac's well-refined compensatory behaviors kicked in.

Her room faced the street and the world to the west. Bare oak floors at his feet. "Your walls, they're hand painted," he noticed, moving closer to inspect them.

"It's a representation of a trip my grandparents took to China."

Fading village scenes and landscapes were connected with flowers and leaves and the spreading arms of trees. He followed a river around walls, found himself visiting other small villages of water buffalo and huts. Mountains and farms. A chubby panda hiding in a glade of bamboo. Peaked red roofs and barbed dragons and a rushing river of bicycles when he rounded the corner and reached Shanghai. Her room had been, in those days, the master suite. "How did you get it?" he asked. And she said, "Dad could never sleep in his parents' room. Ghosts of the fornicating elders." So Charles and Adela now had rooms in the other wing.

On the street side were French doors, which opened onto a narrow balcony. Mac unclasped one, looked down at the street through the tree dotted with shoes. "Why are there shoes in this tree?" he inquired.

Carolyn's gaze shifted out the window, and when she spoke, she seemed to be weighing each word. "When Molly was little, when she outgrew them, she'd tie them together and make a wish and let them fly." She told him that when she herself was young, she'd kneel on the balcony and pretend she was Juliet, and the mailman, if she timed it right, would play his part. She had an old wicker chair draped with discarded scarves and clothes, and Mac took a seat on it. On the wall surrounding the bed, over some of the Chinese scenes, were pencil portraits.

"Did you do those?"

"They're not very good," she said. "Look at the nostrils—they're awful."

"For nostrils, they're pretty decent." He recognized her mother, and Molly in numerous portraits from her childhood, and even her father, and there were a number of other impressive-looking heads and still lifes as well. His eyes came to rest on a fading, neo–Art Deco–style poster from a long-ago FESTIVAL DU FILM, PARIS.

Mac swallowed. "How weird."

Carolyn followed his eyes. "What?"

He studied it, trying to make sense of its presence. "Why do you have that?"

The shallow breathing started, something he could not help when certain things constellated.

"What is it, Mac?"

"That poster's my mother's. It's— She designed it."

Carolyn appeared to wince at this announcement. "I've had that up forever."

Tears were starting down his face. "Sorry," he said, then gulped.

Through the swamp in his eyes, he detected her surprise but felt an arm go around him, a mother's pat delivered to his back. "You okay?"

"I'll never do this again," he said, wiping his eyes. "I swear. Throw me out if I ever do."

"You really think it's hers?"

His heart felt as if it was beating sideways; he was exposed. Call him a basket case—his cover was blown. "Come here." He pulled her over, and just as he remembered, for the poster had hung in various apartments of his youth, the initials C.W. were down in the corner. "See?" He pressed his hands into apelike fists in his pockets. "She was very proud of this. The year before I was born, you see, she had been an art student in Paris, and there had been a competition, and one of her teachers recommended her, and they chose her design." He was rolling back and forth on the balls of his feet. "Tell me why you have it."

Carolyn said, "I found it, snooping around in my dad's office, and thought it was really ethereal and delicate."

"It is."

"You can just stare at it."

"How was your father connected to the festival?" he asked.

"Oh, the glory days," she said. "Let's see, Dad's movie, the French version of *Tangier,* was screened that year. I was about four, so I remember—"

"You're four years older than I am?" he exclaimed.

"I can't help it," she said. "Is it a problem?"

Inexplicably, his lower regions began to tingle and shrink. "It doesn't make any difference," he said. "Go ahead, tell me about the poster."

"The poster. Yes. So let's see, Bill Galeotto was the producer of the film and one of the directors of the festival—you know about their friendship I suppose."

"A little." Who, upon having read *Tangier* in the blush of youth, could forget the buggering scene in the hotel garden, the inferno of the day still held in the clay ground, and the burn on the young man's hands?

"*Des trops bons copains,*" she continued. "The things people want are often incompatible."

"Meaning?"

"Well, he married my mother."

"I'm lost now. You're here, and Molly's here—"

She shrugged, not looking at him. "For quite some time when I was growing up there was no place for any of us in Dad's life. His reason for living was *William Galeotto.*" She dug into her pile of laundry, plucked out a pair of childish underpants, and creased them sharply down the middle. "It's instinctive in children to resent their parents' obsessions, don't you think?"

"Obviously. Then what happened?"

"Life went on, and now they don't speak."

"Really? The famous friends don't speak?"

She took a deep breath and said, "My father doesn't want anyone to know it."

Mac said, "Does anyone care? I'm still thinking about my mother and the festival."

"Maybe that's our connection." Carolyn was back to her chore, rolling clean socks into little balls. "My dad and your mother met at the festival, got to corresponding a little. That's not hard to imagine."

"It makes sense, sort of. That time period's of interest because I was born the following spring, so she would've gotten pregnant around then."

"Oh, but not with my dad—"

"No, of course not—"

They looked at each other and laughed. "Thank God, right?" she said.

"Yeah! Thank God!" *Yet what would be so bad about it? It might ensure a lifelong tie.* "But it's possible he might know something about my—circumstances."

"He might."

Maybe his mother's interest in Charles Ware and *Tangier* grew from seeing the film at the festival; Ware had been famous, married, freckly and red-haired, and Mac's mother had been nothing more than a runaway kid with a musette bag full of art supplies.

"Your bed looks just like mine," he noted, and coughed. It was a mangy lump of blankets and sheets on a mattress squat on the floor.

"So you might be able to embrace the side of me in disarray."

"I'd like to. Right now."

"And how many girlfriends are you juggling?"

"Ha!" He sniffed. "I'm hoping maybe one."

"One's usually enough."

Poor, crippled elation stirred in him, and he managed something like "And you?"

"Not much has been sticking lately."

"So, what should we do today, besides weep and fold clothes?"

She tossed a sock ball into the air. "I can't go upstairs empty-handed. I look around and make sure I'm taking something with me to where it belongs. I feel compelled to accomplish something every time I move. What I'm saying is, I can't leave a room unless I make it *count*. And I scorn others who don't do the same. Is that normal?"

"Doesn't sound very relaxing," Mac said.

"It's not."

They were standing in the middle of her room. The light was fading as the fog wrapped around the house like a coat. He wanted to kiss her again. The poster was making him nervous.

"So, want to go out and have a drink, or dinner, or something?" he asked.

Just then there was a knock. Carolyn said, "Yes?"

"Want to talk a minute," her mother said in that sticky voice.

"Now?"

"Is that young man in there?"

Carolyn grimaced. "I don't want her to start talking to you," she whispered. "Do you mind?"

"Can you open up a moment, please?" called the mother.

Carolyn ushered him into her closet, and he played along, nestling back among her outfits and shoes as she shut him in.

"What is it?" he heard Carolyn say.

"What are the arrangements for tomorrow?" came Adela's voice.

Their conversation receded down the hall.

Time goes very slowly in closets. There was some kind of shoe rack cleaving his buttocks. He shifted his weight, held in a sneeze. And when his eyes failed to adjust to the absence of light, he groped for the string he'd seen hanging by the door. And yanked it. At least he could keep himself occupied by the sight of Carolyn's clothes.

What a collection. And she clearly liked shoes. Strange little beaded shoes, and boots— Damn! Where was she?

Then Mac noticed something sticking out of a crack in the wall: the outline of a miniature door. He reached and pulled it open. Warm air blew along the rafters into his face. Sure enough, there was a nice straw hat, crunched in the hinges, ruined. Then he saw stacks of books, and when he moved aside to let the light shine in, it looked as though years and years of hats and books and other items were backed up in this black hole. A burial ground. At the top of one pile of books was a volume that had been torn to bits, its pages and signatures ripped from the binding. He leaned in and picked up the loose, mangled cover: it belonged to the *Inferno* of Dante's Divine Comedy.

Feeling unsettled, he shut the door and squatted down to wait. Snooping wasn't his desire. His mood was darkening. In short order, the situation he found himself in reminded him of the infamous rat episode from his childhood.

One night, he'd heard a scuffling behind the heater vent in his bedroom wall, and he'd sat straight up. The sound grew louder, the vent began to shake, then stretch, and moments later it clattered and burst from the wall, and a large, wiggling *Rattus norvegicus* torpedoed into Mac's room. He screamed.

It ricocheted off a chair leg into his closet; he slammed the closet door.

For three days and nights, the rat scratched and gnawed. Lying in his bed with it scratching, Mac felt torn in two. His mother said a rat in a closet was better than a rat out of one, so he tossed and turned to the desperate sound. Day four and all quiet; he jumped from his bed and opened the closet door. Maybe the rodent had escaped, was now sunning on the banks of the Charles. But moments later he found it, curled up in one of his slippers—even pests wanted to be comfortable when they died. He was a killer. He couldn't believe he'd sentenced such a robust creature to die in such a lonely way. It was too late now, forever. That night, after they disposed of it, Mac heard his mother and some guy laughing. He came out and told them to shut up; they looked at him as if he was very young.

A new concept crossed his mind: that all these years, he'd been as trapped as the rat. Locked in by events beyond his control, doomed to shrivel and die. It was time to break out, move on! For God's sake, where was this woman he barely knew? It's not hard to chew your cuticles to the point of bloodshed. The air was growing tight. One must be patient at the start of a relationship. One was learning to navigate the other person's world, pileups and wrecks all along the way. Would he die in her slippers? Just then he heard her fumbling with the door, and she opened the closet and released him.

"What's up?" he said, shaking himself out like a dog.

"Nothing. She just wanted to know about Molly getting home."

"Hey, not to pry, but why does she come to *you* to find that out?"

Carolyn said, "I seem to be the one keeping track of everything around here."

It didn't make sense, and he couldn't hold back. "Why are you letting your mother get away with being such a space case?"

But he'd gone too far. "Do you know anything about my mother?" she said. "You don't. She was a great actress, in college had all the leads. She could sing and dance, and she was wonderful at Shakespeare, too. And of course she was very beautiful. *I* look like my father."

"That's great, but so?"

"Well, she could've taken herself seriously, and she didn't."

"And what happened?"

"My father was becoming more well known by the day, and that's kind of overwhelming."

"Why are you so upset?"

"So my mother needs some help—so what?" And she took up

her brush and began to rush it through her hair. She was tearing her beautiful hair.

She had him. He clearly knew nothing about relationships—especially with parents. He stood there a long time, staring at her back, before he finally made himself say: "Carolyn, that was all stupid, what I said. Sorry. I just want to know everything about you. I mean it. Really."

She looked around at him. "Stop that!"

"Stop what?"

"You're looking at me—like you're thinking something different from what you're saying."

"Can I blame it on the closet?"

She tossed down her brush and grabbed a scarf from the chair. She pulled it through the air. Was it true what her mother had said to him—that she had no other friends?

Wasn't that what he liked about her?

"It seems you wanted to find out about your mother, but I'm burying you in stuff about mine." She was peering at him through the scarf. "I take it all for granted, and propose stupid theories."

"It's okay."

"Do you know anything about your father at all?"

"Nope."

"Not even his name?"

He shook his head. "West is my mother's name. Can I smoke on the balcony?"

"Be careful, it's narrow."

He edged out the French door, looking through the tree full of shoes. A delicate scent hung in the moist air. "The thing about the father stuff." He felt as if he was speaking to the universe. "People over the years have said to me, 'That must feel like a big hole' or 'How do you know who you are?' But you accept it. You don't fathom what you're missing."

"You really are alone."

"Not that alone. My cousin's like a sister."

"Too bad I'm not going to see you for a week," she said.

"A week! How come?" He flicked his half-smoked butt over the top of the tree.

"Because when school lets out in June, we take a trip to New York, and we're going tomorrow."

"Oh, man. Just say you'll come back," he said, and he reached out for her, and they began to kiss. "Sorry I taste like a cigarette."

"For some reason I love that taste," she said; then he worried his face was scratching her raw. They moved toward the rumpled bed.

As the evening came on, the light drifted through the high west windows, four moving prisms on the opposite wall. The light moved like a slow spotlight. As it crept up the wall, the smell of warm lacquer scented the room. Burnished the moment. Blue coolness came next as the daylight faded away. Her face went from warm to gray, languorous, then chilly like a fresco.

"I love the way you kiss," she said, but she kept his hands out of her clothes. "I'm not quite . . . ready yet." It didn't stop the kisses from going long and deep, or his hands from going farther into her hair. And lying against her, he saw how she could easily become a hot sliver of meaning that he might cling to as if to a lifeboat. And that he would consume his lifeboat to keep his life. To become his own floating boat of life. To become someone again at all.

He sat up abruptly in the blue light and looked at Carolyn Ware. He said, "I can't stand it anymore." He tried to muster a smile.

"Why?"

"I'm about to explode."

Did she glance at the nearby timepiece?

"In a good way," he said. "Have to go somewhere?"

"We have a lot to do."

"But I just got here."

"I know. It's all so unexpected."

"I thought we could have dinner or maybe take a walk."

"I wish I could. When I get back. Okay?"

He noticed the pile of books by her bed, the *Decameron* by Boccaccio on top. "Is that readable?"

"Very. It's funny. It takes place during the black plague; everyone's dying, and a group of noblemen and -women are hiding away at a villa, waiting for it to pass." She proceeded to sum up a story from the hundred tales—about a band of cruel brothers who murder their sister's lover, and how the sister takes his beautiful head and puts it in a pot and grows basil from it with her tears.

"That's funny?" he said.

"That's one of the sad ones."

"Is my head going to end up in a pot?" he asked.

"I hope not." She laughed. "It wasn't a warning, just a story."

"Will you tell me a new one every day?"

"I hope so."

"I hope so, too."

He thought a hundred days before he'd even had one with her sounded worth aiming for; but he also knew that a hundred days pass very, very quickly.

3

In the car, his tongue felt dry and his lips burned. He reached between the seats for old candies to dust off and suck. He wondered how long it would take before she realized he was a sewer rat. Balding sheepskins covered the seats in his car. The dashboard was cracked into deep canyons of foam. Garbage rattled from every corner of the floor.

With time on his hands, he stopped at a bookstore on Clement Street, plucked off the shelf a new edition of *Tangier*. He wanted to have something more of her, even distantly part of her, to make it through the week.

On the back cover:

Upon its publication nearly three decades ago, Charles Ware's classic novel defined what it meant to be young and dispossessed in America, and it continues to enthrall readers today. In this thinly disguised autobiography (based on Ware's friendship with publisher William Galeotto), Jim Bright, the privileged, confused son of a San Francisco industrialist, meets free-spirited

Nick Macchiato and travels with him to North Africa, where the two become street junkies, flirt with underworld characters, and discover, by the time they return to the U.S., that they can relate to no one but each other. . . .

The girl at the cash register had short pigtails sprouting from the top of her head like baby goat horns. "You like Ware?" she said, laying her hands on his pick.

"Not sure. Need to read it again."

"He lives around here, you know."

"So I hear," Mac said.

"He comes in and buys his own books sometimes."

"That's weird," Mac said.

"No matter how many times I see him, I'm always, like, 'Wow, everyone, it's him.' "

"Ever talked to him?"

"I can't talk to people that smart," she said, which annoyed Mac a little because she was talking to him. *I'm actually enormously gifted myself, but when people don't recognize it on account of my lowly clerk-dom, I feel so angry I could snap* was what she seemed to be thinking.

"It's good to work in a bookstore," he offered.

"Yeah, we get to borrow whatever we want."

"Cool."

"And interesting people come in. Let me know what you think of Ware," she said.

"All right, see you around."

Carrying Carolyn's father's book out to his car, Mac felt a little ashamed for buying it when Carolyn had clearly asked to be known for herself. It was almost as if he'd bought porn. Well, curiosity was inevitable. No harm done.

And for the first time in ages, his loneliness felt less fatal as he wound off the highway into Redwood City, still radiating heat like a pit of embers, to his cousin's little house. Hard to believe it was going on thirteen years since he'd arrived at the Los Angeles airport on a hot June afternoon like this one.

It was supposed to be a short vacation, that trip away from his mother. Not a whole new life. Aunt Helen, his mother's twin, greeted him with hugs and kisses, while Uncle Richard said, "I'm putting you to work, young man." They all waited together at the luggage carousel, and Mac wondered why it was that his cousin Fran was looking at him with the serene, conciliatory look most often seen on the faces of social workers and nuns. What had she been told? His California cousin was short and a bit rotund, wore pleated plaid shorts and a white blouse with a small pin on the pocket, of a poodle carrying a school satchel.

They drove to Tres Osos that summer evening, late sun glimmering all the way. Where was the water? Why were the hills dead? He came to like that golden color, by the way. He hoped his mother would have a good time in Paris—she needed it. He knew he was a burden. He knew that when he got to jabbering (he was fascinated by military invasions, from ancient times through World War II, and liked to draw decisive battles, cavalry and infantry going this way and that, then analyze and conjecture) he was driving her nuts. All his needs seemed to drive her nuts, come to think of it. Having friends over, making too much noise. Gilt with guilt he was, a boy unsure what rightfully was his.

All the way back, Fran and Helen chatted cheerfully about the fun things Fran and Mac could do together. Soak envelopes for a stamp collection, build Father Serra's missions with Popsicle sticks. If that was how they had fun in California, he'd give it a try. Glancing up at Helen, he almost called her Mom every time he let down his vigilant grip on the moment. And continually, for years, he'd bluster into a room and start talking to her that way; there was no doubt in his mind that faces were there to mock and deceive.

Uncle Richard, a large man with tiny white hands and a surprisingly narrow head, gave him all kinds of special instructions as they neared Tres Osos about how to interact with his homestead. The Solder house was like a grounded intergalactic space station. First they entered the detox chamber, in which they took off their shoes, set down the bags, and breathed the modified air. Then they were ready to enter the life-support system. Uncle Richard opened a second door, which emitted the whooshing sound of a broken seal. One socked foot at a time, they crossed the white shag wall-to-wall carpet that cost something like fifty dollars a square yard, as Richard often reminded everyone. "No interior decorator did this," he liked to say. "Picked out everything myself."

Mac looked around. The couches and chairs were all huge, bulging and unwrinkled, and looked as though not a particle of dust, let alone a human being, had ever lit upon them. There were a few stock pictures on the walls, of ships and fruit and hunting; nothing like his mother's manic scribblings. Then he noticed a low hum: this was the System, a massive conditioner that purified and circulated the air in the house and maintained each atom at the proper temperature as well. "We don't open windows here," Uncle Richard said. "Keep the good things in, the bad things out."

Mac was led to his bedroom. It was bigger, brighter by far, than any room he'd ever had. An oak headboard dignified a real mattress, and on the mattress were sheets, pillow, and comforter, all matching, with launching rockets on them. The curtains had rockets on them, too. About twenty rubber-coated hangers waited in the closet for his unhangworthy clothes, and there was a small desk and a new reading lamp, and a clean shelf for his books and microscope. "I hope you like it," Helen said modestly. "We've never made up a room for a boy before."

"It's really great," Mac said.

As for their first dinner together, Mac completed their square table. He'd never seen napkin rings before. They had a whole drawer of them—brass, wooden, shell, bamboo. Putting them on the table was Fran's job, one thing she did to earn her allowance. Helen served roast beef, potatoes, and green beans—it was delicious. Mac was tired of the headcheese, dill pickles, liverwurst, and the rest of the delicatessen staples his mother swiped at work and brought home.

"So," Richard said. "What do you think of the place?"

"Mac hasn't seen the town yet, how can he answer that?" Helen objected.

"He's full of opinions. I'm sure he's got one already."

Mac was trying to pry a flattened wafer of dinner roll from the roof of his mouth. He sensed the man didn't want a lengthy analysis. "It's practically Umbria," he finally answered.

"This is the best piece of land around. And you won't find a better-built house in this area—"

What was wrong with Aunt Helen and Fran? His mother never let blowhards like this prattle on—she'd laugh at a few of their jokes, then send them packing. Here, it seemed as if Uncle Richard really believed he was the head of the household. Mac's mother had told him petroleum hunters had found oil on the Solders' grazing land one generation before, turning a farm boy into a Little Lord Fauntleroy right before the town's eyes.

By the end of the month, Mac was raring to get home, and by mid-July, he was feverish frantic. He'd soaked stamps and glued Popsicle sticks until he felt as if he was in day care at an asylum, had burned out his best daydreams, and had nowhere new to turn in his mind. The day before his scheduled flight home, Helen said it was off. Cecille had not called. "I'm not sending you to Boston without a note or a call," she said. "Unless we hear from her by morning, we're keeping you here. Which is fine, we'd love to have you."

That night he stayed awake, listening for the phone, which he was sure would ring at some deep hour because his mother would have forgotten how to calculate the time zones. What a terrible night it was! He sat up in his bed and wished on stars. He even knelt beside his bed and prayed. With bleary eyes at dawn, he concluded she'd missed the flight or forgotten the date, and every hour from then on became nothing more than an aching wait.

In later years, he would have trouble remembering what came next. Helen made calls, while he felt an unspoken shame and disgrace. To hide from it, he decided to check out every book from the pygmy Tres Osos library. He read a good one about Scipio and Hannibal and the Punic Wars that summer; *punic* became his slang for everything bad, especially Uncle Richard. He had been used to having his own schedule, coming and going as he pleased, in a city with places to go and people to see, and suddenly, he was plunked in the middle of nowhere under the thumb of Dick-Dick, who acted as if he owned the place. Actually, he *did* own the place.

By the middle of August, the wait was tearing him apart. Mac missed his mother every hour, all the craziness, all the stops and starts. He just wanted to get home. He was starting to overhear Dick-Dick say things like "We shouldn't be too surprised, right? How can she be responsible, she's a nutcase."

"I'm not surprised, but I'm worried," Helen replied.

"If she hadn't been reckless in the past, I wouldn't say it."

"Finding a few oil wells sure helped make you responsible," Mac shouted, running into the room.

"Hey!" Dick-Dick said. "Now you're eavesdropping?"

"At least I'm not all *punic*, like you are!"

"Now I'm *punic*?"

One afternoon, bursting into the cool house and whipping Fran with a towel, Mac found Helen hanging up the phone, looking as if she'd received bad news.

"What's wrong?" he cried.

"I've just been speaking with the State Department. Your mother—last month—she left her things in an unpaid room, and hasn't retrieved them," Helen said.

She left her things in an unpaid room. "I want to go home. Uncle Richard hates me."

"Of course he doesn't hate you!"

"I miss my mom. I need to go home!" *She left her things in an unpaid room.*

"Mac, until we find her, you can't go, and it's much better for you here—"

"No, it's not better for me, it's not, it's not, it's not!"

"I am sorry. I just mean for now it's better."

"It's not better, it's not, it's not—"

"Calm down," she said, and tried to hug him, but he broke from her and ran to his room and locked the door. He'd never do anything they asked him again. He'd turn to stone!

"Mac, let me in!"

"No," he moaned into his pillow, "it's not better, it's not better, it's not better, it's not better, it's not."

Tres Osos. Nine hundred people. Hills the color of lion fur, and cottonwoods growing like scanty pubic hairs around a few dry creeks. Off across the valley, the oil derricks bowed up and down, up and down, the way Aunt Helen and Fran bowed to Richard. His mother never did write, and an investigation was opened, and Helen was devastated but did not want it to show; and Mac's mind soon blackened with squid's ink whenever he thought of her, so that when he celebrated Christmas with the Solders that year and they presented him with a gift they pretended was from Cecille, he pulled apart the wrapping as if it was the shell on a very poisonous nut.

The present was a leather jacket of the coolest kind. Adolescent greed eclipsed his feelings, and he wore the jacket until it looked like a rotten hide on a buffalo carcass; a buffalo that had died without its herd and become a sinewy mound somewhere on the Great Plains. (Which wasn't far from his self-image at the time.) Sometimes Mac wondered if feelings also rotted and died, or if they existed in a terrible vacuum, unkissed by gravity and water and air, full-bodied and grievous forever.

It wasn't until spring that the State Department phoned them again, with the news.

Yes. By now, Mac had adjusted to the idea that a kindly cousin could come in handy. Frances Solder Bixby. A quadrate presence if ever there was one. In her veins ran a bracing blend of impatience and solicitude, and a deep furrow was always undulating her brow. She hovered. She nagged. But no one took better care of him when he was sick, or worried about him more when he took plunges off the map.

When he arrived home that evening, it was not surprising to find her in the kitchen. "Hey, Ho," she said. The nickname she'd given him as a kid, short for Ho-ho, short for "Laugh a little. Cheer up. We'll work it out!" In her arms was a lumpy object, bundled in a dish towel.

"Hey, Fran."

"What did you get?" she asked, zeroing in on his purchase. As if he were real all of a sudden for having bought something. When he pulled it from the bag, she said, "I remember that book! It was one of the only things you had when you came out from Boston."

"No way."

"Yeah, that and *Winnie-the-Pooh*."

"That's a bald-faced lie."

"Mom and Dad thought it was weird. I snuck in your room to read it sometimes, but it seemed kind of homoerotic."

"It's a classic! It's youthful exuberance. I'd say it's more pansexual."

"No wonder they thought it was weird."

It wouldn't hurt her to loosen up, but he was trying to be nice. "I met the guy's daughter," Mac slipped in. "In fact—"

"Who, the author's?"

"Her name's Carolyn. We pretty much hit it off profoundly."

"You mean, romantically?"

"Um, kind of."

"Oh, that's great! That's wonderful! I never thought it possible!"

"Chill, Fran. We'll see."

"What does she do? What's she look like?"

"I can't sum her up tidily."

"I want to meet her!"

"We'll see. I want to play it cool."

"Why don't you bring her here for a barbecue?"

"That's not playing it cool."

"Or maybe we could all meet in the city."

"Yeah, I have to get to know her better," he said, wishing Fran's husband, Tim, was in a full body cast so as to be unavailable into the foreseeable future. "I don't want to rush anything. What's that?" he asked.

"Oh, Tim bought a juicer."

"You're holding it like a baby." The impulse to pick on her was like the need to pick a scab.

"We made some really good juice with carrots and apples, and now I'm cleaning it. Is that against the law?"

"Giving it a bath. Getting it ready for bed. About to tuck it in."

"Some people were over; there's some roasted chicken if you're hungry," she said.

"I'm starving. Who came?"

"Tim's manager and his wife," Fran said.

"I thought Tim was the manager."

She said, "Tim's the Bay Area manager, but Boutrous is the manager of the *Western Division.* He's very easy to talk to and normal."

"I didn't really think otherwise," Mac said, hunkering down with the leftovers. "Oh, Brussels sprouts, too. I love 'em."

At that moment he cast a glance into the "family room." There, Tim, the huge, baby-shaped man with beet red elbows because he always slumped at tables holding his head, was now perched on a chair, about to crown one of his totem poles of merchandise boxes with the box from the new juicer. Six to ten high, the packagings from a popcorn popper, an electric wok, a fancy kettle, an air purifier, an ice cream maker, a humidifier, a halogen lamp, an oscillating fan, a food processor, and a special dust-mite-capturing vacuum, among others, were stacked against the wall.

"I know you think this is a stupid thing to do," Tim said.

"Hey, it's your house," Mac conceded. At least Tim wasn't indulging in his other hobby, staring into space and fondling his rump.

"Giants won tonight," Tim said, but Mac was already retreating with his bowl down the hall.

"He met someone! Hope you don't mind, I changed your sheets today," Fran called after him.

"That's kind of personal."

"I couldn't help it. I don't think you've changed them in about six months."

"That room smells like gangrene," he heard Tim say.

He locked his door. God! It was so strange what happened to people once they married. Marriage seemed romantic in theory and damning in practice. Two creatures neutered by their union. And yet it was his own mess that struck him tonight as even worse. Books, in sloppy stacks up the walls, contributed to the must. Bottles of wine and bourbon on the table, next to a couple of resinous shot glasses, lent a biting smell. A large plastic cactus, once his only possession, sat in a phony terra-cotta pot, spines trapezed by cobwebs and dust. On one wall hung a few of the grisly sketches and prints wrought by good old Mom. (These likely had no odor.) They were of prison inmates and the wards of asylums, and the largest and most grabbing was of a disemboweled torso—in the mode of eighteenth-century anatomy texts. Yet his favorite poster was the one Cesar and he had created together, in violent streaks of black paint. It hung directly over his bed:

The Stench of my Soul
Wafts to my brain
My brain, my brain!
Yes! The rancorous, fetid bulb!
Chaotic promoter of the turmoil within!

They intended this masterpiece to rip out of Central California as the first verse of their postsurrealist gospel. They both grew cacti in order to say the cacti were mirrors of their souls. They were proud to think their souls were so prickly and stenchful.

And whenever Fran saw the poster, she looked as if she'd been poisoned, which was most of the fun of keeping it there.

He uncorked a half bottle of rancid red wine and took a long swig. Coughed. Placed his new book by his bed, ready for when he turned in. Held up a few rumpled shirts and pants that had been flattened on the floor like rugs and shook them out, as if it might soon matter what he wore. He snorted his upper lip to his nose, and it smelled like a Bacon Thin he'd eaten in third grade. Then he looked at his teeth in the mirror and rubbed them. He chewed up a candy bar, hiccuped in a spasm, started to leaf through Ware's book, then sank to the floor. There was a tap on his door.

"What?"

Fran tapped again.

"Come in!"

She peered in through a crack. "Interrupting anything?"

"Like?"

"Okay, from now on I'll just burst in no matter what you're doing." She threw herself down on the end of the bed. "Tim and I just had a fight. He is such a pack rat."

"How about making him rent a storage space?"

"When we first met, I thought it was strange that he'd order two dinners for himself in a restaurant. He wouldn't eat it all, but it made him feel secure."

It was true, Tim did seem especially stubborn about his habits. "What's his trip?"

"You've met his parents. They're in a death lock of misery. So I think, deep down, he's afraid it's not going to work out between us, and he holds on to stuff for protection. And I wish you'd be nicer," she added.

"I'm nice."

"Not *that* nice."

"I don't know how to be nicer."

"Remember that time Dad brought a turkey home a few months before Thanksgiving, and all the chickens in his chicken house were pecking it?" she said.

Mac did remember. The chickens had seemed bent on bringing down the larger bird and were pulling its feathers out in turns, and its poor, bare turkey butt was soon a raw field of stubble and blood. "We could even see the peck marks after we roasted it."

Fran said, "Remember how we couldn't figure out why?"

"I think they were scared of that red thing on its nose."

"Well, maybe, but what I'm trying to say is that you're like those chickens, and whenever any male figure comes into your yard, you peck at him. You did it with Dad and now you're doing it with Tim."

"Why would I do that?"

"Well, maybe because you didn't have a father, so they seem like intruders to you."

Mac said, "Maybe it's because they seem like turkeys."

Fran stared at him as if she wanted to attack. They used to have huge face-offs as kids, rolling and snarling and kicking until someone screamed "Spitfire!" which meant "Enough."

"By the way, I'm still not pregnant," she said, rising from his bed with an expansive yawn.

"Oh." He felt guilty for how little he ever thought about her concerns. "I'll try a fertility dance."

"I'd like to see that."

"You're young, what's the hurry?"

"Mom was twenty-two when she had me. I always felt proud of how young she was."

Mac had once felt proud of his mother's youth, liked to shock people with it back in Boston, loved to grab her thick braid in the morning and hold it like a rope, but her youth and immaturity had backfired on him. "Why do you want to have a kid with Tim when you're not even getting along?"

"I love him. We're married. What do you mean?"

"I don't get it, and probably never will."

"I'm excited about your girlfriend. Give me your dish."

He handed it up to her; a rejected, wormy Brussels sprout rolled out and bounced on the carpet.

" 'Night, Ho-ho." She leaned over and kissed him on the top of the head. Long-standing habit. Made him feel docile, like a pet.

After she'd left the room, he picked up his old coat and slipped it around the shoulders of a hanger, placed it on the vacant rod in the closet. It swung freely a moment, with nothing in its way. A single swinging coat in a closet made him want to cry. So he fell into the book, which, by contrast, smelled fresh and full of promise. What did Carolyn see in him? How long did they have, before she vanished in the night?

4

"If I told you the only happy family I'd ever seen—"

(said Mac's mother, one gorgeous May morning in his youth, as they moved along the duck-waddled bank of the Charles River in Boston where it begins to widen to merge with the Atlantic, and only a month before he was sent away to California)

"—was a trio of snowy owls, what would you think?"

She had heard them as a teenager one Christmas Eve, communicating: about sightings of fresh mice under the stars. Next morning, her father was not in the house. The note on the table said MERRY CHRISTMAS TO ALL, AND TO ALL A GOOD NIGHT.

—Told you he wasn't happy around here, said Cecille with her usual know-it-all savoir faire.

—What do you know about it! cried her mother. I am his wife!

They sat and opened their presents darkly by the tree, and then Cecille, restless in the gloom, talked her twin into a romp in the snow. Maybe they could find the owls.

Helen was disheartened about the paterfamilias, wanting to improve the day with cooking and games.

—It's too cold, sniffled she.

—Come on, Hel! cajoled Cecille. We need some air. Let's take our skates down to the pond.

—What about Mama?

—I'll have a good cry while you girls are outside, the poor woman replied.

The air was stinging as the twins crunched through the shimmering fields. The inside of Cecille's nose was dry and prickly, the outside of her scarf soon white with crust. As they went tractoring through the bristly face of the cornfield, something caught her eye.

The Connecticut River adjoined the property. A naked willow guarded the white bank like a witch over a ghostly bed. And that's where she spotted them, the huddled lumps high in a tangle of twitching boughs. The skates went down in the snow.

—Helen, look!

Cecille tossed up a snowball to make them fly. Nothing so beautiful ought to live here. And they swooped from the tree, wings wide, the young one wobbling behind.

But Helen was whimpering and shivering. —It's too cold. I'm going in!

Cecille snapped off a willow switch and whipped it at her sister. She loved the sound it made, slicing invisible curtains of air.

—Move a muscle or two and you'll warm up, she said.

—My side hurts, said Helen, on account of the broken rib that had not quite healed.

—You still mad at me? said Cecille.

Helen shrugged. —Maybe a little.

—You should be!

Cecille chased her twin around the trunk but tripped, fell on her knees. And there she noticed the curved leather tips of her father's boots sticking up through the snow.

—Oh no. She dug through the powder with her mittens.

—Daddy? Helen cried.

Cecille had not called him Daddy for years. She preferred a cool, crisp John. At once the volatile face that had loomed through their days bore out their deepest fears. For never before had the sisters seen human eyes frozen flat like skating ponds. Pupils fixed on the sky. Red ice ran like ribbons through the ringlets of his hair, and a big, livery thing had formed outside his ear.

Cecille wrestled the cold pistol from his tight hand. They were both familiar with the weapon, for he'd waved it around before, threatening to do himself in.

—He's crazy, Cecille cried, understand? Nobody's fault but that!

Don't say that! cried Helen. Don't say that ever again!

"Mac," his mother said to him that memorable day, on which he heard the story for the first time, "you're made of something bigger and more wonderful than two people linked by empty vows; you're like lightning that only strikes once. Fathers are overrated. You'll be safe out there, and you'll wonder why I couldn't live that way. But don't, all right? Tell them we did some great things. Mac, will you tell them?"

"But how long?" he asked, already sobbing.

"Mothers are overrated, too," she said. He'd never told anyone she'd said that.

"You're not overrated, Mom. You're my favorite person in the world!"

"Stop crying! You're going to go to California and grow up!"

Grow up? He was only nine. He looked bleakly at the purposeful scullers, all elbows down the Charles, and began to gather all the golden, glimmering things about his youth and his mother he would say, in time.

~

$\mathcal{J}$t was a sunburned afternoon in Redwood City, the kind of day the world turns on, the day to slip on your favorite new shirt; the first day of summer, and Fran and Tim were employing all their latest purchases and throwing their annual barbecue. New gas grill, tumblers, trays, and tongs—from a catalog, they'd ordered the works. Mac's cousin scurried around inside, her hair wrapped in pink worms. She always became agitated before guests came over. Tim was out cleaning off the lawn furniture while Mac chopped vegetables in the kitchen to keep her from blowing her top.

Then Mac pulled out the bags of meat for the grill. Twenty-five pounds of chicken backs.

"*Fran?* This is all you got?"

"Chicken, yes."

"Chicken *backs*!" he screamed.

"No wonder they were so cheap," she called. "Well, that's too bad. Could you chop off those things?"

"What things?"

"Those diamond-shaped nubs, the pope's nose. Hurry! People are coming, and there's someone I want you to meet."

Mac pried a frozen chicken back from the clump in the bag. Fine, he'd cut off the nubs and fry them in chili powder and serve them as delicacies, hope someone would ask for the recipe. Just then a woman wearing a gauzy white dress drifted past the stove.

"I'm Danielle," she said. "I'm sorry, I was looking for the bathroom, and I stumbled into a room which Fran said is yours."

"Yeah, temporarily. Probably not for long."

"I hate doing laundry, too," she said, sipping from her glass. "If you're not out rolling in the mud, you can get a lot of wear out of things. If I get a spot on a blouse and the rest of it's clean, I can dab it off. You shouldn't overwash most fabrics anyway."

"My philosophy," Mac said.

"I always get this way at parties. I drink too much too fast. Then I blurt out mundane things about myself. Naturally, working at the library, I read a lot. Guess what I'm reading right now."

"What?"

"Anaïs Nin's diaries. Don't get the wrong idea—it's not like I'm poring over erotic literature in a pile of dirty clothes. God, I didn't make myself sound very appealing." She turned her head to the side and gestured with one of her hands as though talking to somebody else. "Remember that thing mothers used to do—they'd grab your hand and say, 'Stop hitting yourself!' and force you to hit yourself? I believe that's a German tradition. But you'd laugh, because it was *attention*. I do nice things for myself, too. I make a bubble bath every night after work. I burn candles and space out. How do you relax?"

"I don't," he said. "Anxiety is the key to success."

Her expression changed. "Are you . . . mocking me?"

"No, not at all."

"I thought we were communicating. I really can't take any form of rejection right now," she said.

"No, I didn't mean—" Mac said, but she had fled.

Whoops. He must have been glaring at her without realizing it. He flexed his smile muscles a few times. He remembered with a jolt how in the old days he always liked meeting new people, how friendly he used to be as a boy, how good a host he was, helping his mother entertain the endless parade of strangers who came through their apartments, and how, like his mother, he prided himself on being able to talk up a storm with anyone.

Once, in the subway under Arlington Street in Boston, an old man from Jamaica Plain revealed to him the secret of his success with people. They had been talking, leaning against the tile wall, for almost an hour. The man's pockets were jammed with the miniature bottles of liquor they give people to placate them on airplanes. He handed Mac a vodka, told him how good a woman his wife was to him and what a terrible bear he was to her. That was why he was drunk in the subway: he couldn't face her anymore. She'd packed him a meat loaf sandwich for lunch every day for thirty years. And he'd never bought her a present, no anniversary pins, no pretty dress for church, nothing. All he ever brought her was "a handful of dandy-lions," he said. "In spring I bring her hard yellow suns, in summer it's soft white moons." Finally he turned to Mac and said, "You know why I tell you all this, boy? You got a nice face. You got a nice face that don't say, 'I is better than you.' You listen to an old man feel sorry for hisself, and you don't say, 'Go away, old bum.' You not a big judge like all the rest."

So that was how he did it, how he elicited these spontaneous confessions. As the old man said these things, Mac nodded earnestly and listened, and inside he was judging whether or not the man was making it up about having such a nice wife, and worried that he might be, seeing as how he'd noticed the guy slumped in the subway for weeks. What nice wife would let him do that? He liked the old guy anyway. He invited him home.

"You want an old bum follow you home?"

"Sure," said Mac.

"Well, I be damned. If old Ralph stands, old Ralph comes along glad, boy."

Mac tried to help him up, but the man wasn't able to get to his feet. He remembered how later he'd begged his mother to make some meat loaf sandwiches he could deliver in the subway.

"Ready?" Fran came in and asked.

Sure enough, he'd completed his chore. His hands were frozen and covered with chicken fat. "I predict these will go like hotcakes."

"Come on outside. There's someone waiting to see you."

"Woman named Danielle?"

"No, someone else."

"I don't want to meet anyone."

"Why not?"

"I've met someone already."

"You can stand to meet more than one person."

"Okay. But I don't want to *meet* someone, as in *really* meet them."

"Just come out here."

He was biding his time. He was driving to the city soon to see Carolyn and to meet, at last, Charles Ware. After he washed up, he looked out the window at the group of people Fran and Tim had invited, which included a few of the neighbors he liked (a friendly old woman who walked her trusty spaniel and waved at him as if he was arriving home after a journey across the tundra, no matter how many times a day she spotted him) and some of the ones he despised (a family who scolded him once for stepping on their lawn). Mostly, it was Fran's librarian friends. He came outside and fished a piece of cauliflower off a tray, crunched it up.

Moments later, Fran brought over a tall, attractive woman in her thirties. "Mac, you remember Miss Kobayashi, don't you?" He looked carefully at the woman and placed her all at once. No way! It was his fourth-grade teacher from Tres Osos.

"Call me Melinda," she said with a laugh.

"We ran into each other in the library a few weeks ago," Fran said. "I wanted to surprise you. Isn't it amazing?"

"Yes, I left Tres Osos about eight years ago. I'm teaching high school now, here in Redwood City."

"Wow," said Mac. "You look the same, but—"

"You've grown about three feet," she said. "So what are you doing with yourself now, Mac? You're a teacher?"

"Is that what Fran said about me?" Mac snickered. "I guess she tries to hide the awful truth."

"Tell me the awful truth. The awful truth, really, is that I can never get the awful truth from anyone."

"I'm kind of between things."

"I wish I were between things," Miss Kobayashi said. "Actually, in the fall I'll have six classes, and I'm already out of my mind about it. When I see all those faces, I stutter and drool."

"You?"

"Yes. Someday I'm going to write a book called *Classroom of Darkness.* The instructor goes insane and dies, and they find a stack of her students' papers, and across the top of the pile it says 'Exterminate the brutes!' "

He laughed. "I didn't know you were thinking things like that, back in fourth grade."

"It was different with the younger kids," she added. "I didn't feel as self-conscious."

"You were a good teacher," he said, recalling the cheerful bungalow full of desks and art projects. "I still remember a lot about that year."

"Oh, tell me! Like what?"

"You read out loud to us. *Chitty Chitty Bang Bang, A Wrinkle in Time.* I loved that! You'd do the voices. And you never got mad."

"That makes me feel so good, like it counted! You were having such a hard time," she added.

Her words startled him, and inside, he cringed. What, had he been pissing all over himself or something? Picking fights? Or just his nose? He didn't remember not fitting in.

"Any sponsors yet?" An older woman joined them. "I'm up to twenty-five."

"This is Marjorie, who teaches with me. We're signed up for a limpathon," Melinda said. "It's a real thing, like a walkathon, but for people with knee injuries."

"You have a knee injury?"

"Can't you tell I'm kind of gimpy? It's from running."

"Miss Kobayashi—"

"Please, it's Melinda. The age gap thing changes a lot, doesn't it?"

Miss Kobayashi, his fourth-grade teacher, was smiling at him in a way that was very attractive. Was it okay to think so? He felt a little strange. Apparently he went for the gimpy type, for Carolyn had that strange walk, too. "Yeah."

"Let's have coffee sometime, and catch up, what do you say?"

When your teacher suggested you have coffee, you had to have coffee. What if she told him to do other things?

"Good idea," he said.

He lifted his cup in cheers and now had the luxury of surveying Fran and Tim's backyard and feeling nostalgic for the days (only a week ago) when he had nothing else but this. The fence into which he practiced throwing tomahawks—that was really fun. The lumpy vegetable patch Fran worked at like a dog, yielding its tough-skinned tomatoes, mildew-tipped zucchini, and anemic green beans, which crawled up bamboo poles to choke and die. The smell of backyard grass, the hulking form of Tim turning chicken backs over the billowing flames of his grill. Perhaps it was more special and fleeting than he had realized. He often stopped in a given moment and calculated how many more times he might experience similar moments in his lifetime. If they continued to have summer cookouts every year until they couldn't move out of bed—what, say fifty or sixty more? Enough to spare. He skulked toward the house. *So long, farewell. Auf Wiedersehen, goodbye!*

Back in his room, he flossed his teeth, picked up the pint bottle of George Dickel he'd purchased for the occasion, as well as the stack of envelopes in question, and, hoping he wouldn't be noticed, stole out the front door and peeled away in his unsightly barge.

Driving out of Redwood City, past the neon martini sign and the do-it-yourself dog wash, past the shrill used-car lots and the diesel clouds of tractor trailers idling on side streets for the night, he happily joined the crowd going north on 101. He never tired of approaching the city. Everyone complained about the summer fog, but these were the complaints of proud parents apologizing with smiles for the brattish deeds of their children. Ultimately, San Francisco did no wrong in the eyes of the people who lived there, and it was true, the summer fog and chill had a charm all its own.

Driving across town, he followed Geary to Divisadero, climbed that 35 percent grade hill. The fog was coming like rivers down the streets. Nowhere to park, and he nosed his car into a fraudulent space at the corner. Then he was up to the porch and one buzz away from her. He pushed.

"Who calls?" The terse male voice on the intercom startled him; he felt pimply and adolescent.

"Um, hi, I'm looking for Carolyn," he faltered.

"Who is this?"

Who should he say he was? No choice. "Mac West."

The connection was severed while the cold air found every warm spot on his skin. And when the door opened, he found himself standing in the presence of the man himself, Charles Ware.

Mac recognized the sensitive face from the back of *Tangier*— a face that had helped create the mystique surrounding the book. The real Ware was now a man who looked rather like an aged boy, a pituitary case—a replica of his former self with too much skin. Puttied, old cheeks crowded his small features; blue gray slugs rested beneath his eyes; thin, monkey red hair sprouted from the roof of his immensely admired brain. The man didn't look so bad, really, once Mac had cleared his mind of the initial comparison. Maybe even kind of dapper.

"And you are?"

"Friend of Carolyn's." Apparently Carolyn had not prepared her father for his visit. "MacGregor West."

Ware looked as surprised to see a friend of Carolyn's as his wife had, the week before.

"Is she expecting you?"

"Yes, she is."

"Then come in."

Two young men were shadowing Ware. One was tall, bearded, and wan, and looked like someone in an old daguerreotype from the Klondike. The other wore a brown velour suit and had a long goose neck with a flickering Adam's apple at the center of it. He said, "Daniel LaPlante." The tall, wan fellow said, "Tom Rothman." And they eagerly held out their hands to shake Mac's, and he had an impostor's discomfort in shaking back.

"Any relation to the Green Street Wests?" Ware asked, motioning for Mac and the others to follow him back to the library and liquor shelf.

"Don't think so," Mac said.

"A very impressive family," Ware said. "I went to school with Donald West in Chicago. Two of his brothers went to Yale. What do you suppose made all of us boys run east like that? And what in God's name made me stop in a town known for its rail yards and slaughterhouses?"

"The Cubs?" Mac wondered where Carolyn was this time.

"Tom has written a marvelous novel," Ware said. "I've just finished it; I'm sure it's publishable."

Rothman murmured something appreciative, and LaPlante said: "I knew it. I knew this would work out perfectly."

"Congratulations," said Mac.

"To San Francisco," Ware said, handing them each a glass and raising his. "Home of lost causes and forsaken beliefs!"

"Manhattan is incredibly alive," LaPlante blurted. "Tom, you'll love it. You'll meet great people."

"I certainly hope he doesn't have to meet 'great' people." Ware chuckled, surveying his small audience. "When I left home for college, I was seventeen. We ran into bad weather, and I missed my connection in Denver, I believe my first trip to Chicago took twenty-two hours. But it felt like a miracle. When I saw Chicago, it was like coming out of a stupor."

Ware seemed to have no intention of summoning Carolyn for him, and pulling out the envelopes didn't seem like a great idea now, either. Mac gulped his drink instead.

"Poor, pink baby I was; I had to scour off that innocence! So did I throw myself onto the blackened streets? Hardly. I went right to the English Department at the university. I unpacked and planted myself for four years. And when I left, I was no longer pink. And not from looking under the skirts of experience, not from seeing its hairy legs and sniffing its musky smell! Instead, I met brilliant people; I was beaten and bruised, and by the best minds of my generation. Then I *discovered* some of the best minds. Do you know where I met Bill Galeotto? On break, not far from here; at the back of a restaurant, peeling the fatty skin off chicken in a tub of gray water. He had to work the knife so fast his hands were bleeding with cuts. I saw this marvelously handsome boy and I started talking to him and I discovered that he was brilliant and ambitious and he no more knew what to do with himself than the poor plucked chicken in the tub."

LaPlante laughed. Rothman said seriously, "'For beauty is nothing but the beginning of terror we can barely endure—and every angel is terrible.' What about *Erlebnis,* Mr. Ware, as in Rilke's afternoon at Duino?"

Ware glowed. "To open to experience, to be receptive, is a far cry from buying the costume of a butterfly catcher before one has studied and knows which are rare and worth catching and which are as common as flies. When young writers set out on their safaris for this *Erlebnis,* as you say, they mostly catch flies!

"Now, in Chicago I wrote poetry first; as Williams put it, a poem is a small machine made of words. We were practical. We wanted to wind up our machines and march them over the world, armies of poetry, World War Three! Because what did we learn from the legions of muse-struck poets who destroyed themselves? We thought all that engineering, the steel girders of classical poetry, could best support our ideas. A little hocus-pocus, and each new contraption could be disguised as a mystical gem, a scarab. But I abandoned my group: I wrote a novel. And I was so successful at it I determined that I'd rather spend my life toying with the loose, baggy monster than scrubbing the scarab's back. So there you have it."

Daniel LaPlante actually sighed; Tom Rothman was too absorbed to generate noise.

"Tom asked me how I started out," Ware said. "I'm afraid it's a subject I can talk too much about."

LaPlante said, "Of course you have a lot to talk about. You should be putting it all into a book."

Rothman said, "Sir, it's your responsibility to literary history to write that book."

"Yes, a memoir's long overdue," LaPlante added.

"Mr. Ware, what are you working on now?"

Ware drew in his breath, in his quietly theatrical manner. "If you'd asked me a month ago, I might not have felt comfortable talking about it. But I'm so pleased with the work I've done so far that I will tell you. But please, it stops here. I'm planning a new novel about Jim Bright."

He crossed his arms and legs, and left it there to be viewed and admired by all. It was as if the name Jim Bright should stand on its own, like Stephen Dedalus or Humbert Humbert. And for these two, Mac saw, it obviously did. LaPlante's neck bobbed, and Rothman shivered. Ware acted as if his character deserved the reception of a cult figure, an American hero making a long-awaited comeback. Deserved? Maybe. But instantly, Mac couldn't help wondering whether Ware had always thought, during his career, *If all else fails I can bring back Jim Bright.*

"What about Nick Macchiato?" LaPlante said. "It's impossible to imagine Jim without Nick. He'll be in it, won't he? He's your tour de force!"

"That's the simple view," Ware said dryly. Mac thought LaPlante had complimented Carolyn's father and was surprised by the fierceness of Ware's reply. "Through Bright's eyes, Macchiato comes alive. Bright creates him. Without Bright's brilliant investment in Macchiato, you'd have nothing but an unplumbed cutout. You'd have nothing! This is an important literary distinction, and you must be aware of it," Ware said.

"You're absolutely right," LaPlante said quickly. "Macchiato is only as fascinating as Bright makes him."

"That's right," Ware went on quietly. "I haven't made up my mind about putting Macchiato into this work." Then he laughed. "I'll have to see how he behaves!"

In motion, bodies make a certain sound. Mac heard Carolyn pushing her sister up from the basement, or whatever lay below the massive domicile. When they appeared in the doorway, Mac saw that the girl's shirt was damp and matted to her chest, and the acrid smell of bile wafted through the room. Mac jumped up from his chair.

"She was in the sun all day," Carolyn announced. "Roasting! How long have you been here?"

"Just arrived," said Mac.

"It was the hamburger," said Molly. "It smelled like horse broth."

Mac watched Ware take a sip of brandy, not budging in the direction of his sick child. " 'A thing wherein we feel some hidden want,' " he intoned.

Carolyn said: " 'She wants a heart.' "

" 'Ah, the foul rag-and-bone shop of the heart!' " Ware said, and Mac moved from their midst.

"Great meeting you all," he said. "Mr. Ware, thanks."

"Yes, you too, you too," the young men echoed.

"One thing," Ware said, following Mac out of the room.

"Yes?"

He pulled Mac aside, his breath and clothes as stale as the pages of an old book. "You're a very nice person, aren't you?"

"I guess I'm okay," Mac said.

"I hope you're a very nice person," Ware said, and he reached over and brushed off Mac's lapel.

"I do my best."

"Yes, you'll have to do your best," Ware said. "Good evening!"

Mac followed Carolyn and her sister up the back stairs, trying to shake off the encounter. In the hexagonal chamber at the top, Carolyn leaned on the door frame of her sister's room. "Sorry about this. I want to get her to the shower."

"I can get in myself!" Molly said. She pushed Carolyn out of her way, closed the door.

"Don't throw those clothes on the bed," Carolyn called. "Put them on the bathroom floor. And wash your hair!"

"Okay" came the muffled response.

Carolyn hesitated a moment, then turned her radiant face on him; despite everything he found strange and ungainly about getting to know her, he felt grand again. "So—are you ready?" he said.

"You must dread coming here."

"Carolyn?" called the sister.

"What?"

"I still feel sick, and—"

"Just take a shower."

"I'm sick, I'm really sick!"

"It's her own fault," Carolyn said. "I told her to stop gorging."

"I never knew having a sibling was such a big responsibility," Mac said.

"I need a break. My mother could be a lot more helpful. So could my dad."

"You're not kidding," said Mac.

"Carolyn?" came the whine of Molly.

"This is awful."

"Hey, don't worry."

"How about this? I'll square her away and get my mother on board, and meet you downstairs."

"Aye-aye," said Mac. "Oh, and I brought the envelopes." He patted his breast pocket. "Too bad those drips are here."

"Maybe they'll leave. I'll be down soon."

"I'll be waiting," said Mac.

Ware and the sycophants were still spouting off in the other room, but now Adela Ware was bungling about in a large pantry in the kitchen.

"You'll be a stupid girl to do that," she was saying with a lavish Germanic accent. "You'll be taking over my business, soaking your hands in curing water when you're fifty years old. Don't you wish you'd had a father with a good living?"

He cleared his throat so as not to startle her. Something fell from a shelf, rolled across the floor. She peered out of the shadows.

"Hello, Mrs. Ware." He scooped it up—a prescription for her, filled by Porter, Isabel, M.D. *Xanax.*

"Hello, MacGregor! I'm mining my memories for material," she informed him. "I'm working on a one-woman show."

"Best of luck," he said, giving her a nod. Adela had probably been giving a one-woman show for some time.

"You see, I didn't want to marry a *father*." Her voice came out indignantly. "Mother had high hopes. I was never quite as disciplined as my sister; but everything I touched I did naturally, with ease. With my sister, you saw the sweat."

"Is that so."

"I won a scholarship," Adela said, "to Northwestern, and over the next three years developed myself as an actress. In fact, I walked away with the leads in every production the Theater Department put on during my time there. I became well known at the university. Still, from time to time, suddenly, just before I went onstage or spoke to someone important, I wondered if I smelled of brine!"

Her voice was squeezing the air out of him.

"Well, it was absurd. Absurd because sophisticated people from Chicago were traveling up to Evanston just to see me perform. One night, the whole lot of us went out for drinks with another group from the U. of C.; I was introduced to a young poet my wonderful professor Marcel DeSimone was acquainted with.

"I was told that this Charles Ware was a very promising writer, a young man at work on a novel that was reported to be very important. I looked at him—he looked young and shy and bland; later, that was what I told my friends. But Marcel and this Ware fellow had much to say to each other—after a few hours of listening to their overheated talk, I wished the poet would go away. I drank a few more glasses of wine, and next thing I knew, I was standing on the table. I began to sing a sultry torch song. They stared. Even the poet had shut up. I kicked off a shoe."

She demonstrated by kicking off one of her slippers; Mac flinched. He felt irritated and uncomfortable, and he could hear Charles Ware now, bidding the young men farewell. The front door closed with a bang.

"The room howled. I kicked off the other and reached for my sash—dear Marcel swept me off the table and carried me to the car. I wrapped my arms around his neck and murmured something in his ear. I might have told him I loved him.

"It all caught up to me. A few days later he told me that his young friend Charles Ware had been mesmerized—by me. 'Anyway, I think he's brilliant. I've read most of his novel. It's spectacular. I believe he'll be quite famous,' he told me. 'Not that he needs the money, like the rest of us mortals. He's extraordinarily wealthy. I hear his father owns a small city out west. Not as big as ours. It's called San Francisco.'

"What matters next is that I was heartbroken that the love of my life wanted to pawn me off, no matter how promising or wealthy the fellow. I had a fundamental insecurity—"

Mac shifted his weight abruptly. "This is fascinating, Mrs. Ware, but—"

"It's Adela."

"All right, Adela."

"Anyhow, that's the story of how I met Carolyn's father."

"It's—riveting. Thank you for telling me. See you around." He took a stride.

"Did your parents meet in an interesting way?"

The unexpected query caused him to flash on his creation myth—a bunch of rancid drifters groping in a Parisian hostel. "Yeah. Probably."

She followed him to the monk's tower. The angel in the fresco hovered over them, as plump as a cloud. Ware had vanished! "I wish I could know everything about a person, just looking at them," Adela said. "I wish I could lay my hands on you and know whether or not you were a good person. Still, I'm getting a good feeling about you all the same."

"I'm not even trying," Mac said.

"Nobody's perfect."

To Mac's relief, Carolyn appeared at the top of the staircase then, in a girlish red tam-o'-shanter and a car coat with brass buttons. He smiled at the sight of her.

"You're going out?" said Adela.

"Mother, Molly's been a little sick. She'll be fine, but she's in bed now."

"So am I to—"

"Just go check on her," Carolyn said.

"Now?"

"She's in bed," said Carolyn. "You can figure out what to do."

The creaking floorboards announced Charles Ware's return. Mac looked overhead and beheld his descent. With his guests out the door, he had made a fast change into his bathrobe. He was up to his ankles in argyle socks, with holes at the toes carved by long, jagged nails.

"Dad, what are you doing?"

"Having my nightly bowl of vanilla ice milk, Daughter."

She said, "Now that you're here, my friend Mac has something to show you."

"No rest for the wicked."

Mac reached for his pocket. "Sorry to spring this on you. Just some old envelopes; I'm trying to find out if—"

In semispastic fashion, Mac delivered the bundle to Ware.

"His mother designed that film festival poster, the one on my wall, from the summer *Tangier* premiered in Paris," Carolyn explained.

Her father produced his reading glasses and placed them atop the bridge of his nose. He peered closely at the flat pockets of paper. He looked up at Mac over the tops of his frames, then flipped through the envelopes quickly, like a bureaucrat. Mac could hear the breath coming out his nose.

"So what can I do for you?" Ware said officiously.

"Do you remember her?" Mac asked.

"No recollection," swore Ware.

"Dad, it's your writing."

Ware looked witheringly at his daughter. "Have you given any thought to the quantity of correspondence I receive each week? And to how much of this stationery I've gone through over the years?"

"I'm—" Mac stopped. He pulled another item from his pocket— a picture of his mother on the stoop of a three-family house, Mac a toddler on her lap.

Ware took the picture, glanced at it, but dismissed it right away. "No, I'm sorry, nothing at all."

He couldn't say why, but he wondered if the man was lying. "Maybe she wrote you fan letters. She liked your book."

"Ah. Many people did."

"Dad, what about the poster?"

"You're barking up the wrong tree, both of you."

"But would you have written a young woman so many times, Charles, and not remember?" Adela joined in.

"I feel as if I'm being grilled on the witness stand," said Ware.

Carolyn said, "Maybe just lightly poached."

"I hardly remember *anything*. Gossip has it I'm half senile." He continued toward his frozen dessert. "Mr. West, good luck with your quest," he said, and trudged on. Mac was chewing on his lower lip so hard it began to bleed.

"Oh, that's too bad!" said Carolyn.

"Yeah."

"He does get a lot of mail."

"I'll bet."

"I wonder why she kept the envelopes but not the letters," said Carolyn as she pulled open the door. The evening mist rushed in on them.

"This will be the first time she's gone out in years!" Adela said, but Mac noticed that she was not saying it to anyone in particular. She was back in the mode of practicing for her show.

*A*nd yet surely, Mac thought, despite his suspicious nature, despite the swift and decisive letdown, nothing could be nicer than to spend the rest of his life plowing the fields between Redwood City and San Francisco, cultivating a relationship with Carolyn Ware. He had an escapade to impress her with now, steering across the Bay Bridge, with the lights of the city over his shoulder, the salt water sweeping beneath him full of whitecaps and frigates and freighters from everywhere in the world, with a girl in a car coat beside him, and not another thought of that troublemaking mother of his in his mind. *This girl* was there, *she* was sucking a cinnamon drop, probably so that when he kissed her, soon, *she'd* be proud of the way she tasted. Her green eyes were gleaming in the evening light. And he smiled a crooked smile.

"Now that you've talked to him, are you through with me?"

"Not quite," said Mac. "Is it possible he was holding something back?"

"Very possible. He holds everything back. What else was in that box of your mother's stuff?"

"Weird junk. Incense burners, things I made in school, some of her paintings and drawings, some snapshots—nothing else that looked too promising."

"Don't be discouraged, okay? You'll put together your colossus somehow."

"You think?"

"I do. I know it. So where are we going?"

"First stop, Oakland. I hope you like Indian food."

"I love it, and I hardly ever have it."

"There's a place I discovered a while back. It has great naan, especially the onion kind." He couldn't let go of her hand.

"And I never go to Oakland, so that'll be something new."

His crummy car seemed like an asset all at once, a crazy but lovable old pal, and something to remember him by. Fran had borrowed it recently, when her car was in the shop, and left some brochures from her doctor's office on the dashboard; Carolyn happened to pick one up entitled "Detecting Rectal Cancer." "That's not mine," Mac said. Cans and bottles rattled in the back as they bumped over the joints in the bridge. "My cousin's always looking for new things to worry about."

"God! How old is she?"

"Just a few years older than me—your age—but she's always been middle-aged at heart."

"What's she do?"

"Works in a library in Redwood City," Mac said. "Know those rings cups make on things? She's obsessed with those. She sees a beverage come into a room, and it's like, *Okay, we've got a situation here, find the coasters!* And splinters, too. She's *really* worried about splinters. It's like she got a splinter once and it was the worst thing that ever happened to her."

"You know what's really terrible are *glass* splinters," Carolyn said. "If they're small, you can't see them, so you're digging around with the tweezers, and it's excruciating."

"Hmm," Mac said, trying to superimpose Fran's head onto Carolyn's body. Didn't quite fit. "Actually, my cousin's very nice. I feel guilty casting aspersions on her character. How do you think it works—is being nice learned, or just a matter of brain chemistry?"

"Sometimes when people wake in the middle of the night," Carolyn said, "they seem different, like they haven't remembered they're nice yet."

He wondered, badly, who she had seen in the middle of the

night. More to the point, what *she* was like. "Sounds like we're say-ing no one has a genuine self," he concluded.

"But I think you can trick a consciousness into *forgetting* things it's learned. Such as old gripes and feuds."

"Like, could an Armenian wake up forgetting he hates the Turks?" said Mac.

"Uh, do they still hate each other?"

"Good question." He was mad that he didn't know.

"And what about love?" she went on. "Do you wake up loving someone, or do you have to remind yourself?"

"I think you have to keep a cue card in your pocket, and look at it every five minutes," said Mac. "Hey, it's my favorite song!"

He turned up the radio.

I found a picture of you, oh oh oh oh
What hijacked my world that night . . .

He felt wildly happy all of a sudden, ready to take on anything.

But first, he had to find the restaurant. It was on an obscure cor-ner in Oakland, and he'd stumbled upon it almost by accident. From the outside it didn't look like much. It was actually part restau-rant, part movie rental store, part candy shop. Inside, on a TV mounted near the ceiling, music videos played: feckless maidens threw themselves at blubbery rajas, opening their mouths to emit erotic shrieks and yodels. Mac and Carolyn sat in a booth and or-dered big, burning bowls of lamb vindaloo, salving their mouths with mango lassis and beer. "Of course," Mac said, hoping to dazzle her, "I've traveled extensively on the subcontinent."

"You have? Wow."

"After I was in France, that was my big splurge. Got a few thou-sand dollars when my grandmother croaked. Ever been?"

"No."

Making it to India was probably his life's chief accomplishment to date. Even though he'd stayed in the country only three weeks, he had gotten a lot of mileage out of telling people about it. "It's very intense—the colors, smells, faces, coming at you. If you're alone and depressed, it can snap you out of it or push you over the edge. Or maybe a little of both. One day I was in some village, about to walk by this guy with no legs who was sitting on the hot sidewalk, and I was just thinking what a sad, horrible, reduced life he had, and how he was human misery incarnate—and right when I passed him I slipped on a banana peel, like in a cartoon, and I was lying on my back, and my eyes were, like, two inches from his stumps, all black and shriveled, and suddenly he reached over with these sinewy, powerful arms and lifted me up. Next thing I knew he was holding me like a baby."

"A legless man picked up your whole body, without toppling over?"

"Yeah, no kidding. He kind of rocked, but then he regained his equilibrium."

"What did you do then?"

"Tried to keep my cool, because I didn't want him to feel like I was repulsed by him, and then I actually started to relax. It's not too hard to regress to infancy, you know. And later, I realized the whole thing was a metaphor for Western hubris. I mean, here I'd been pitying him, when on some spiritual plane, that guy had it over me, ten to one."

"Maybe so, but I like you more," she said.

"Gee, thanks."

He felt like pounding his chest like a male silverback anyway.

"By the way, how was New York?"

"Not as kaleidoscopic as India."

After dinner he took a detour for the second part of his surprise, down the highway farther south, until they were beyond Hayward, in Union City, where he turned off the freeway and drove through an industrial zone, then went bumping over a dirt field behind a warehouse, agricultural fields rolling on to the salt flats and the bay. It was warmer there, and when he parked, an earthy smell drifted through the windows.

"What's out there?" she asked.

"You'll see. I think you'll like it."

"We're getting out?"

"Here."

He felt around in the backseat. The bourbon was nestled in a soft, rumpled bag, and he undid the top and offered it. She shuddered upon swallowing some. The crickets were raucous all around.

"Oh, and I brought these, too," he said, reaching into the glove compartment. He had two U-No bars.

"These are hard to find, and I love them."

"Whenever I see them, I buy a bunch," he said.

"They're very delicate."

"Yeah, they melt easily."

In the crickety, warm air they peeled the foil wrappers, and the aroma of chocolate supplanted the loaminess outside. For a while they simply nibbled on their bars.

Then she was fiddling with her seat belt, plucking it with her thumbs. "Can I admit something about myself?"

"Sure."

"I think I'm sort of a square," she said.

"You seem to lead a quiet life these days," he granted her. "Baking cakes for your sister, stuff like that."

"I think I can trace it back to a crucial moment with a dental hygienist," she said, crumpling her wrapper.

"Go ahead, throw it anywhere."

She looked into the backseat, then tossed it. "My hygienist was cleaning my teeth one day, nothing out of the ordinary, but I was gagging and ripping the tools out of my mouth. I needed to have total control. I was insisting that she let me hold the little spit vacuum myself. After a while, she set down her pick and took off her mask and said it was clear there was some reason I was so protective of my mouth, and that maybe I should get real and think about it."

"You don't seem all that guarded with your mouth," he reminisced cheerfully.

"See, you're helping me." She flipped the mirror down from the visor and examined her teeth in the dark.

"So—did you come up with anything?"

"The whole thing bothered me. I started to feel like maybe I had a horrible secret. Like a repressed memory. And then—" She hiccuped. "Then one day, I got to talking about it with my mother. Know what she told me?"

"What?"

"She said that when I was about four, I actually tried to swallow one of my dad's pens. It was lodged in my throat, and I went to the hospital."

"Oh, man," said Mac, nearly gagging. "So the hygienist became your guru."

"Yes. I bought her a parakeet to thank her."

"That's thanks?" Parakeets shrieked.

"It was a very pretty blue one, with a yellow head."

"Did she dig it?"

"Yes, she loves that bird."

"Swallowing your father's pen," Mac mused. "Sounds pretty Freudian."

"It does. It was because it was so important to him. See, I always wanted his attention, and I never saw him without it. The psychiatrist I used to see called it triangulating."

Mac batted at a mosquito. "You were triangulating with a pen?"

She laughed. "Among other things."

"And you gave up having fun and started baking cakes?"

"I still have fun."

Mac nodded. The past was deeper than the sea.

"You know what Molly said about you?" she asked.

"What?"

"That you seem really nice."

"Nice?" Mac said. "That's it?"

"I thought it was a nice thing to say."

"Have you ever considered moving out of your family's house?" Mac said.

"Someday I will."

"Like I'm one to talk. Maybe we should move in together," he said, which paved the way for a deathly silence.

"It's hard to live with people," she mused. "Let's say I want to do something eccentric, like find a farm and raise animals. Let's say miniature donkeys. That's not every person's dream."

"No. But you could *maybe* find one person on earth who wants that."

"What if it's not the person I want?"

"By the way, how miniature?"

"Like this," she said, indicating something so small Mac didn't believe it.

"A donkey the size of a squirrel?"

She started to laugh. "You know what my biggest problem is? It's that I always start to feel bad when I start to feel good. So don't make me feel too good," she said, kissing him.

Trapped behind the wheel of his car, Carolyn in the seat beside him, the insects rasping, flashing green lights passing in the sky on wings coming in to land by his bay, his San Francisco, here he was— *Don't ruin it*—here was his new girlfriend, his. And they kissed, and then some more, and then some more, until he'd actually crawled over her and pushed her door open and they'd rolled out beside a row of flowers, bunting each other into the soil, hands and elbows in it, pollen flicking from the flower stalks onto their cheeks and chins.

"Can I?" he asked clumsily, because he actually had a Trojan thin-skin in his pocket.

"I want to, but not yet."

"Please, my darling."

"I know it would be nice. Oh, I love your face!"

She kissed him. He wanted to go inside her more than anything.

"Are you enjoying the earth?" he asked.

"Earth is our mother planet."

"Oh my God, this is very difficult."

"Then look at the moon."

He had his back to it.

"Come on, get up, look," she said.

And with that he said, "All right. Moon." Approximately fifteen thousand more chances to see it, but fine. He sat up all in a mess. The lunar face was hanging over the eastern hills. Up on his knees, to his feet. He held her hands.

They were at the edge of an industrial-size field of gladiolus flowers. The special thing was, now they were all in bloom. Union City was the glad capital of the U.S.A. While driving around on one of his solitary expeditions, his first few months in the Bay Area, Mac had stumbled on this, acre upon acre of the luminous bayonets.

"You said you liked flowers."

But her reaction wasn't what he'd imagined. "They're blooming," she said. "Once they bloom, it's too late; it means no one will sell them."

"It's okay, they're not for selling cut. They're for the bulbs."

She tripped down the furrows, spangling in the silvery light. He followed her, found her snapping off the stalks one after another. She had an entire armload of them. The moon cast a colorless sheen on everything. To his surprise, her cheeks were glistening with tears.

"They're wasted," she was saying. "No one will ever see how pretty they are. No one will ever *know*!"

He said, "But hey, Carolyn, we will. We know." He stopped her and brought his mouth to hers, and took her down on the ground right then, and tried to chase away this strange feeling she was having, and this time, she made no call to wait for what he wanted from her, and the flowers slipped all around them like a soft bed; nothing from then on was only in his head.

PART TWO

W.G.

Let me come back again to the
waking state. I have no choice but
to consider it a phenomenon
of interference.

—André Breton,
Manifestos of Surrealism

5

He dreamt Carolyn was giving birth to huge, ripe strawberries and feeding them to him straight from between her legs. He woke with a pang so hard it surprised him.

He had a hard-won respect for the place he'd come to live. California. Mighty from bottom to top. He even liked the shape of it on a map, a burly sailor's forearm, holding back the sea. Before he bought his car, he used to ride Tim's bike up to the summit of the coast mountains and shoot them north and south. He honored the existence of Ansel Adams but wished the camera-crazy pest had never been born so that he, with his trusty lens, could have been the one plastering the world with calendars. The redwoods, those old, hairy trunks, had once shaded all the peninsula, "Redwood City" becoming a scathing oxymoron as the township had devoured its namesake.

Thanks in part to the camp Molly had gone off to, Mac was getting to know San Francisco, and Carolyn, faster than he could have hoped. They walked arm in arm around North Beach, slurping espressos in crowded cafés, and they attended the opera, because her family had excess tickets, which otherwise went to waste. The music Mac heard in that hall came instead from the braiding of their arms and legs and the reception in her long hair, pressed against his, picking up all the electricity in the room. There were cavernous, popcorn-crunching movie matinees, and at night, martinis in clubs. Mac wasn't much of a dancer, but Carolyn could throw back some drinks and let loose on the floor. What a difference with her sister off at camp! Late at night they'd sneak into her room, and she seemed to want him more—and again and again—than he could even keep up with. But he managed somehow. They made love seven times one night.

The hitch to hanging around with Carolyn Ware, he discovered, was that she threw money everywhere—she threw it like crumbs for the birds. For cabs, for tips, at musicians; for every movie, in every restaurant they went to. And while he'd fumble with his tired wallet stuffed with a few twenties and ones, she'd open her change purse and pull out her magic platinum card.

Mostly, however, she was extravagant for herself or her sister, to whom she was sending care packages at Four Winds. Once they were out on one of the piers, and she stopped at the table of a jewelry vendor, picked up three bracelets at a hundred dollars apiece. Two for Molly and one for herself. Just like that. Nothing to it. Five minutes later and she was putting a twenty-dollar bill into the hat of one of those human statues, and that cracked his silver spray-painted concentration fast. She picked up bouquets whenever they came upon them—roses and daisies and stock and lilies and irises and dahlias—she wanted to own every flower. When she saw a new hat in a window, a pretty scarf around a mannequin's neck, an old-fashioned brooch, or an antique valentine, she bought it for herself or for Molly. When she saw a book or a CD she liked the cover of, it was quickly snapped up. If she saw something apropos of penguins, which Molly collected, she didn't hesitate—she'd purchase the item on the spot. Her purse was an eternal spring, which he gradually came to look at with cautious eyes.

"Ever dream of having a job?" Mac asked her once.

"I have one. I do freelance editing for the press."

"For Galeotto House?"

"They're reorganizing right now; there's a new office opening in New York. I'm taking the summer off."

"Oh." He couldn't believe she'd never mentioned this. The privilege of having such a job was nothing to her.

But how about this for a reprieve—during the time Molly was away at camp, Charles took off for New York and Adela went with Isabel Porter to Carmel to visit a friend. Mac and Carolyn had the house to themselves!

Those days, his only sense of time came from an old clock on her shelf. Could use the fog as an excuse and never go out. They weren't much hungry, though he yanked some lemons from the tree by the path. Slipped a segment into Carolyn's mouth—she laughed and spat it out. In the evening the light dimmed the windowpanes while the low drone of foghorns reached them from the bridge. At night the room was damp and dark, and they fogged up the windows near her low-lying, unfoldable bed.

By day he roamed the place. Examined every painting and artifact downstairs, found it a qualified museum. She gave him a tour of the parents' wing—big rooms, separate lives. Adela's was like a starlet's bedroom in a black-and-white movie—vanity table, tortoise-shell combs lined up in a row. Charles's room looked east to the downtown skyline but was drafty and cold. A number of suits were strewn on his bed, as if it mattered so much what he wore.

Dressing, Carolyn tore through her closet and tried on different clothes. One blouse, one sweater, one skirt down. Nothing for that day right. Another wrap of silk and linen down. She had her clothes made by a tailor on Greenwich Street. An Italian woman who knew just what to do. She had simply to drop off a few yards of fabric there. So the fabric cut to cover Carolyn thundered down from her hangers to the floor. And Mac lay back in her bed, watching. When she found what she wanted, she undressed and ironed it on an old board by her closet door.

Sometimes he thought about the episode in her closet and all the abandoned things beyond the little door, but not for long. And sometimes he thought about Charles Ware and his curt response to the envelopes addressed to his mother, but not for *too* long. Paranoia was the weed of the psyche, too easy to sprout and grow.

And he thought, during that time, about Carolyn's apparent isolation—her age, her lack of friends, her house, protecting her from the world. He wanted to ask but felt it was delicate and not to be talked about. Even with him, there came a time when she wanted to be alone, and she'd drift away inside herself, cease to be company. He would pull back, too. He knew the signals without watching for them, for he'd been alert to his mother's every day of his life as a child.

Very little dampened his happiness now. Especially not the fog, which could begin anywhere just north of Redwood City. He felt as if he was on the inside. Of something big. He was making promises to himself by the drove. One was to re-create himself into someone she would always want to know. He interviewed at an art supply store, a gym, and the bar association (mail room). He cleaned his nails more. He got a haircut and was doing chin-ups and push-ups, and had even taken up fooling around with Tim's power tools, with which he was hoping to turn a pile of scraps into a rustic drafting table she could make use of, for becoming indispensable to Carolyn was at the forefront of his plans.

"Want to hear something endearing about the great general and two-term president Ulysses S. Grant?" Mac asked her one day.

"Definitely."

"Okay. He was born Hiram Ulysses Grant, but it embarrassed him so much, the thought of having his initials put on his trunk, that when he went off to West Point, he changed his name."

"HUG?"

"He was a very modest guy. He always had to change his clothes in his tent."

"I can understand this very well—my middle name torments me."

"What's your middle name?"

"I've never told anyone before."

"How bad can it be?"

"You won't laugh?"

"I can't promise."

"Gee, this is a milestone—it's Ophelia."

"Carolyn Ophelia Ware—COW?"

"Moo."

He couldn't help laughing. "We'll never speak of it again. What's your father's middle name?"

"Owen."

Mac said, "Same initials—that's mean. He knew!"

She said, "That's him. He knows but does it anyway."

"What's Molly's middle name?"

"Doesn't have one," she said briskly.

Her parents would be back tomorrow. On that last foggy evening, Carolyn stood by the window; he saw her silhouette in the fading light, like a ghost. To snap out of it, he did a push-up on the floor. He did some more. Carolyn? She joined him. A bowl of scented leaves and crumbled flowers by the bed made everything smell nice. And her statuettes, rabbits and geese and bears, gathered around the window to watch. When they made love, they forgot the hard floor.

The dream he had that night was harrowing: he was standing on a dark riverbank, searching the water for his mother, who could not swim. All at once she came on the current, bobbing and rotating like a log. Quite dead. He called out to her anyway, and woke rigid as a board in Carolyn's bed.

It was typically chilly one afternoon when they met on dating terms again—the clouds and the waves were high. They had decided to take a walk on the beach where Golden Gate Park ends; she wore a red beret pulled over her ears against the wind. Around her neck were her pearls. Always. On the sidewalk by the sand, they came upon an improvised arcade of old mechanical games of the type that used to reside under the Cliff House. In a spangling circus jacket and with a gray, unshaven face, the proprietor had run a power cord from his van, parked nearby, to the machines and now sat slumped on the seawall. Mac would have walked on by, but Carolyn lingered and said, "Oh, Mac, look at this one! It's from Dante."

Mac gazed with her into a bell jar. It contained a turn-of-the-century Love Meter and had a slate jutting out from beneath it on which the hands of a man and woman were to be placed. Inside the glass was a delicate garden filled with cracked trees and fruits. A porcelain woman and a waxen man sat on the tawdry grass, clasping a book together, all the while gazing into each other's eyes. In gold script on the glass were the names Paolo and Francesca.

"Have you read the *Inferno*?" she asked.

Another lesson in medieval literature. "No," said Mac, feeling paltry and uneducated. "Should I?"

"Yes. This is from Canto V. Dante's going through Hell with his teacher, Virgil, and they're in the second circle—they meet Paolo and Francesca, who tell them about how they fell in love and are doomed to be together forever just for *wanting* to be together.

Which is kind of a sad metaphor for marriage, if you think about it. See that book?" When he nodded, she said, "The book was their excuse. They pretended to read it when all they really wanted was to jump each other. Know what it's called?"

"No again," said Mac.

"It's a Galeotto!" she said, transported to some special delight in her knowledge. "The name appears in Canto V. It's a very famous name. In French it's Gallehault, which has come to have its own meaning—kind of a panderer, or go-between. See, Paolo and Francesca are reading about Lancelot, who fell in love with Arthur's Guinevere. Gallehault, or Galahad, was the character who encouraged Guinevere to fall in love unsuitably, so the book is 'a Gallehault indeed,' because it also works for Paolo and Francesca as a go-between."

He couldn't help noticing how much of a charge these specifics carried for her. "Neato."

"The whole thing goes on," she said. "It was such an interior part of Boccaccio's connection to Dante, he gave the *Decameron* an alternate name, which was 'Prince Galeotto.' "

"Is that so."

She said, "Do you like hearing about this, or is it boring?"

He flashed on something he'd spotted in the crawl space inside the closet that time—hadn't he seen an old, leathery copy of the Divine Comedy ripped to shreds? "How come you're so into this stuff? I thought Galeotto was your father's obsession, not yours."

She appeared to blush. "No— I mean, he was a charismatic person. It's true, I had a girlish fascination with him—for all the same reasons my father did."

"A go-between," Mac said quietly. "Kind of like swallowing the pen all over again."

"You're right. It was about connecting with my father, in the long run."

He was about to say "What else did you swallow?" but stopped himself. Just as she was ready to put the quarters into the machine, he said, "Let's not do it."

"How come?"

"It might say something cryptic that'll freak us out and change the course of everything natural and decent between us." He was joking, but he meant it. The machine suddenly seemed evil. Panderers, go-betweens, go to hell.

"It's just a game," she said.

"Not to me."

The day's silvery light flickered on the breaks in the waves. "Okay, never mind." The coins rang as she dropped them back in her bag, and she pulled on his arm, bringing him up the hill like an irritable child to the next amusement. There they found the home of the camera obscura. Before he knew it she had paid their admission to a hunched man in the glass booth and entered, past a display of holograms, which followed their progress into the dark chamber. Mac couldn't tell how many other people were inside waiting for the demonstration, but he smelled warm breath and felt the heat of bodies. From one corner of the room, girls giggled and hissed like little geysers; from his right came some heavy wheezing. Across the darkness, a small child asked his mother if "it" was happening yet. Inexplicably, the child began to cry. And then the voice of the barker crackled from a public-address system on high.

Mac listened at first. The camera obscura is a glass lens so deep and so cut that it pulls in—as a periscope does with mirrors—the panorama above the viewer. But unlike a periscope, this thing actually projects the image onto a convex screen. A living movie. They were told to imagine the wonder of this in the fifteenth century, when da Vinci designed it. This was the kind of presentation he normally enjoyed. But he felt the sudden, intense presence of uncharted depths in Carolyn's life, and uneasiness got hold of him. And she had dropped his arm. All at once, the light poured into the dish at the center of the room, where they could see a wide arc of sea and gulls and waves foaming and crashing, and small human figures climbing the rocks.

He looked through the faces hovering over the dish—no sign of her. Had she left him? He lost his breath, began moving along the wall toward the promise of an exit sign. The room was packed; he thought the ticket taker had malevolently jammed them in beyond the limit. "Excuse me, pardon me." He accidentally pushed someone. "I need to get out." But then Carolyn was beside him, wrapping her arms around his shoulders.

"Too stuffy?" she whispered.

Like some kind of underworld queen, she managed to glide easily through the throng, pulling him toward the bright image of the world up above. All the puny people, doing puny little things. They looked like game board pieces—frail, and ready to be knocked on their sides. He held on to Carolyn, held on tight. He didn't want to spend his life guarding himself and mistrusting people; he'd wasted enough time already at that. "Amazing," he agreed. "Absolutely . . . amazing." The lens now swept the exact spot where they had been standing only minutes before, and he was sure he saw, as if by tape delay, the two of them, holding hands.

"Look, isn't that us?" he said.

Us? The precious word fell from his lips like ripe fruit, sure to rot on the spot where it fell.

6

"Hey, babe, I'm real now." Mac was washing his car out in the front yard in Redwood City, a universally approved activity. Neighbors he'd never seen before were coming out and waving at him. *You're not the malevolent pervert we were thinking. Welcome to the neighborhood!* "I got a job."

"Where?"

"Piano moving. Three or four days a week to start. I saw the ad this morning, called up, owner said, 'Come down right now,' hired me on the spot." "Strong and experienced" said the ad, and he could claim both by fudging a little.

"We're having so much fun," she whined.

"I know it, but I'm low on cash."

"Molly's only at camp one more week—"

"I won't be working all that much. I'll still be fully available."

"No you won't, you won't at all."

She was mad? He sprayed the car one last time, whipped the hose into the grass. "Carolyn. Did you know that I used to play the piano?"

No answer. "Carolyn?"

"I used to play the lute," she replied.

"That's what angels play in paintings. When did you stop?"

"I was just about to say, 'When I stopped being an angel in a painting,' but I don't know what I mean. When did *you* stop?"

"A while back," Mac said. "I've always wondered how my mother paid for my lessons. We were so poor she couldn't even buy me shoes."

"No! A good pair of shoes is number one on every parent's list."

"Not mine. She tried to *make* shoes! She took apart my old tight ones, used them as a pattern, cut out this weird piece of leather she scrounged somewhere. They were gross, man. Looked like goblin shoes."

"Sounds kind of arty."

Mac sat on the front steps, his wet feet covered with blades of grass. "When you're a kid, who wants to be arty? I'd take them off and wear my socks around."

"Your mother had a job, didn't she?"

"Just shitty ones with minimum wage and tips."

"Making shoes sounds more like a choice, if you ask me. She was an artist. Maybe into the Pre-Raphaelites and William Morris?"

He was impressed. "Actually, yes. You called my bluff." He didn't want their poverty to repulse her, so he backed down. "We'll go out tomorrow evening and negotiate a labor agreement, okay?"

"You won't miss the party, will you?"

The party at Galeotto House. Her parents would be there. He shuddered. "I'll make it."

"I was planning— I really want you—to be there," she said.

"You okay?" Her voice sounded strange.

"Fine!" she said before they hung up.

It felt bad not to have a job, but bad to have one, too. That night he drank a beer but slept restlessly. In the night he thought more about his encounter with Carolyn's father, and in the night, when thoughts were thick and woolly, he felt annoyed by the man's bad memory and chagrined by Carolyn's perverse fascinations and aroused by her anyway. He wondered why Ware had reacted so mechanically to the envelopes. He wondered how he could go further, looking into it.

At dawn, a blue jay raiding a nest woke him before the alarm. Mac pushed himself from bed, roughed the bristles on his cheeks, ground his palms into his eye sockets, sniffled, coughed, pulled on his jeans, a T-shirt, a sweatshirt, favored socks, and his old work boots—then stumbled out to his car and drove down Whipple to 101, north to San Mateo, and found the warehouse east of the freeway.

A small office had been jerry-built into the front of the warehouse. It contained two desks, several steel file cabinets, two cracked orange plastic chairs, and a ratty love seat stained by beverages of various hues. The owner of this business was named Dwight Dixon, and he was already at it, staring into his computer and wearing headphones attached to the telephone.

"Got your own gloves?"

"No," said Mac.

"Take these today, but get your own." He yanked open a drawer in his desk, pulled out an oily-looking pair, and tossed them to Mac. "You're starting with the Africans, and they're ready to go."

"Okay. Thanks again," said Mac.

The Tanzanian was named Ahmed and the Kenyan was named Henry and they waved Mac straight into the cab of the shiny red Iveco, which was sending the smell of diesel into the warehouse, deposited the clipboard with the day's bills of lading onto his lap, drove right from the lot to a café, ordered three lattes to go, then set off in the bobtail for the city. They had one conveyance stop on the way, as well as an upright player piano in the back, coming out of storage to an old man who had relocated and was ready to crank it up in his new place.

The cab shook like a rock tumbler, and while his bosses enjoyed their hot drinks, Mac knocked a few shots straight up his nostrils, spilling the rest across his knees.

"Piano moving," explained Ahmed, "is a complex task which demands a great deal of strength and dedication to the art of transporting the value, beauty, and essence of the instrument. Each is crafted differently, therefore is one of a kind and cannot truly be replaced if damaged. We must always attempt to understand the customer's attachment to their piano and treat the precious cargo as if it were our own."

Mac was impressed by the man's delicacy of expression. "I'll do my best."

"And yet it's nearly every time a melodrama, no matter how well it goes," Ahmed added.

"So how'd you guys get into this?" Mac asked.

Ahmed said, "In a previous life, I was an engineer. I wanted more control."

Henry said, "Now he has more control. I was a high-ranking party official. I wanted less." The men laughed.

"What about yourself?" asked Ahmed. "How did you come to the trade?"

Mac said, "I think I just want to see some pianos again."

The men nodded with appreciation.

They chugged into the city and stopped for their first job, at a music school on 19th Avenue. A straightforward task. Here they harnessed a baby grand to a rolling thing in one building and moved it to the next, through wide doors and ascending only three steps. Over and done in less than an hour. For this they were treated to pastries and orange slices, and the man who had contracted them gave them each a tip of ten dollars. "The day begins well," said Ahmed.

Back in the cab, taking off again, they lurched through the lights and traffic of the city, and Mac soon realized they were approaching Carolyn's neighborhood. In fact, they came to a stop just a few blocks from her house, on Presidio, and parked beside a pollarded row of sycamores. Kind of French-looking, which always made him flinch.

Ahmed said, "The chock blocks are located behind the seat."

Mac found the wood chunks—a couple of short four-by-eights—and wedged them under the front tires. The San Francisco hill rose steep and fast, and Mac gazed up at the building before them, a sheer white face of windows like a jury of judging eyes. Henry rolled down the ramp and called him into the back while Ahmed buzzed the door. Mac helped loosen the various straps restraining the player piano on the side wall. It was wrapped like a pupa in quilted blue blankets.

"I cannot stress enough," Henry said, indicating the shiny, well-maintained equipment on the floor of the truck, "that this is a very dangerous procedure, and not to be undertaken lightly. An inexperienced young man was crushed last year."

"You now have my full attention," said Mac, thinking of the release form he'd signed when taking the job. Yes, he might be maimed or even killed. Fifteen dollars an hour.

"At heart, I am still a government official," said Henry.

Ahmed emerged from the building, his face a picture of stress. "We have a problem. Dixon has made another bad telephone estimate. We need to consider a hoist."

"I would rather stick a bull for his blood," said Henry.

"Come see for yourself," said Ahmed.

The piano sat at the base of the ramp; Mac was assigned the job of guarding it. Guard it he did.

A chilling wind blew from the damp foliage of the Presidio. Mac shivered, lit a cigarette.

He had never seen a player piano, so he peeled back the moving blanket, loosened a strap, bunched up the cloth, and managed to lift the lid off the keyboard. The keys were real ivory, with the swirling grain of wood. He rolled up his sleeves and dared to touch them. Then tried a few scales, considering the noise. Not too offensive. The soundboard was muffled in the blanket but still audible, so he wiggled his hands, cracked his knuckles, and continued. Shortly another idea occurred that he couldn't resist, and he wrested his phone from his pocket.

To his delight, Carolyn Ware answered right away, her voice friendly again.

"Hey," he said. "You free?"

"Pretty free. Why?"

"Can you walk over to the corner of Presidio and Washington? Like, right this second?"

"Right this second? Okay."

"Terrific." He liked how she didn't ask why.

Like trace elements of lead poisoning, the music was still inside him, wasn't it? A few easy pieces sprang to mind, such as Chopin's Ballad No. 2 and Mozart's Fantasy in D Minor, but he was warming up for something even better. A friendly girl on a passing white Vespa paused to listen to his serenade. This emboldened him. Shortly a car pulled up alongside, a mother and a boy; she lowered her window and smiled. He must have sounded decent after all. It wasn't hard to think back to his mother's pleasure in his keyboard artistry, to the sight of her face during recitals. She used to say, *"This is all that matters to me, all that ties me to the ground."* So he'd hammered away. She'd had a passion for old, crackling recordings of Scriabin and Rachmaninoff, and even an original 1955 vinyl of Glenn Gould, and they'd listen to them on a flimsy stereo.

Now, as soon as he saw Carolyn's forehead rounding the building on the corner, he attacked his all-time personal favorite, Beethoven's "Waldstein."

How puffed up with pride he'd been, learning this difficult piece back when Beethoven was his hero. The curse of Ludwig's hearing problem, his grumpy persona, his mean, thrashing old dad, all aroused in him the greatest sympathy. The heartfelt Heiligenstadt Testament—*"Oh you men who think or say that I am malevolent, stubborn, or misanthropic, how greatly do you wrong me. You do not know the secret cause which makes me seem that way to you. . . ."*

Carolyn paused by the side of the truck. He stumbled and made some mistakes, but his hands were good little servants. He was standing on the street, but he was back in the recital room, his mother following his every move, clinging to every note as if it would save her, as if he, young MacGregor, was her only chance, her life raft—

Then, as used to happen in the old days when he felt too responsible for his mother's happiness, he saw that hands were little more than contracting tendons and bones operated by some chain reaction issuing forth from a bunch of spongy matter in his skull, and he seized up.

Carolyn's mouth was in a strange and perfect o, with zipperlike creases on the sides.

"Show's over." He closed the lid and quickly pulled the moving blanket over it, tightened the strap.

She was wearing a pink sweater set with a striped skirt that reminded him of the upholstery on lawn chairs, her bare calves scattered with goose bumps. "Who *are* you?" she said.

"It's good to have a few tricks up the old sleeve."

"Did your mother play?"

"Ha! Not a musical bone in her body."

"Your father must have been musical."

"No, Carolyn, I worked really hard at it. Not everything's inherited."

Her arms were folded over her chest. "We had a beautiful piano until Dad gave it to Bill, who destroyed it. Would you like to come for lunch?"

"God, Carolyn, I'm working, remember?"

She said, "Couldn't you hire someone else? It might clear up—we could have a picnic in the park."

He started to laugh. "Hire someone else?" He hoped she was kidding.

Just then Henry and Ahmed came hustling from the building. "All right. We're taking it up the stairs. Dwight has called an extra, and let us pray he shows. We will double-pad the end and stand it on the refrigerator dolly," said Ahmed. "We will take the stairs one at a time."

"By the way, Ahmed and Henry, this is my friend Carolyn."

They gave her a nod.

"I'll call you when we're done," said Mac.

He leaned in to kiss her, but she pulled away from his reach, and he watched her stroll away. Then he focused on the sidewalk and the front steps of the building instead. Inside the lobby, the carpet was spongy and bunched up under the weight around the wheels of the dolly. They shoved and wheeled the thing inch by inch until they reached the bottom of the flight.

"Five floors," said Ahmed. "Ten flights. Very narrow up top. Are we ready, boys?"

And then there came a grueling, protracted struggle the likes of which he'd never known. A player piano generally did not want to go up stairs.

"These are the heaviest of all pianos," said Henry. He and Mac had the bottom; Ahmed was trapped in the stairwell above, pulling and guiding with the strap.

After forty-five minutes, they had ascended five steps. Each heave-ho depleted Mac's entire body of any stored force. He was gasping for breath.

"One, two, three, *heave*," called Ahmed, and with his shoulders and body Mac pushed, so that the piano could climb yet another step. Then he collapsed, coughing and sweating.

"Call Dwight," said Henry. "Find out when the hippie will arrive. He is a hippie but also a super mover."

"Good," gasped Mac.

"This is an outrage," said Ahmed.

"You're getting paid by the hour, right?" said Mac.

"No. We are subcontractors. We must go by the estimate. Dwight's estimate for this job was two hundred and fifty dollars. We will end up paying you and the hippie almost all of that."

"Can't the estimate be adjusted?"

"By only ten percent. We don't wish to gouge people, anyway."

"They're gouging you!"

"This is an old man who wants to see his player piano again," said Ahmed.

"He didn't have to move to the fifth floor," griped Henry.

Mac's muscles were stiffening. He started to blame the whole day on Margaret Sullivan, his childhood piano teacher. They heaved and pushed and struggled for another hour before "the hippie" arrived. He had a shaved head and a lightning bolt tattooed on his neck. Perhaps Ahmed and Henry didn't know what a hippie was.

"Jesse," he said, shaking Mac's hand.

With the help of his brawn, they were able to raise the piano up a few steps without stopping. But after Jesse's initial burst of energy, he too fell to the floor, winded. Mac's trapezius muscles and biceps were bunched into fists.

"This next flight is narrow, and the steps are not as deep," in-structed Ahmed from above. "This will be far worse than what we have endured already. And be careful of the walls. I will guide you. Don't push until I say."

Mac looked at his watch. Four o'clock!

"I'm going to miss my date, too," said Jesse. "With destiny! As long as I get over the bridge, I'm all right. I've been saving a little money and sleeping in this graveyard over in San Rafael, where it's pretty friendly and no one busts you, or at least they don't notice."

"Boys, *heave!*"

They hefted, fell spent.

"On your feet! One, two, three, *heave!*"

They hefted again. The stairwell smelled like sweat.

"Damn it!" yelled Ahmed. "The wall! Go down!"

They brought it back down.

"Damn this, the wall is freshly painted. Move to your right as you lift."

They tried.

"Don't break the wall!" Ahmed cried. "Do not go so fast!"

"Fast?" said Mac, gasping. Pain shot through his shoulders and around his ribs. His knees were shaking. "I gotta make a call."

He took his phone a flight down and tried Carolyn, and when she didn't answer, he left a dignified apology. He'd never failed her before and wondered what the consequences would be.

Back in the stairwell, Jesse was saying, "Locals always dig me. I was visiting this town in Nebraska, this farmer brings me home for a meal, and next thing you know I'm living with them, got a room upstairs, the Frau is cooking for me, I'm working on the farm for my keep. Well, the Frau is a beautiful woman, and the farmer's never home, and when he is he's burned out and muddy, and the Frau and I start fooling around. I know it sounds unethical, but she was lonely. This boring you yet?"

"Not me," said Mac.

"Anyway, one night I wake up in my cot, all in a sweat. And there's these icons on the wall, and they're all staring at me, and I'm shaking, and this voice in my head yells at me, 'She's going to have a baby—you have a son! A *son!*' And then suddenly there's this knock on the door, and the farmer comes into my room, and his hands are covered with blood! I jump out of my cot. I'm screaming, man. And he says, 'Hurry, hurry, the cow is having her calf. I need you to help.' I rush down into the yard, and we go into the barn, and I help him pull the calf. *Stillborn.* I left the next morning."

"One, two, three, *heave!*"

"Unnn," said Mac. The piano had become like a horrible problem that loomed and obscured all the pleasures of life. Kind of like looking for his mother.

"Turn more to the left now," said Henry. "The railing is going to break."

"One, two, three, *heave!*"

"I'm going to heave if he keeps saying 'heave,'" Jesse said.

Time blurred as they continued their ascent. Each discharge of energy drained Mac to the core. Surely, this was the hardest work he had ever been enlisted for. *Oh, for man, the tether was never far!* He thought of the sweating slaves dragging stones to the pyramids. He thought of the endless legions erecting the great walls. All for the next meal. The next roll in the hay. His brain settled into a dull pattern of oblivion, heave-ho; in his delirium, Mac began to register the timbre of a new voice.

"Damned old thing's a bugaboo, isn't it!"

"All's well that ends well," Ahmed said.

"Well, I've waited a long time for this beauty," the old man said.

"We've done our best. It was very difficult."

Now on a flat surface at the top, the piano moved down the hall and into the man's apartment. Mac caught a glimpse of a clock. It was midnight. *Damn!*

"I'm not complaining. I have all the scrolls—you boys want to hear some Gershwin?" The man's eyes were sparkling with excitement. "Haven't seen this old thing since my wife passed away."

Among the dusty scrolls in the basket he had: "The Steamboat," the "Whoa Nellie," and the "Temptation Rag," "The Georgia Giggle," and "Waiting for the *Robert E. Lee.*" After they removed the blanket and straps and positioned the piano against the wall, he inserted a cartridge and plugged in the cord, and the ivory keys began to move in ghostly fashion. It was "The Entertainer," which Mac used to play, on demand, for his mother.

He slept until noon, which meant that he missed the next job in the morning. He grabbed his phone and called in.

"Good morning, Dwight," he croaked out. "Sorry I'm late—"

"Where are you?"

"I just woke up. I didn't get home until after midnight."

"Neither did the Africans, and they were here bright and early."

"Did you know what that job was going to be like?"

"Shouldn't have taken that long, and shouldn't have required another man."

"What the hell? I hear you underestimated the bid and they weren't going to make any money at all on it."

"Well, neither are you, because you're out, and don't come anywhere near here again, or some of my guys'll beat the crap out of you."

"What? I killed myself yesterday, and so did Henry and Ahmed!"

"Go kill yourself today," said Dwight Dixon, and the line went dead.

Huh? He fell back on his sweaty pillow. Why did people take such pleasure in firing him? Was it a reaction against expectation? On first impression, maybe he came off firm and solid, a go-getter, a guy with a future, so when he faltered or strayed, they lashed out at him harder than if he'd just looked mediocre to begin with.

Carolyn would be happy. After a while he got up and smoked a cigarette and kicked a pile of clothes and papers away from his feet. He'd clean up the place today. He was supposed to go to a party tonight with the Wares for Galeotto House. But after he stumbled into the kitchen and made a strong cup of coffee, his first order of the day was calling information in Boston and asking for a certain Margaret Sullivan. The Margaret Sullivans of Boston were multitudinous, but only three lived in Watertown, where she'd lived. He took down every number. And called the first one on his list.

"Hello?" said a woman.

"Is this Margaret Sullivan the piano teacher?" he asked, already suspecting it wasn't.

"This is Margaret Sullivan the oboe teacher," the woman replied. "You're thinking of Margaret Sullivan on Mount Auburn. I can give you her number. This happens all the time, don't worry."

Mount Auburn, that was it. "Thanks," said Mac. She gave him one of the numbers he already had.

Taking a deep breath, he phoned again.

"Yes?" came the familiar voice. He wondered why he hadn't tried her sooner.

"Miss Sullivan?" he said. "It's MacGregor West, your former student. Remember me?"

"Yes, of course I remember you," she said. "How nice to hear from you!"

"How are you?"

"Very well, thank you. How old are you now?"

"Twenty-two," said Mac.

"Oh, how time flies."

"Are you still teaching?"

"Yes, I have twelve students right now—mostly beginners." That voice! It reminded him of the bowl of dusty butter mints sitting on the top of her spinet.

"And, you're still in the same house?"

"Yes, I am," she said. "Where are you living now?"

"California," he said. "Bay Area. Listen, the reason I'm calling—" He stopped a moment. Perhaps she'd never heard the news. "You knew my mother passed away, didn't you?"

"No, I didn't. I'm sorry to hear it."

"Yeah. Tragic. Because—" He stopped again. There was no need for a *because*. "Anyway, I've been trying to figure out some stuff, and one thing I don't quite get is how my mom afforded my lessons with you. Did you two have any special arrangements about that?"

"You were my only student who didn't have his own piano," she said, and boy, did he know it—all those afternoons he'd duck into the meeting hall at the nearby church.

"Somehow I thought maybe you gave her a cut rate. We barely had enough money to eat."

"Now that I think of it, I believe she had to wait on some money coming in before she could pay me, and sometimes it was late, so she'd send along a note instead."

"You mean her paycheck? Or something else."

"None of my business. She didn't share the particulars of your home life with me, though I wondered. Seemed to me you were quite on your own. At first I thought you'd been sent to me by St. Jude's! You'd show up here like Huckleberry Finn."

"Oh!" The voice was pulling him back. "My mother had some strange ideas about clothes. So you didn't get to know her very well?"

"No. She was— No."

This woman was a gold mine. "Go ahead, say what's on your mind. I'm piecing things together. Say whatever you want."

"All right, I suppose I do remember a few things. One day— oh, this must've been a few years after you'd come to me—a man showed up to give you a ride, and you'd never seen him before and you wouldn't go with him. You came back in while I was giving my next lesson, sat there and refused. I went and spoke with the man— kind of a ratty type; he was to take you to a dental school for a free cleaning. Well, I decided to call your mother and make sure. Do you remember this at all?"

"Not exactly," said Mac, staring at a spot on the floor in dismay.

"I couldn't reach her. But when I looked out the window again, the man had taken off. Hours later her car pulled up, and you ran out there with your music bag, and I witnessed her reading you the riot act! Yelling her head off at you. I thought it was my fault, and felt very sorry about it. But how could I have sent you off with a strange man you were afraid of?"

Sometimes friends of his mothers were asked to pick him up, and if he knew them, it was okay, but if he didn't, he hated the smell of their breath and the crummy small talk in the front seat. Leading who knew where. One time, one of them tried to hold his hand.

"I'm not wanting to stir up bad feelings," she said. "She was young and unreliable. I could never pin her down to enter you in competitions. I'd send home notices, the day would arrive, and you wouldn't show up! It was a pity. You were definitely handicapped by your situation, but you did very well, all things considered."

He didn't remember it that well; this was slightly shocking.

"Nice talking to you, MacGregor. Have your own piano now?"

"No, but I moved one up some stairs last night, and it got all scratched and gouged up." For reasons he couldn't fathom, he had some satisfaction in telling her this.

"Oh, heavens!" she said.

He had to laugh, thinking of her thin wrists and pilled cardigans, and the velveteen davenport where the next child always sat.

7

The thirtieth anniversary of Galeotto House was an occasion of note, a cause for celebration, for the press had started whimsically but had thrived, and thrived well. In those years, the colophon of the shrunken head—once considered rebellious and sly—had become as ordinary and often seen as penguins and roosters and Russian wolfhounds and all the rest. This gala had been long in the making. Elaborate invitations—Mac did not receive one but saw the small bound books—announced a soiree not to be missed. Contributors, employees from over the years, writers, editors, and friends would come from all over to make merry and pay their respects. But Galeotto?

"He's not coming?" Mac asked Carolyn.

"He's a shut-in these days," she replied. "He has some health problems."

The party was being held in the editorial offices of Galeotto House, on the fourth floor of an old building on Jackson Street in North Beach, where the press had been for years. Mac met Carolyn in the lobby. She had arrived early, with her parents. She was wearing a soft blue sweater with a wide neck that showed her collarbones. "You look beautiful," he told her, and she said, "I'm glad you wore that coat." It was his "Edwardian" coat. His shoulders were bunched and sore, and his back felt as if he'd carried cargo over a mountain like a yak, but pride would not allow him to complain about any of that. He told her he had quit the piano job, and this made her feel he had done it for her, which was probably not a great idea, but what the hell, and they kissed, and he escorted her up in the elevator, watching a certain mild anxiety play on her features before the lift came to a halt and they arrived in the big, bright, jostling room packed with guests. No sooner had they entered than they were presented with glasses of wine by a white-shirted waiter with a tray. The clip on his pocket said MR. BACCHUS.

"Thanks, Mr. Bacchus," said Mac.

"Mr. Bacchus is the business. I'm Craig."

Mac downed the wine like a shot. He spotted Adela Ware, across the room, in a nubby brown dress like a naked field in winter, alone on the fringes of the frontier—for what else was a room full of strangers? And then he saw Daniel LaPlante and Tom Rothman together, LaPlante craning his long white neck to scope the crowd.

All at once, Carolyn said, "Freddie!"

A sandy-haired guy with Dumbo ears was giving Carolyn a kiss on the cheek. He looked like a shortstop, or somebody's freckly, nondescript brother. Carolyn said, "Mac, this is—"

The guy held out his hand. "Freddie Heald. Say, I've heard all about you." He kept shaking Mac's hand. "You've really swept her off her feet."

"Well, you know, you give it your best shot."

"I know, believe me, I know!" he cried.

Was this the ex? Carolyn wasn't listening. She was already being preyed upon by LaPlante and Rothman. "I don't think your father realizes we're here," Mac heard Rothman say. "We'll try to talk to him later, when he's less besieged."

"Don't worry," LaPlante said. "Tom's nervous. His novel is outside, waiting in the cold."

"Bring it in," Freddie spoke up. "This is the local shelter for lost novels. I'll show you where to put it. There's a room here stacked to the ceiling with them."

LaPlante looked at Freddie with contempt. "He is expecting Tom's novel."

The din in the room made speaking a small effort, and the five of them settled into mute observation. To be mute alongside them apparently made LaPlante and Rothman feel more at ease, for LaPlante's neck ceased to crane, and both he and Rothman embarked on a steady, nervous rocking on their heels. The walls of this room, Mac began to see, were covered with nude women. Dozens of them. A gallery of lips and eyes and breasts and thighs.

"Who's into this stuff?" he asked Carolyn.

"That's right, it's your first time here. I don't notice anymore."

Just then, the sound in the room shifted. They turned their heads to the source. From the center of a dense core, Ware's figure was trying to emerge. As he moved through the surge, he was stopped and grabbed, and Mac saw his ears being filled with secrets and salutations. Ware laughed in the way Mac envied—a laugh that made one man his own audience.

LaPlante and Rothman braced for the encounter; the effort was not required. Ware hardly appeared to notice them. He wrapped an arm around Freddie. "I want you all to know that this is our best. A fantastic editor; a superb businessman—" Freddie beamed. "Freddie has been a wizard with the books for years," Ware went on. "With the reorganization, he has a new title."

"It's embarrassing." Freddie grinned.

"Freddie Heald," Ware boomed. *"Controller!"*

"Isn't that too much?" Freddie laughed. "People will ask me what I do. And I'll have to answer, 'I'm the Controller.' Spoken like the true megalomaniac I am." Ware nodded, and Freddie said, "I'm honored, sir, really."

Ware shook his hand again and said, *"We're* honored." Then he nodded to the rest of them and continued to make his way through the crowd.

LaPlante was heard to say, "It's okay, Tom, it'll happen later."

Craig of Mr. Bacchus made his rounds with goblets of wine, and Carolyn was caught up talking with two older women; Mac was ready to discard his fast-emptied glass. He saw that their friends, LaPlante and Rothman, had found a target. They were now engaged in flaying Freddie Heald—Mac gathered by his expression that he didn't mind.

"What about Ware's books?" LaPlante was asking.

"Oh, he's our bread and butter!" Freddie said cheerfully.

"All of his work?" Rothman asked. "I mean, are they still a go— *Parnassus? The Chicago Papers? Satyrs of San Francisco?*"

"Sure," Freddie said. "They're workhorses. I'll tell you something, though. This will impress you. You know what our top title is? Year after year?"

Rothman nodded reverentially. *"Tangier,"* he murmured.

Freddie smiled. "You know it."

As though in a stupor, Mac had been listening to this gossip and staring as he did at Adela Ware, who swayed in her own lost repose against one of the niches containing a breast-clutching maiden. She seemed ineffectual and broken in this crowd. How did she feel about her husband's relationship to Galeotto? Had her husband ever mustered for her what he had for his friend?

Mac battered through the room and found a place beside her.

"Hello, Mrs. Ware."

Her eyes came up to his. They were as deep and wet as pools. "Hello, Mac."

Carolyn was wrong, absolutely wrong, that she did not resemble her mother. Something about the way Adela and she held their heads when they talked was very alike. Carolyn and Adela Ware weren't balancing pots on their heads in finishing school; they were letting them slide off and crash to the ground. Mrs. Ware seemed glad to see him.

"Enjoying yourself?" he said.

"I can't, I just can't." Her voice was deep and sticky. "I can't stand it here."

"Don't like parties much myself," Mac said.

"Why can't they do something fun? These parties have no plan."

"You mean like a game or something? Speeches?"

"I mean, people who enjoy each other," she said.

"Well, I guess we can try to enjoy each other," he offered.

"Yes, we can. What I really need is some help. I have a small job for the right person."

"What is it?"

"Transcribing my tapes. I've made quite a few of them. Probably nonsense, but I'd like to sort them out and see what's there."

"Yeah, sure," Mac said, thinking such work could be strangely fascinating, and also unaccustomed to being offered anything.

Then she remarked, "It's hard on me, being here, because, you see, Chloe was once my closest friend."

"Galeotto's wife?"

"Yes. I feel her presence here, still; but in a sad and sorry way. This room is filled with things she bought and collected."

"His wife collected this stuff?"

"Oh, yes. She was out at auctions at dawn; and she searched all the galleries and studios. I went along with her, I ought to know!

How much nervous energy does it take to get a woman up at dawn to look for things she despises? She hated these things, all of them."

Mac followed the explicit canvases around the room. "Then why—"

"For *him*. Everything always for him."

"Mrs. Ware," he said, "did you tell your friend she wasn't doing a very sensible thing?"

"We didn't know anything! We were ninnies. We were fools. We were afraid."

"And now?"

It seemed she wouldn't answer—she drank her glass to the bottom, and the wet eyes gazed away. But then she spoke. "Chloe is long dead. No, Mac—now I'm very brave. Too late!"

And at that moment Carolyn joined them, braided an arm through his. "I want to show Mac around, Mother. Have you seen Lorraine Ogier? She's here tonight. Go over and say hello."

"I loathe Lorraine Ogier," Adela said. "Where is she?"

And with that Carolyn interrupted what was the most unnerving conversation he'd had so far with anyone in her family, pulled him away, down a corridor and around a corner and through a door, and together they entered another party, a secret party. "This is Bill's office," Carolyn told him. The room was long and low and had paneled walls, cool and dark like a fox warren. Charles Ware sat at the head of a long table cluttered with empty bottles. Three people flanked him. Ware was pouring burgundy into glasses reaching for him like the frantic, stretched mouths of baby birds.

He was laughing. "Who are these people? Why are you telling me this?"

"I know, I know!" said a woman, who had bright red hair cut like a mixing bowl. "Whenever I see you, I end up telling you the most god-awful things!"

The man next to her said, "Say 'book' and it's written."

"Are you kidding me?" Ware laughed. "No one actually writes; I have to say 'dollars and cents' before anything gets written!"

Then he seemed to notice them. "Welcome to the inner sanctum. Away from the madding crowd!"

"It's *your* madding crowd, Charles," the woman said.

"Come, come." He beckoned with the wine bottle, and they extended their glasses into his reach.

Carolyn said, "This is Marci Croudther and this is John Medders and this is Samuel Groom. Everyone, this is MacGregor West."

Marci Croudther's dress crawled with paisleys, John Medders was the man at her side. Samuel Groom had the puffy face of an old lush.

"Carolyn Ware, are you flaunting this man?" said Marci Croudther. "He's very good-looking. And tall."

"No, you're just short," said Medders. "I ought to know, I'm shorter. That's why you never flaunt me."

"You're going to scare him away," Ware said. "This is the rude room."

"I'll control myself," Medders said blandly, and lifted his glass. "Here's to Galeotto House. Long may it prosper. Long may it never take a risk on my work."

"Is Carolyn in love?" Marci interrupted. "I think she is. I think she must be!"

"That's what they're saying," said Groom. "Everywhere she goes."

"Tell us about him!" Marci said.

"Oh, come on," Carolyn said. "You're going to make him sick!"

"Here," Ware said dryly, passing on an empty glass. "Be sick in here and keep it for your scrapbook."

"Did you hear that?" Marci said. "You said 'crap book' instead of 'scrapbook.'"

"For those who believe doomed attachments are all that count," Ware said.

"My God, anything helps!" Marci exclaimed. "How's Bill, anyway?" When no one answered, she said, "Carolyn?" She began to laugh. "You've given up riding his leg and calling him Daddy, haven't you? I don't think MacGregor would understand."

"Marci, you're a disgusting drunk," Carolyn said, though Mac felt his hair stand on end.

"I was never sure how healthy that was, Charles," continued Marci.

"Vigilance," Medders roared. "Keep her on the straight and narrow!"

Ware interrupted. "Tell us, Carolyn, is it true, have you found happiness the old-fashioned way?"

Everyone turned and awaited her reply. Mac wanted to hear more about Galeotto. Just then Craig stuck his head into the warren. "It's time for the toasts, sir," he said. "They're demanding you!"

"Do they always get what they want?" Ware shouted. "Yes, I guess they do!"

"Nice show," Marci said.

"Bravo," said Medders.

Ware was first out. Passing Mac on his way, he gave him a thump on the back that could have passed for a blow. Mac stumbled.

Marci came next and said, "I think you showed up just in time." And Carolyn said, "Get a move on, Marci." After the room had cleared, she went to the table and filled her glass again, knocked it back in a few seconds flat.

"Why did we come in here?" he asked.

"I'm sorry, I kind of hate these people. They're blithering idiots! Don't pay any attention to them. Dad used to have a literary group that would meet—every week or two—at our place. I'd sit in. Marci and John were part of it. I'd practice all week in my room, memorizing verse or prose to recite, like it was my big break or something. For people like them! How stupid of me."

"Show me," Mac said.

"You mean, what I did?"

"Yes."

"Well," she said. "Something like this." Without further ado, she kicked off a shoe the way her mother had in the kitchen a while back and climbed up on the table. She paced a moment, getting into character. She punted an empty bottle off the table, and it flew against the wall. The neck broke off.

"Come, you spirits, unsex me here!
And fill me from the crown to the toe top full
Of direst cruelty! Make thick my blood,
Stop up the access and passage to remorse!
Come to my woman's breasts,
And take my milk for gall, you murdering ministers!
Come, thick night,
And pall thee in the dunnest smoke of hell!
That my keen knife see not the wound it makes,
Nor heaven peep through the blanket of the dark,
To cry 'Hold, hold!'"

"Jesus," Mac said, chilled by her murderous intensity. There was something damned authentic about it. He had the immediate thought they should make love on the table. When she climbed down, his hand slid into her sweater.

"You're quite an actress."

"A great one," she said, collapsing into a chair.

"So what's the story with you and Bill Galeotto—was that a joke?"

"Of course it's a joke." She dropped her head on the slab. "A huge joke, a joke the size of the world. Fill me another glass."

He didn't mind having more himself. The wall was littered with memorabilia, with clippings and photos and awards, theater tickets, and other tokens of obscure significance, tacked one over the other into a collage the size of a highway billboard. Studying one upper corner of it, he noticed a fading print of Carolyn leaning against a tree, her lovely brown hair as long as a yardstick. The photograph was wedged between postcards and book reviews and profiles of William Galeotto, who in his younger years stood well over six feet, head high like an emperor's. He had favored tailored Italian shirts with large cuff links, and had worn an enormous ring. His black hair had been thick and unruly.

"Let's go listen to the toasts," Mac said.

"Blah blah blah," she said from the table.

"Herrre's to thirrrrrty years of fine publishing!" he slurred, lifting his glass. A portrait of Galeotto and the woman Mac assumed was Chloe caught his eye. Chloe had been, not surprisingly, a beauty. A black-and-white shot of Galeotto and Charles Ware, buddy-buddy, in front of what might have been a Moroccan marketplace. Chickens in the road. Galeotto and Ware balancing on a train trestle who knew where. A valuable dust jacket from the first edition of *Tangier*.

Mac drew up closer to examine a shot of a younger Ware family standing on a beach somewhere. Isabel Porter was there. Charles Ware posed in the foreground. Carolyn, her breasts larger then than now, wore a one-piece bathing suit with a skirt attached to it, barely disguising a tubbiness he'd never ascribed to her. Adela showed up a knockout figure in a bikini. Isabel held up the dark-haired baby girl.

Then his eyes drifted to another dated print. He inched closer to it, made a noise like a laugh, then felt as if the room had detonated in his face.

"Mom" was what he said.

8

Brittle and cracked, the black-and-white surface flaking in tiny shards, the snapshot was mostly of Galeotto, who sat posed before a stone wall. But Mac's mother was right behind him. She had her arms around his neck, and Mac could see her hair and her eyes peeking out over the top of Galeotto's head. He could see the striped scarf around her neck, and that her hair poured over the scarf and was caught in it, bulging out in bumps. Just like her. She always looked a little bedraggled.

"Carolyn, come here," he said. He gently peeled the photo off the corkboard. The tape on its back side was yellow and powdery. Nothing written on it.

"Why'd you take it down?" she said, lifting it off his hand.

"See this woman?" His heart was galloping against his ribs.

"Barely."

"There's a woman here." Just plain unbelievable, what he was about to say. "It's my mom."

Carolyn did something then that he would turn over in his mind for a long time to come. As if on guard lest she say the wrong thing, she cleared her throat and tucked her hair behind her ears. "Are you sure about that?" she said with some pique.

"*Am I sure?*"

"You can't see much."

"I see enough. There's no doubt."

"Well, great, but she may not have *known* him."

He looked into Carolyn's face. "Are you kidding?" He took the print back from her.

"It's just, they went through a lot of people. They were basically on a mission to meet everyone on earth."

"*They?*"

"Dad and Bill."

"They weren't Siamese fucking twins, were they? What's the matter, are you jealous she knew Galeotto?"

"Hardly."

"You said you had a crush on him."

"I told you it was a vehicle—to my father's earthly love."

"Okay, whatever. I still want to talk to him, see what he says."

"Don't get your hopes up," she said.

"Why the hell not?"

"He doesn't see *anybody.*"

True, Galeotto wasn't attending his own party. "Not even your father?"

"Not anymore."

"Why not?"

"He just doesn't, okay?"

"What's wrong with the guy, anyway?"

"He's sick, I told you! Diabetic."

Mac was annoyed that she was annoyed. "That's it? Lots of people are diabetic."

"He's diabetic and eccentric!" she said.

Mac felt that lots of people were probably diabetic and eccentric yet still saw visitors. "Okay. What should I do? Call him?"

"Definitely not."

"Write him a letter?"

"Do what you must." Carolyn shrugged.

"You'll give me the address?"

"Write it, I'll mail it for you."

"Wait a minute, how come you're the gatekeeper?"

"It's unlisted. God, it's not my fault!"

"It's your fault you're not giving me special privileges."

And he didn't want to dredge up his hateful sob story for nothing, but maybe this was the time. Maybe she didn't understand, never had.

"Carolyn. Come on. This is a huge moment for me." He began to itch, and sweat had sprouted all over his head, and his hair felt damp, and his throat felt dry, and his eyes were raw and stinging. He caught his voice before it cracked. "You know, I found the file they had on her case, which took weeks because, believe me, the red tape in France is thicker than blood. From the State Department I had the name of the lieutenant who handled it, so I track him down, he agrees to meet with me in this little room, he looks in the skimpy file, and you know what the jerk says? Something about how this was the fate of *une telle personne*—someone like her. That's the response I got looking for my dead mother. I'm going to take this, if it's okay," he said.

"What were you hoping for?" Carolyn asked, glaring at him.

"Just—whatever they had. I mean, he'd interviewed a few people on a party boat," Mac said quietly. "The last people who saw her alive were a bunch of coldhearted strangers."

She was polite enough not to speak for a moment, but then she said: "I'm sure this is another dead end, and I'm only trying to warn you, that's all. Now I'm going home."

"Now? No dinner, nothing, that's it?"

"I drank too much," she said, adding, "and it's out of your way. You can just go from here to the freeway."

"What, are you mad about this?"

"No, I'm just— I want to go home."

He fought to contain his irritation as they emerged from the back office and returned to the thick of the party. Moving through the crowd, they ran into Daniel LaPlante. He was holding a flat parcel. He grabbed Carolyn's arm and implored her with haunted eyes.

"Tom has been completely ignored; I'm sure it doesn't mean anything. Could you give this to your father?"

Carolyn laughed and said, "Oh, don't give it to me! The *Controller* is over there."

"The Controller?"

"That's right, he's out there!"

Mac looked around the room for Adela Ware; he thought she might shed light on the photo. But he didn't see her.

"I'm going to throw up soon," Carolyn said.

"Here, sit down."

"I don't want to sit down. Sitting down's the last thing I want to do."

"Okay, Carolyn, then I'll say good night." And with that, he summoned the elevator, and she moved out of his sight. If she'd been callous about his discovery, perhaps it was because she didn't respect his search for someone who had abandoned him. Perhaps Carolyn was his greatest advocate yet! But after he joined the scrimmage on the streets, tasted the garlic and sewage in the air, something big was stirring in him, some long-forgotten sadness, and all at once a poignant image crossed his mind. He saw a pretty girl up on a table telling some jaded, mauling group a story for her life. It was in Boston: the girl wasn't Carolyn but his mother. How easily they seemed to come together in his mind right then; he quickly put the strange, sad comparison to rest.

~

When he arrived home that evening, his cousin was in the kitchen, eating a bowl of cereal in her russet-colored pumps.

"You just get home?"

"Staff development meeting."

"I'm glad you're up. Look." He produced the little miracle.

"It's—" She peered closer. "That's Cecille back there, isn't it?"

"Yep."

She looked at Mac with wonder. "Because she always wore her hair straight! Mom used curlers. Where'd you find it?"

He told her the whole story. And she said, "It's amazing. I have to call Mom and tell her."

"The guy may not remember her," he said, echoing Carolyn. He was trying to keep his hopes in check. "I'm going to write him and see what he says."

"So she was getting letters from Charles Ware, but here she's with his best friend? What do you make of it?"

"Enough to keep me busy."

"How's everything going with Carolyn?"

"She's moody and irrational—I can't get enough of her."

"Melinda Kobayashi likes you."

"As a boy or as a man?"

"Isn't the boy within the man?"

Mac pictured a collapsing telescope, each segment of life disappearing inside the next. "The squalling infant's in the man, that's for certain."

Fran was gazing down at the picture again. "Look how young she is here. It must be right after she ran away from home, wouldn't you say?"

"Yeah. And I'm thinking this is France. Look at the wall."

"Mac, this guy looks an awful lot like you."

"No—you think so?"

"Look at the brow, look at the jawline."

"This guy's really well known, he's Ware's best friend, he's practically—"

"Dad?" Fran said, gritting her teeth.

"We're getting carried away," Mac said. "Forget it."

He retreated to his room and looked at the picture and then in the mirror at himself. Then he pawed again through the box of the things Helen had given him. He pulled from it this time a little drawing he'd done as a kid—when and where he could not remember. A vast willow weeping over a stunted house. In his own thick and childish scrawl at the bottom, it said: I LOVE TO LIVE IN SUMMER!

To love to live in summer—that was the height. To be a child again in summer, to truly *be alive* in summer. That was something to love, all right.

Once, at a yard sale in Medford, Mac's mother had spotted a tribal kilim spread out upon the grass, on sale, with various items also up for grabs scattered haphazardly on its surface. So excited was she by the carpet, into which had been woven the crude figures of birds and goats, and best, bearing a price tag of twenty-five dollars, that she single-handedly pulled the thing out from under everything on top of it, a feat of uniquely focused strength.

"Hey, lady, whatcha doing?" the man conducting the sale yelled.

"Buying your rug," she said.

"You just made a disaster area outta my yard sale!" the man barked. Cups, saucers, and kitchenware, and all kinds of junk rolled into the ragged summer weeds. She gathered up the rug and hauled it to their car like a leopard with its kill, then carried on about it for weeks. She checked a book out of the library to identify it. She proudly showed it to everyone who came by. She washed it on the hot sidewalk with nothing more than a hose, had seen rugs cleaned this way on her travels, before he was born.

Mac carried on the tradition. No matter where he was, he always noticed the rugs. He felt attracted to carpets in a way he wasn't attracted to any other material thing. Along with the box, Helen had recently given him the rug, and he was considering bestowing it on Carolyn. It was rolled, standing on end in the corner of his room, sagging and leaning like a midget at a bus stop.

He'd been poring all night through the pages of *Tangier*, examining the parts about William Galeotto. The midget image was a steal from the final chapter. Jim Bright (Ware) puts Nick Macchiato (Galeotto) on a bus in Chicago bound for California and has a skewed chat with a suicidal little person as the great Macchiato disappears into the sunset. Macchiato is hope, possibility, life; the dwarf, quite unfairly, stands for the reduced options Jim Bright feels he is left behind with.

William Galeotto as Nick Macchiato was the hero of this cult favorite; it could be said that Ware's character didn't exist without Galeotto's. It could be said that Jim Bright was a complete cipher. In criticism, it *was* said. (The opposite of what Ware had pronounced to the sycophants.) This new edition had a modish cover; and it included a lengthy introduction by P. G. Blackman on precisely that subject. The novel "glorifies the narcotic effect of one young man on another," Blackman said. But Blackman pointed out that Bright, too, had a charming façade, an allure. "Bright's education and moneyed refinement empower him; Bright alone enables the never obviously acquisitive Macchiato to indulge in his fabulous desires and dreams."

Mac was agitated, his mind crawling with ideas. He was departing from the track he was on with Carolyn and it would feel like a betrayal. It was like clubbing your guide in the catacombs and charging off into darkened, untraveled, possibly even dangerous passages alone. It was a betrayal because Carolyn had allowed him in in the first place.

But it was his mother, after all, who had given him his first copy of *Tangier*. Not stolen from a library, or picked up for a quarter at a yard sale. She'd bought him a brand-new copy, before he could even read.

"Someday, maybe, you'll understand."

Oh, the things he'd endured, on account of her! That time in the bathroom, how old was he? It still caused him discomfort, remembering it. He had needed to take a leak while she was in the shower, and he couldn't wait. *"Mom, can I come in?"* The tub had a thick old shower curtain, so mottled with mildew it looked like a street map. *"Yes, come in,"* came her siren call.

Her showers were as long as an afternoon, it seemed to him as a child. Waiting for her forever while the water gurgled in the drain. A deep-throated sound you could hear from every corner of their place.

After he was done, as he washed his hands, the water abruptly ceased. He said something about dinner, turned off the taps. Just then she pulled back that wet drape. And all of her was revealed, bejeweled with droplets and mist. He stood there trapped, no chance to look away from her breasts dripping with water, her hair wet and dangling around her shoulders like seaweed; yet it was her face that seemed most bared. She measured his gaze with her eyes.

Jesus! Needless to say, he cut out of that steamy bathroom as fast as he could move. What did he do to deserve it? Watched TV that night without facing her. Didn't even say good night.

Then his mind played with him, forced him from time to time to remember her that way, to focus on the smooth pink skin around her nipples or the sprinkling of hair at the top of her thighs. Felt like a sicko. Struggled to block it out, one half of his mind battling the other.

He could never be sure what in the world had possessed her to do that. A mother with bad motives is too frightening a monster. He would never let himself think it had been with purpose.

His best guess? She had a lot to live down, she did. Father blowing his brains out when she was a teenager, finding his corpse in the snow. Put that in your pipe and smoke it. Try that on for size. Anyone think that's an easy one to live with? She'd spaced out, that's what happened. Forgot she was even naked. Forgot he was a boy rinsing the soap off his hands.

He sat straight up in his bed. The light on the table felt warm on his arm, and the digits in the old clock radio flipped. What if—what if. His thoughts took him down a rabbit hole to another world, where he discovered the man who was his father. Would it make a difference, to know? Of course it would, how could it not! For in this place, this world, his father beamed and was exceedingly glad to know him. And in this place the father rejoiced at knowing his son and deemed him worthy by dint of his *quest*. For in taking up this quest and finding him, the son hath proved himself a man. And as a man come to him, worthy of his love. Failing, ill, in poor health, he had a place for such a son. In the ruins of his life he hath need of this son. And in the ruins his need brought him great joy, for the son was not withholding in *his* love. The father then gave his son what the son did not even know he wished for, which was providing the world with his name. *This is my son,* he went and told the world. *And you will accord my son what you have accorded me. . . .*

I must see him, Mac decided. *I must know who he is.*

9

"Seven children?" Mac said. "No way."

With Carolyn's telescope, he peered down at a slim and attractive woman with hips like a teenager's, striding up the street. And yet Carolyn claimed she had borne from her body seven children.

"I saw it happen," she said. "Every year, for seven years."

"How old is she?"

"About thirty-five, but doesn't she look great? That's sixty-three months of pregnancy."

"Hard to conceive. Or maybe should I say, believe."

Carolyn pointed the instrument the other way. "The mailman's coming."

Mac bent over and squinted through the tube. The sight of a postman pushing his canvas cart reminded him of the letter he'd given Carolyn the week before, for her to address and put in the mail to Mr. William Galeotto.

"Still no reply to my note," he mentioned. "You didn't hear anything, did you?"

"No."

"You mailed it, right?"

"Of course."

"I wonder if he got it. I guess it's still soon." His excitement about contacting Galeotto had already spiked—as soon as he sealed up the envelope with a copy of the picture inside, he had reexperienced the dismal, groveling nature of his position. And yet.

That day, he had come prepared to the city with ropes and an old blanket, which had puddled up together on his backseat. Arriving at the Ware house, he removed them from the car in an updraft of jute particles and dust. And sneezed. The blanket was one he had held on to fiercely until he had seen it one day for the miserable thing it was—thin as paper, gray with grime and age. And then he had fully rejected his attachment to the blanket and abused it, relishing how the fibers weakened and broke down. Taking it, he spread it over the roof of his car, and he and Carolyn, who had been kissing under the fresco because he thought no one else was home, now found themselves struggling out the door with the bulky fold-up bed all over again.

"Careful," Carolyn said. She was wearing a pair of gloves.

"Ouch," Mac said. The frame knocked him on the chin, and he protected his hands from the pinching, flapping legs.

"Are you sure he wants this?" she gasped from the other side.

"He's waiting for it right now."

"Maybe we should clean it up first." In the light of day, the bed smelled mustier than he had noticed the night he met Carolyn.

"Where are you taking my bed?" came a fractious voice.

There stood Molly, squinting at them from the steps. He had not seen her since she returned from camp.

"We're taking it to a boy Mac knows," Carolyn replied.

"What kind of boy?"

Mac said, "Around your age."

"What's he want it for?"

Mac felt protective of Filipo's modest wants. "This bed's a curiosity, a tragic hero, a marvel of function and form; now but a simple soldier from the closets of time, and—we'll see if he wants it or not."

"He won't."

"It's also the wave of the future," proclaimed Mac. "I've found all my furniture in the garbage."

"You have?" Carolyn said.

"Garbage reeks," said Molly.

"Molly, want to come along?" Carolyn said.

"Is the boy going to be there?"

"He's there."

"Does he know about me?"

"How could he know about you?" Carolyn said.

"If he doesn't now, he soon will," Mac said.

The girl ran inside.

By the side of the car, Mac and Carolyn hoisted the fold-up bed into the air and, with some exaggerated grunts and laughs, pushed it onto the blanket on the roof. The net of wires that supported the mattress scraped through the blanket. With the frame in place, Mac began to weave the rope around it, as if stitching it on for good. He secured it through the open rear windows, ran another end from the rear bumper up the back of the car and around various brackets of the bed, and then cinched it around the base of the antenna in front. Then he tried rocking it. Tight.

"It's good luck, this bed," Mac said. "Imagine, it's twenty years from now, and there are no political parties anymore, just a few huge corporations who battle it out. The ruling party is called Crockery Shed. When Crockery Shed is in power, everyone must buy all their household goods from their catalogs and stores. When inspectors go into rebel neighborhoods, they find homemade furniture and old hand-me-downs under counterfeit slipcovers, and the penalty is death. Miss, my question to you is, how do we avoid a future like this, and what would you do to prevent it?"

Carolyn began to speak like a Miss America contestant. "I would try to help educate the young on the dangers of rampant consumerism and corporate greed, despite the fact that I'm being sponsored by some of the biggest of them."

"All the best to you, young lady."

"Why, thank you."

"By the way, at the party—that Freddie guy—that guy was seriously your old boyfriend?"

"Sort of, yes."

"The Controller," Mac said with some malice.

"He's not that bad."

"Kind of dorky. How long were you an item?"

"Now you're the jealous one?"

"Not at all. I can't even imagine it."

"Want some?" She produced a U-No bar from her purse and broke it in two. "I guess he was more like an escort. He'd take me to concerts and movies."

Pods were falling into his hair from the tree. "He definitely didn't seem like your type."

"No such thing as a type." She added, "For some reason, Dad doesn't think you're my type."

"Damn. What did I do?"

"He liked Freddie, so go figure."

"He's mad I'm not related to the Wests on Green Street."

"I'm telling you so that if he acts unfriendly, you won't take it personally."

"Wait. Of all things, shouldn't I take this a little personally?"

"But I don't care if he likes you or not."

Molly emerged from the house just then—she had significantly upgraded her attire. She sported the latest faddish pants and a sky blue T-shirt studded with rhinestones that spelled out ICE QUEEN across her chest. For the benefit of Filipo? The girl climbed into the backseat on her knees and said, "This car is really dirty," as she kicked away some rubbish to place her legs, and off they went.

Rounding the corner, they could see Alcatraz rising from the bay. "My camp was like a prison," Molly said, "because it was on an island and we couldn't escape. But I did sailing, and jewelry making, and archery and drama—and I met a girl from South Dakota, and she said where she lives there's only twenty-two people in the whole town. Did you ever meet anyone from South Dakota?"

"They move undetected amongst us," said Mac. He was feeling a little gloomy.

"Next summer if I don't go to camp I want to go to Spain," she went on. "Have you heard about the human pyramids? They have human pyramids, and that's what I want to see. Oh, is it okay if I sleep over at Saki's tonight?"

"She's back?" said Carolyn.

"Yesterday. Oh, you know what? Brownie's being put to sleep."

"Poor Brownie!" Carolyn said. "A sweet old quarterhorse."

"I don't like Brownie anymore," Molly said. "She always stops and dangles her lips."

"You'd dangle your lips if you had a bit in your mouth," Mac said.

"Omar never dangles anything," declared Molly. "Omar is deluxe."

They cruised down Franklin, jagging across Market into the Mission, the fold-up bed holding to the top of the car.

Molly said, "Is this boy, the boy for the bed, is he very, very poor?"

Mac flinched. "He's doing all right."

"Is he so poor he doesn't have a bed?"

"He has other priorities."

"This might not be a good idea," Carolyn said, digging her

hands into his ripped upholstery. "What if he gets his finger caught in it, like you did?"

"Hey, when you were planning to give it to the Goodwill, you didn't seem to care who got their body parts severed."

"You're right; now, with a name and a face, I feel like it's not good enough. Why don't we buy him a bed?"

"No way."

"This is the boy you're teaching to read?"

"No!" Mac said. "He knows how to read. He's learning to read *literature.*"

"Where is he from?" Molly asked.

It was starting to feel as if he was taking two corseted Victorians to view a wild man in a loincloth. "El Salvador. His father was a lawyer, part of the antigovernment insurgency in their civil war. Made some enemies, evidently. After everything settled down, when Filipo was a baby, his father went to work one day and never came back," Mac said, his voice trailing off.

"Sounds like a movie," Carolyn said.

"Well, it's not a movie; it's real."

He double-parked in front of Filipo's building, and they all piled out. Molly stood brushing her hair in the reflection she discovered in the car window. She had transformed herself from a tomboy into a girl who looked a lot more sophisticated than twelve. It was alarming how irksome he found her. He unknotted the rope and threw it back in the car, and he and Carolyn lifted the bed down. Carolyn still wore her gloves. They marched the bed across the sidewalk, and Mac buzzed the cage. In moments the door opened at the top, and Filipo came charging down, arms and legs flying in every direction. He threw open the metal door but frowned when he saw Mac's companions.

"Filipo, this is my friend Carolyn—and her sister, Molly. I think you two are in the same grade."

Molly stepped forward. "What school are you at?"

"César Chávez," said Filipo.

"I'm at Sacred Heart," she said. "It's the best school in the city."

Filipo shrugged. She was taunting him, or was it flirtation? It seemed hideous.

"Okay, Filipo, here it is," Mac said. "Turn it into modern art if you want."

Filipo moved stiffly. He grabbed the folded bed, testing its wheels.

"How's it open?"

"Let's take it up, I'll show you," Mac said. The daily throng pushed past on the sidewalk.

But Filipo was clever and dexterous, and moments later the latches had been sprung and the bed opened. The buttons on the ticking rolled around in their indentations like old-fashioned doll eyes.

Molly was adept in her annoying ways. She kicked off her sandals, climbed onto the mattress, and began to bounce. "Come on," she said. Filipo watched her, rising and falling; Carolyn said, "Molly, get off!" But Molly had no intention of doing anything of the sort. "Try it," she said, luring Filipo into her game. To Mac's surprise, he removed his sneakers and joined her on the collapsible bed. With her long, flying hair and sparkling chest, she was stupefying him. And Mac imagined them falling down a long hole into an Eden where all things were equal, and where they would start over with nothing but their wits.

"Look at your socks!" she cried. There were holes in his heels, big as chestnuts. Mac felt a pang of embarrassment for the boy.

"Okay, come on, let's take it up," Mac said impatiently.

Despite his socks, Filipo bounced with daring, higher and higher. The bed rocked and groaned dangerously.

"Hey," Mac shouted. "You want to break it?"

Molly said, "It's for hunchbacks! We only used it when hunchbacks slept over!"

The bed creaked and gyrated; Mac and Carolyn took a few steps back.

"We're witnessing a strange ritual," said Mac.

"Yes. Bizarre."

"Baseball?" Molly was saying, her face flushed.

"Nope," Filipo gasped.

"Soccer?"

"Yes. And I'm good."

"Horses?"

"Nice animals."

"Have a blog?" she asked.

"No way!"

"What's your . . . address?"

"Yeah, I got one."

"I have a bunch . . . some for real letters, some for fake ones."

Mac said, "This is progressing rapidly."

"Very," said Carolyn.

"Mac. Remember that game, we say words we hate?" Filipo called.

"I'll . . . tell you one," huffed Molly. *"Girl."*

"Girl's not bad," said Filipo.

"How would you like to be called a *gurl*?"

"I don't . . . like *meal*," said Filipo, flying in the air.

"What's wrong with *meal*?" asked Mac.

"The next *meal*," said Filipo. "Sounds . . . foul."

"I'm not crazy about *colloidal*," Mac threw in.

Carolyn said, "I hate *people*. I hate the way it sounds, I even hate how it's spelled."

"Very revealing," Mac said.

"Where'd . . . you . . . watch . . . the fireworks?" Molly was heard to say.

"Up," panted Filipo. "The . . . hill."

"We had . . . fireworks at camp. You know . . . the ones . . . that look . . . like sperm?"

"No."

"They have . . . little tails, and they fly . . . around in the sky . . . all weird . . . and going crazy . . . like sperm."

"I've never seen that flying in the sky," said Filipo, slowing down.

Mac heard the girl laugh wickedly as Filipo sat down and reached for his shoes. "I don't need someone's old bed," he said.

"No, wait," Mac said. "I'll help you fix it up, it's going to be good."

Molly climbed down, too, and groped for her sandals with her prehensile toes.

"Nice going," Mac said.

"What's going on?" Carolyn was saying to her sister.

Mac and Filipo latched up the bed, then Filipo started forcing it down the sidewalk.

"What are you doing?" said Mac.

A big, fat receptacle for all things rotten and discarded sat in the alley between Filipo's building and the next one, and Filipo was making a beeline for it with the movable bed. "Hey, wait," called Mac.

"I don't want it," Filipo said. "Understand?"

"Yeah, but—" He watched as the boy pressed the bed against the side of the dumpster and, using it as a fulcrum, tipped the bed up and into it. It fell down onto a rancid carpet of plastic bags and other stinking mulch, casters facing the sky like the stiffened feet of an animal well into rigor mortis. *So long, ye bountiful fold-up bed.*

"Filipo." Mac looked back at Carolyn and her sister. "I know it's hard to believe, but in some sick and twisted way I think she was trying to make friends."

"No. Don't think so."

"Is it because you think she's pretty?"

"She's pretty, but she started talking about sperm."

"That's what did it?"

"I don't know her good enough to talk about sperm," Filipo said. "Even if I knew her, it's the last thing I'd want to talk about." He wiped his hands off on his shirt. "We gonna meet Saturday?"

"Yeah, we're going to meet."

"I need some new books."

Carolyn and Molly were sitting on the hood of his car, indolent as cats. As he and Filipo came back that way, Mac saw the two as through Filipo's eyes—haughty and advantaged and untouchable. He felt a hopeless pain in his stomach.

Opening the cage, Filipo slipped back inside. Then he turned to Mac. "Dump her, before she dumps you!" he whispered, hurrying up the steps.

"Egregious misunderstanding, Filipo! *Egregious!*"

Why did he always hit this red light? Mac hated this intersection. It had left-hand-turn lanes from every direction and took forever. And whenever he was detained there, he had the same thought. It was always his impulse to cut to the right lane, which in fact was an illegitimate lane, and then speed ahead, beating out the other car when the light turned green. And why? Because the *illegitimate* person always had to make up for something, *try a little harder.* The one in the regular lane, nothing to prove, took off at an absentminded pace. Just like in life! Because Mac felt marginal and ill at ease, he always had to go at everything with a running start. Try harder. He was probably trying too hard with his new girlfriend.

"It's better," Carolyn was saying. "Really, I would have worried he'd hurt himself."

"He didn't know how to handle me," said Molly.

"It wasn't nice to make fun of his socks," Mac said. "Anyone can have holes in their socks. Including your father."

"He thinks of his toenails as part of him," said Carolyn, "so he's afraid to cut them off."

"Oh, really? I hear that's the same reason infants like to roll around in their shit."

In the rearview mirror, he could see Molly, staring at him with disgust. Bull's-eye!

He drove them back across town, viewing the city with less affection than usual. As soon as they parked in front of the Ware house, the baboon jumped out and ran inside. Once she was out of hearing range, Mac said, "I'm sorry, but that was grotesque."

"Why? It was good for her!"

"She humiliates a nice guy, that's good?"

"Don't take it so seriously. She's as inexperienced as he is. I thought she was flattering him."

"Flattering?"

"Are you coming in?" she asked. "Mac?"

"I guess. Your loving father around?"

"I think he's at the press."

"I don't know. You might try to flatter me."

"I can do that." She reached for him and kissed him, and though he felt cold toward her in his mind, his body reacted predictably. He had never wanted anyone more in his life than he did this woman.

He followed her inside, chased her up the stairs, they were kissing on the bed, things were getting a little better, when that winged gnat of a sister came knocking on the door, and he wondered if Carolyn would push him into the closet this time, but she didn't. She yelled through the wall for Molly to *wait*, but then the knocking started up again and Carolyn rolled her eyes and growled and he knew that she would go to the surly girl and that there was nothing he could do to stop her. It was in that cloud of dissatisfaction that he goaded himself into taking a peek into the hiding place in the closet, because he had a horrible hunch about something that might be inside it. His dark side was leading the way. So now he was a spy, pushing past the silk garments and the mountains of shoes, lunging for the little door, yanking it open and feeling the warm, musty draft on his face, narrowing his eyes and blinking. In the bare-bulbed light, he reached for the closest pile and placed a hand on what he wanted. The letter he had written to William Galeotto, in its unaddressed envelope, was right on top.

He shoved it deep in his pocket, withdrew from the closet. By the time she came back, he was examining her drawings on the wall.

"I'm sorry," she said. "Kind of ruins the mood, doesn't it?"

"Very much so."

"Can I make it up to you?"

Lies peel away like a bad coat of paint. Later, he realized that this was a time when he should have said something, that in a way she needed him to shake her up. But it was hard to interpret her that way when he still imagined she had all the advantages. "You know what, I have some stuff to do at home. I'm gonna head back." His voice came out thickly.

She tried to kiss him; he gave her a quick peck. Did he really know her *at all*? Her smile came apart from her and flew his way. But her smile didn't have a corresponding crescent in him to nestle into; her smile would not find shelter with him, he would not know how to nourish that smile. He would kill it the way he'd killed the rat in his closet. He would lock it up until it died. And when he opened the closet, he'd find the dead smile, still smiling.

"Hey, is something wrong?" she asked.

"No! I'm just . . . a little cold. The fog's finally getting to my bones."

"It lifts in the fall."

"Yeah, I know."

up, and sped away, trembling only at the burden of softening Wendy's rock heart, of rowing to her lonely island.

Does it occur to a seventeen-year-old that all his jumping adrenaline can transform itself into a sleeping potion in a matter of moments? He was wide-eyed and alive through Santa Maria, but a few miles later he nodded off and the car plunged off the road and rolled. The roof caved in. Mac didn't die. All he could remember was a highway patrolman cussing as he wrestled Mac out the window of the wreck, filling his hands with the cactus spines that were poking out of the upholstery everywhere. The crushed bottles of wine were like marinade, and the Lincoln was like a pounded flank steak soaking in it. Helen and Richard and Fran showed up as fast as they could get there.

"Sorry, Dick-Dick," Mac said deliriously. "But I've got to get to L.A.!"

"Stop calling me Dick-Dick, you little punk!"

Since this wasn't long after his "spell," the few months during which Mac's tongue was paralyzed, no more was said about the incident lest it tip him over the edge, and magically, a new Lincoln appeared in the driveway the next week. Richard had a hard time disguising his infantile pleasure in getting his hands on a newer model.

Mac then wrote single-purposed Wendy twenty or thirty letters over the next couple years before he finally heard from her again. He was in Boston by then, trying to dig up his past. Wendy was in some dance troupe, living in West Hollywood, and wasn't speaking to her stage mother anymore; her plans were to marry an older man, a studio pianist. Evidently she liked a man who could tickle the ivories. She told Mac that she could never communicate with him again, because Boris was the jealous type and opened her mail and was violent if provoked. She said she was happy. She said she thought of him whenever she heard the term *rumpus room.* (How often was that? he wondered.) At the end of the letter, she wrote, "Mac, it's been nice." He wadded that letter up on the streets of Cambridge and jammed it in the daiquiri blender of the first tavern he came across and whirled it into a million wet bits.

(Nevertheless, a few weeks later he received an "Edwardian" knee-length coat, with a note: "I know it's cold out there and I know you don't have a good coat," and he held on to it, he held on tight.)

Should he throw his letter to Galeotto in the blender, too? Forget about it? Fran had at least three blenders to choose from. Liquefy. Whip. Puree.

"You look like someone I used to know," Mac said to his plastic cactus. "Don't I know you? Say, haven't we met? I've seen you before. You look like a friend of mine. You look so much like a friend of mine, it's— You know what it is? 'S *uncanny.*"

10

For the first year, tooling around the city, he didn't recognize Angel Island as an island at all. It rises from the water precipitously but at a glance blends in with the hilly country on the north side of the bay. Later Mac would fixate on the small island right under his nose, beautiful and exploited by various authorities over the years. It was like so many other things in his life right then.

At noon it ranked as the warmest day that summer in the city. Still no sun. Dry hills north of the bay were burning, and the sky was strewn with smoke and bits of pale ash, fluttering down and irritating the whites of all eyes. In the Marina, ashes fell like snow on a forest of masts. He hadn't seen Carolyn in several days.

He found her sitting on the dock next to a whale-size sailboat, in jeans and a large man's shirt. Long sleeves dangling over her hands. She wore the darkest glasses made.

"Hey there," she said. "Wasn't sure you'd show."

"I always show," Mac said. They'd spoken a few times by phone, but it wasn't easy to be false with her, and he had cut the conversations short. It was when she lifted her arm to push the hair from her face that he saw her hand was wrapped in an Ace bandage. "What's that?"

"A slight injury."

"What happened?"

She said, "Oh, nothing. Socked my dad."

He smiled, despite himself. "What did he do?"

"Nothing unusual."

It was hard to conceal his joy.

Isabel Porter came down the dock then, rolling an ice chest stacked with cushions. She wore a Cal Bears T-shirt and was strong-looking for her age—eighty-two, Carolyn had told him. He met her in time to gallantly lug the chest a few whole feet.

Carolyn said, "Isabel, do you remember my friend Mac?"

"Of course I do."

"Nice to see you again," he said.

They all stepped onto the boat, and Isabel invited them to help her take the sails out of their covers, which they commenced to do with the seriousness of purpose that makes activity so stabilizing for the soul. He thought maybe Carolyn and he should go into construction work together. As they leaned and unfastened and unfolded, they grinned at each other. And this time it felt good. *Punched her dad! Bravo!*

Isabel said to Carolyn, "Tell me, dear. I don't know if I've ever heard how you met."

Carolyn said, "It was an act of God."

Mac said, "Actually, it was an act of Molly. Carolyn was folded up—"

"Molly and her friends—"

"—in front of her house, sideways, in a bed—"

"You know that old fold-up bed we had? It was a trap," Carolyn said. "I was the bait."

"I swallowed it, hook, line, and sinker," Mac said.

"What luck." Isabel laughed. "Do you know how many generations of Carolyn's family I've known? Charles's mother, Mary, was my dearest friend. I've known Charles longer than anybody."

"Isabel's dad's godmother," Carolyn said.

"Charles was a wonderful boy," she went on. "Do you know, he was very clever with arithmetic and the sciences; I thought he would go into medicine. He had an elaborate chemistry set, and he was always collecting specimens and looking under his microscope, and he had all kinds of white mice he would build mazes for. He was so earnest—I've never seen a more earnest boy. He designed and built all the birdhouses in my yard. And he built that beautiful chest I keep all my photography equipment in. Those terrible thick owl glasses Mary picked out for him—how he hated them! Do you know, I saw him smash them once. He picked up a cobblestone from the garden and smashed them to bits. Told Mary an elaborate story about birds dropping rocks from the sky. But could you blame him? The pressure the boy was under. His father had no interest in his temperament, no faith in his writing, and had Charles not found a woman to marry, I think his father would have disowned him."

And no sooner had she said the words than the man himself pulled into the Marina parking lot in his little black car.

"He has arrived," Mac said. "Where's Adela?"

"She doesn't like water," said Carolyn.

Mac saw that another car had pulled in next to Ware, who was now busy helping three older women out of it, like a do-gooding scout.

"You will meet my three best friends today," Isabel said. "Sal, Winnie, Bess, and I go back years. Now that they've lost their husbands, we depend on each other as much as we did in high school."

And finally a car pulled up at the gate to the dock, letting out Molly and another girl.

Charles and the old-time gals made their way over, Molly and her friend carrying their bags and parcels. Mac was introduced first to the three women, and they all shook hands with stronger arms than he would have given them credit for having. They climbed onto the boat gamely, and Charles Ware greeted him in his usual fashion, but he had a bruise on his face that almost resembled a black eye. "Mr. West! I'm glad you found your way." The phony bastard! *I'd love to throw you overboard when no one's looking!* he was more likely thinking.

Isabel said, "What happened to your eye, Charles?"

"I have been sleepwalking lately. My unconscious is restless. I'm making my way east. I made my way last night straight into a bookcase!"

"Mac, this is Saki Harrison," Carolyn said.

"Sorry about your horse," he said.

"Now he's in a little box."

"She's getting a new one," supplied Molly.

"Nothing like getting something new," said Mac with some venom.

Shortly they set sail. Isabel turned on the engine and took the wheel, and they putted out of the Marina past the other shimmering crafts, joining the promenade of rigs and masts and booms on the bay. Mac did not tell Carolyn, but he had never before set foot on a sailboat. Her beauty was incandescent to him that day. The possibilities of how their love might flourish if he could control his demons went through his mind like a time-lapse film of a bean stalk—growing, growing, growing!

They tacked out toward the Golden Gate, met choppy open sea, turned about, took in that breathtaking view of the city, which he could never get enough of. At one point Molly complained of seasickness, and Carolyn rooted around forever in the hold for a ginger ale to bring her.

As they hit smoother sailing, Charles Ware moved over beside him. "Now then, boy. I want to ask you something."

"Like what?" Carolyn interrupted.

"We've never had a chance to talk. That shouldn't be! I want to ask him about his music."

"My music?" Mac laughed.

As the bracing sea air met his skin, he marveled at how he had traveled in his life to this strange moment. From his scattered, proud childhood in borderline slums, through his anticlimactic teen years in the veritable outback of California, to his swinging early twenties in Redwood City, he'd had the most wasted, obscure career he knew of. If someone had told him, as he wondered about his future in Tres Osos and smoked skunk weed and scribbled with Cesar, that he would one day be questioned by Charles Ware about his endeavors, he'd have used it for collateral to buy all kinds of dreams. He would have borrowed against it all along.

Ware said, "I hear from my daughter that your piano lessons paid off."

"Not exactly. I gave it up a while back."

"That's very bad of you," Carolyn said. "You're too good to give it up."

"She's trying hard to make me respectable," Mac said.

"Just as well," said Ware. "Music's a terrible profession. I wouldn't recommend it to anyone."

"What would you recommend?" Carolyn said. "Being the only child of a real estate magnate?"

"Ah, but a sea captain's life is mighty fine," Ware said cheerfully. "Shall we give it all up for the gorgeous 'snotgreen sea? The scrotumtightening sea'?"

Mac winced. The boat gleamed as it rocked through the waves, with scarcely a mark on it, like some exquisite, carved tusk. To own such a boat was not just the boat, he calculated. It was the maintenance, the slip; the expenses alone could probably feed a family. Would he be torn in two forever, half of him loathing any luxury item, half of him wanting to relax and have fun? He didn't know if he belonged out on the deck or down in the hold, peeling spuds.

"What's that from, Dad?"

"Joyce. *Ulysses.* I'm so very tired of my own diction, I could cut out my tongue."

Here's the knife, thought Mac.

They passed Alcatraz, and that was when he looked ahead and said: "There's another island."

"Angel Island," Carolyn said.

"All this time, I never realized."

"We should go there."

"What's there?"

An idea was suggesting itself to her. "Isabel," she called, "could you sail to Angel Island and drop us off?"

Ware said, "What on earth for?"

Molly said, "No! It won't be fun if you get off!"

Ware said, "She can't stand me, even in the open air."

"Would you stop it for once?" cried Carolyn.

"I'm a martyr, what did I do?" said Ware.

"We'll go, too," said Molly.

"Girls, I need your help," Isabel said. "I won't have you leave me."

"*She's* leaving you!" screamed Molly.

"You're not leaving," Carolyn said. "I don't feel like sailing. I'm tired, I'd rather take a walk. We'll see you all in a couple hours."

"Let's give them some time alone," Isabel said.

"This isn't fun," sulked Molly. "It's not fun at all!"

"How can you say this isn't fun?" yelled Carolyn. "Dad, would you say something?"

Ware shrugged.

Isabel tacked toward the small jetty, and Mac liked the idea that Carolyn wanted to be alone with him. They docked briefly and agreed to meet the group there in two hours. They were continuing on to an inlet in the north bay to meet with another old friend. *Bye-bye.*

"God, I couldn't stand it," she said as they found their land legs and straggled up the hill. "I hope you don't feel cheated out of a sail."

"No, this is great."

"I just can't be around my father right now; he's really annoying."

Once again Mac bit his tongue. *No kidding.*

They strolled arm in arm. Tall eucalyptus rustled and spiced the air. They passed some of the old barracks and even some half-buried artillery battlements.

"Well, Isabel's a character," he tried next.

"God, yes. She was one of the first woman surgeons in San Francisco," Carolyn said. "She's traveled everywhere; she knows artists and scientists all over the world. She speaks seven or eight languages, including a dialect of Inuit."

"Superwoman." It was funny how some people could grab hold of life so much better than others. "What privileged lap did she spring from?"

"Self-made. Her father was a shoemaker. She's wound up tight as a clock and works as many hours. She's very fond of money."

"Who isn't?"

Carolyn shook her head. "Isabel more than most."

"Hmmm. Wound up tight as a clock and works as many hours," he repeated. "Who said that?"

"I did."

"I thought maybe it was a quote."

"No, I made it up."

"Pretty good," he said.

"Sometimes I have good ideas."

After they had covered more ground, Carolyn led him down a path off the main trail, to a secluded cove with a great vista across the water of the skyline. Of course, to Mac, all vistas of San Francisco were great. They sat perched on a sandy slope and sipped from the flask he had brought along in his pocket.

"See how it's all a big system of cooperation?" he said. "The order of the streets, the rows of apartments and houses, the evenly spaced trees, the lanes of traffic—it's an agreement among the masses on how to live. I find that miraculous."

"Cool. Now that you mention it, it is pretty amazing."

"Someday, when there's anarchy, it'll seem like a fairy tale. Now I'd like to ask you what the name of this mountain is," he said, for he had noticed it on the map in the cove.

"Oh, yes. I think it's called Mount Caroline."

"There's an idea."

He pushed her back against the ridge. She smiled and rolled over and crawled up to the umbrella of a leafy bay laurel. He followed right behind. The sun burned through the suspension of ash and smoke, and she had a look in her eye that let him know what he could do, and he could see the tree and shadows reflected in her eyes, all the while; there were imprints of broken shells and pebbles stuck to their arms when at last they sat up, and she pulled the bits off him that stuck, and he brushed sand off her neck, one little grain at a time.

"When I was a kid," Mac said, and he picked up her bandaged hand, and kissed it, "I memorized a poem for school. In this A. A. Milne collection *When We Were Very Young*. It was called 'Disobedience.'

James James
Morrison Morrison
Weatherby George Dupree

Took great
Care of his Mother,
Though he was only three.
James James
Said to his Mother,
'Mother,' he said, said he;
'You must never go down to the end of the town, if
*   you don't go down with me.'*

"Anyway, the mother goes to the end of the town and never comes back. Here I was, running around spouting off this poem about my own destiny! The clues were all around me, I just didn't know it."

"Like what?" said Carolyn.

"Well, she was communicating to me somehow that she was sick and needed a rest. She'd leave me with this long-faced old woman named Bridie Durkin, who'd been a nun at one point." All his memories about those times centered on an incident involving a sugar bowl. A violated sugar bowl. An angry face towering over him. The big shiny sugar bowl stood in the way of retrieving anything more about the cold gray house, which smelled of cleanser. "I'm not sure how often I went there or what my mother was doing. But all the while, I guess my brain was making sense of it."

"It's true, kids know things, without knowing how they know them."

"Not just kids."

Carolyn nodded thoughtfully, and said nothing more.

Walking back to the cove in the ash-laden air, holding Carolyn's unbandaged hand, he loved how her hand was warm, squeezing his as though she liked him. As if everything in the world made sense. And thus it was all the more surprising to hear her say, "I meant to tell you, Molly and I are flying to New York next week."

They had reached the trailhead; several sailboats were in the process of mooring and unmooring, and not too far off, he thought he picked up the outline of Isabel's yacht clipping along at a furious pace.

"Kind of last minute."

"I'm taking her to look at a school."

"This has to do with *Molly*?"

"Why are you saying it that way?"

"Can't her parents take her to see it?" he snapped. "But you probably enjoy going to New York." He was struggling to say something that sounded reasonable, and it came out like this: "I don't understand the division of labor in your family."

"Division of *labor*?"

They were veering in the wrong direction now; maybe there was no turning back. "So, I guess I'm not invited."

"It's not that," Carolyn said. "You're not the only one who's had a hard time. Molly's had all kinds of problems, you know!"

"What kinds of problems?"

"Do you know how hard I have to work to make her feel normal?" Tears had formed in the corners of her eyes. "Everything I do is for that!"

"What do you mean, *normal*?"

Carolyn was hiccuping, mashing her eyes on her sleeve. "Forget it!"

"Please."

"Oh, that she's not aware! It doesn't matter, we've talked about it before."

"Aware of *what*?"

"She's just—not aware," Carolyn said, and let out a short, bitter laugh.

The very girl in question had spotted them and stood waving and yelling from the prow of the approaching boat.

Carolyn waved back. *What the hell?* Molly seemed normal, maybe too normal. She had friends. She was nice-looking (but not as pretty as her sister).

"Come on," he said. "Carolyn."

She shrugged and wiped her eyes. "It's just that . . . my parents couldn't care less about her."

The words were so simple, yet explained so much. They also appeared to undo her. "She's such a sweet, darling person," she said. "Can't anyone see that?"

"Sure, of course they can!"

"She's solid as a rock, and when I used to have nightmares, and I had *a lot,* the poor kid, I'd go crawl in bed with her in the middle of the night! This big person curling up next to a three- or four-year-old for comfort. Sad, don't you think?"

He nodded and followed her down the trail, kicking up dust and leaves. He saw that, in speaking the truth, she had shocked herself. Yet the story of the Ware family was as confusing to Mac as ever.

Climbing onto the boat from the dock, he saw a bag full of empty wine and soda bottles, and corks scurried around the deck like mice. Ware's face was flushed by the wine and wind.

"Ahoy," he called. "Those who abandon ship must walk the plank!"

Carolyn put on a good face; in short order she described their jaunt around the island in such cheerful terms that Mac wondered how often she wore this mask. It was a stunning performance, and she smiled at him without the slightest hint of what had passed between them. The wind had picked up, and the water was choppy. The plan was to dock at the Marina and have an early dinner there on the boat, and after a tossing ride over, this was what they did.

Isabel seated everyone in the cockpit, on slatted wooden benches on either side, and managed to put Charles next to Saki. He had been engaged in conversation with Bess and Winnie.

"Isabel, dear," he said, "don't part us!"

But the table was already filling, and his request was drowned out, and Charles Ware stood there helpless as a child, doomed to dine beside quiet little Saki on one side, his younger daughter on the other. Mac watched his face while he took stock.

"Charles, sit down!" Isabel called to him.

Like a scolded schoolboy, he collapsed in his seat.

Molly said, "We'll entertain you, don't worry."

It was a moment to be savored. Ware was someone who let out a constant stream of emotional flatulence; Molly didn't notice. Carolyn and Mac sat across from Ware and Saki and Molly. Isabel wouldn't let anyone help and wanted them all to stay put. Shortly she produced baked artichoke hearts and salad and a basket of bread and a big bowl of linguine with clam sauce. Bottle after bottle of wine came around, and Ware soon realized that no one was entirely out of earshot.

Later in the meal, he again found his stride.

"Now, you asked me about Winston Defries. He lived near Bapaume, in a wonderful stone house with a spectacular view of the valley and the fields and rows and rows of poplars. It was right off the train line from Paris to Calais, and interesting people were always stopping in—I'm sure the entire University of Chicago crowd stopped in. Winston had explicit instructions to hide me away so that I might finish my next novel. I was, of course, working on *Parnassus*. We found my young wife a flat in Paris, and she did some theater work—she knew Roberta Richards and Lois Springkeet and Renata Monroe—and I'd come into town, and here I was, flanked by the most beautiful women in Paris. Then back to Bapaume to work. Winston would say, 'Charlie, you're richer and younger and more famous than anyone I know. You know why I let you live? I've seen more beautiful women since you've been around than in all my paltry life.' So he'd gladly entertain these silly young people who stopped by to meet me while I pounded my keys upstairs.

"And then, of course, I'd get my mail—Horace Conrad wrote me dozens of letters. And Townwater Fitzgerald and Clebo MacLeish and Fay Atrose and Reinhold Gurtzbein all wrote. But I'd be waiting to hear from Bill. One little word, and he knew it." Something in his tone changed. "Do you know how many letters I wrote him? Nearly every day. Some would say I had been preyed upon by the cleverest bloodsucker around—which they did say, of course. And that he had begun to grow tired of it. All that we'd built together, he seemed out to destroy. I had to take the business back from him, before he ran it into the ground!"

"Dad, come on." Carolyn looked embarrassed.

"My daughter thinks I'm a bitter old man."

"Why do we have to keep hearing about this ad nauseam? You were close and then you weren't. Can't you just get over it?"

"We *are* close, in the way of brothers. Our attachment is deep and abiding. His devotion to me has been undeniable! It's one of the great friendships of the ages. They're writing about it, you know. The book will draw on decades of correspondence, and set the record straight for all time."

"Who's writing it?" Mac blurted out.

"Do you know them? Mr. LaPlante and Mr. Rothman."

"Those guys?"

"Isabel, tell them what happened when I was born," Molly interrupted.

"Is there any stopping you?" Ware groaned.

"I want Saki and Mac to hear it!" Molly said.

Isabel said, "All right. When Molly was born, I was looking her over stem to stern, and her face was screwed up red as a beet, but all of a sudden she opened her mouth and said, 'I'm here.' It was obviously a complete fluke, but I heard it clear as day. 'I'm here.' "

"It wasn't a fluke," Molly said. "I was a genius. I could talk from the minute I was born!"

"You could talk, but what did you have to say?" asked Ware.

Mac noticed, in the light from the lanterns surrounding the table, the look on Charles Ware's face. His distaste for his younger child was expressed in every feature.

"I've got an interesting one," Bess said. "We heard this on the radio this morning. Down near Gilroy someone's been dumping surplus cheese. Tons and tons of it. They're reporting a forty-thousand-square-foot cheese slick back in the mountains."

"How on earth!" exclaimed Isabel.

"Why would they dump cheese?"

"Couldn't they dole it out?" Sal asked.

"It's still under investigation," Bess said. "Nobody is coming forward."

"I have something." Ware turned and looked at Mac as if he had an announcement. "Better than cheese patches and nattering newborns. It came to me—I seem to remember something about your woman."

"Huh?" Mac didn't fully register what the man had said. It came out of nowhere. "My *woman*?"

"He brought me a picture of a young woman the other day, an old picture. It put me in mind of a time." Ware was addressing the table at large. "You say the girl is your mother?"

"I do," said Mac.

"Funny she should have been in that line of work. But we all fall on hard times!"

"Dad, shut up!" Carolyn said.

"Christ," Mac said.

"Now, sit down, everyone," said Isabel.

"You've got to be kidding." Mac was trying to yank his legs out from under the table.

"What did I do?" asked Ware. "We were all libertines, back then."

"You were sending her letters," Mac said. *"What about all those letters?"*

Ware's face softened, as if he was practiced in breaking the news. "Letters, no. But I remember now that she was one of my charity cases," he said in front of everybody. "It's the truth! I had a miserable little soft spot for certain types, and she was one of them. Lost and alone. I'd like to believe, now that we've met, that you benefited from that."

"Everyone settle down, let's have some of that brandy!" Isabel said.

"It's a lie," said Mac, and he was out of his seat, stepping behind Bess and Winnie and through piles of rope and life jackets and bags. He wanted to club the man with a steel rod, over and over, until his body was soft like a sack of mud.

"Mac, don't go!" cried Carolyn, who tripped trying to catch him.

"He lies all the time, why should I believe him now?"

His mouth felt hot, his hands were warm, but the coldest winds of the world blew through his ears. He balanced on the stern and stepped onto the dock.

"You can't leave now."

"Carolyn, sit down with your family and think about what you want in your life."

And then he saw Carolyn do the strangest thing. She sat on the side of the boat and bit down on a dish towel and began to wail with it in her mouth like a gag. Mac was torn in two. Stay, go. He went.

He could hear Ware saying, "I didn't mean to upset him."

So there he was, stumbling to his Cavalier; as he left the city, all the shape of it flattened out behind him and blurred into one big, cruel knot of light. Good God, what had he let himself in for? He found himself saying, "Screw it! Screw it! Screw it!" He said it all the way home. He said it so hard he thought he'd push his teeth out of his mouth. He'd never forget the welling of his feelings, the quick fall through the vortex of hope to despair, when he parked in front of Fran and Tim's, looked up to the front window, and saw, as if it were the Annunciation and she the angel come to him, his own mother. "Mom?" He let himself out of his car. "Mom?" She didn't evaporate as he ran from the street to the house. "Mom," he cried, jamming his keys into the unyielding knob, shaking the door in the dark. Tim came and fidgeted with his shiny brass locks. "Hold it," he griped. And when the door cracked open, Mac pushed his way into this hermit crab's home of his and fell on his knees in the living room at the sight of her.

"Mac," she said kindly. And the tire iron dealt its blow. It was Aunt Helen. He wept.

11

When did he start to do things wrong on purpose? His instincts, if he admitted it to himself, had been perverse all his life. His earliest memory was of a beloved stuffed cat toy, which he intentionally left behind in some bed so that he could suddenly "remember" it and cause his mother inconvenience having to go back. But it backfired! They were miles away when he "remembered," and she wouldn't go back! He cried until he was hiccuping and sick. He cried for losing his cat and cried because what he'd done made no sense even to him.

And you know what? If I ever have a kid, I'll go back no matter how far that cat toy is. Even if it's in another state, another country! I'll go wherever it's necessary to get back your cat toy, kid—stick with me!

He remembered jumping up from bed when his mother's key rattled in the lock late at night after work, for the purpose of spreading himself out pitifully in front of the television, disheveled and malnourished, so she could bark at him for not being in bed and then curdle with shame. He'd put on his clothes backward, just to dare her to twist them around. Later he took change from Uncle

Richard, grabbing coins from the neat bureau top where his uncle was sure to miss them. He wanted the family man to blow his top. As if in the punishing Uncle Richard would debase himself more than he could possibly debase Mac. After he lost Cesar, Mac made a point of insulting anyone who so much as spoke a word to him. He'd stay locked in his room with his books. And then he began to drink a little too much, night after night, to push away anyone who cared, if only a bit.

Recently, he had overadjusted. He'd put on a disguise. He'd rammed his head into Carolyn's life wearing the mask of a well-adjusted suitor. But he was prickly and bitter and resentful so close to the surface. It took a lot of work to push that down.

Was he bent on self-destruction? Only once, on a howling, windy day in Tres Osos when he was about fifteen, had he made a plan for his own end. He ran into the hills with a rope. He knew Dick-Dick alone wasn't worth killing himself over; but this waste-land—brown and crunchy in all directions, empty of beauty and hope and love, and as alien to him as a moonscape—this wasteland was doing him in. Would he become one of those drooling hicks who raped barnyard animals and bragged about it? Who watched his cousin undress through a keyhole? He didn't even have a pet to love; Dick-Dick said animals made him itch. Nothing for miles to attach himself to. Was he destined to stay in this barren landscape forever? A single oak grew at the top of the hill, a broad, tired oak overlooking the town. That day, he thought about hanging himself from it. He threw the rope over a low branch and watched it wiggle in the wind. He wanted his mother, in the heavens, to see what he was doing. And that was how he knew it wouldn't work. He wanted *more* from his life, not less. He really didn't want to miss anything. It was just that the anger in him had nowhere to go. The anger he carried made him worthy of a freak show. *Come and see the Angry*

Man! Step right up. The one and only—the greatest! Keep the children away!

"Mac, Mac." Helen was on her knees, wrapping her arms around him. Fran was patting him on the back. "Mac? What is it?" she said. "Mac?"

"I thought you were Mom," he said. "I thought you were Mom—"

The rounded forehead, the long, straight nose, the wide cheeks; these features had once been the standard by which he judged the world.

"I'm sorry, Mac," she said. "I'm sorry I'm not."

"Let me make something to eat," Fran said. "That'll make us all feel better."

"I'm fine," he told them, pressing his eyeballs with his palms. "Really. Sorry."

He followed them into the kitchen like a matted animal. He was sick of himself for wanting his mother so bad, even now, and for showing it.

Fran poured some soup in a pot, chicken and vegetable, served it with tortillas covered with melted cheddar cheese on the side and some strong coffee, stronger than she made it for herself. The combined smells relaxed him, yet he felt sticky with sea salt and low as ever.

"Why are you here?" he asked Helen after a few gulps. "Is everything all right with Uncle Richard?"

"He's fine," Helen said. "Can't I come visit without a reason?"

"You should visit more."

They stared at him.

"What?" he roared.

"What's wrong, Mac?" said Fran.

"Who says something's wrong?" He didn't feel like talking about his sour personal life.

But then he said: "Okay, something's wrong, all right." He took a big, scalding slurp of coffee. "I was just told by my girlfriend's sweet, kindly father . . ." He couldn't go on.

"What?"

"It's sick."

"You have to tell us now," Helen said.

He was panting. "It's too much! I don't want to expose you to the guy's evil machinations."

"He's evil?" Fran said.

"Yeah. He said that Mom was, like, a prostitute or something."

"Who is this man?" said Aunt Helen.

"The author!" yelled Fran.

"What author?"

"The one who wrote that book Mac had when he came to live with us, the *Tangier* book."

"*That* book? What a sick man. A thoroughly sordid person," said Helen.

"What a jerk!" said Fran.

"I'll say," agreed Mac. Their anger was warming his heart.

"It's not true," said Aunt Helen.

"No, it can't be," Fran said.

And then a pregnant silence filled the room.

"You sure?" Mac said.

Helen looked at Fran and then at him. "I'm reasonably sure."

"A lot of guys used to come over," said Mac wretchedly. He felt like such a child!

"But that doesn't mean—"

"That stuff you gave me last time, that's what got me into this mess."

"The things in the box?"

"It's a Pandora's box."

"Oh my. I shouldn't have given it to you, then."

Helen, who spent much of her time reading psychology and self-help books, had one childish characteristic: when nervous, she grabbed her hair and pulled on it rhythmically as if milking a cow. She had come for a visit back in May, full of the goodwill of her mission in presenting him with his mother's rug and the other odds and ends.

"Why did you wait until now, Aunt Helen?"

"You couldn't have it," she said, "until you had a place to live."

"It was a *material* consideration? Just the old 'get a house, get stuff' routine? Wasn't based on my emotional development or anything like that?"

"Getting a roof over your head is part of your emotional development, I believe," Helen said.

"Maybe I wasn't ready for it," he said, pushing away his bowl. "It's obviously because of me, whatever she had to stoop to. I'm a sucking louse."

"What's that?"

"A primitive parasitic insect perfectly adapted for siphoning body fluids from its hosts."

"No, you aren't," said Helen. "You are a delightful boy with normal needs!"

"Get me a beer," Mac barked, and to his surprise, Fran fetched one and popped the top.

"You know how to neutralize the enemy, don't you?" Fran said. "Pretend he's right and think, *Who cares?*"

"Yes, and even if she was, she was probably the very expensive, clean kind," said Aunt Helen.

"I'm just saying, there are all kinds of prostitution," Fran said knowingly, making Mac wonder about her inner life more than usual.

"How would he know, unless he was a *customer*!" spat Helen.

Mac's brain was spinning. "What does it matter." He rubbed his eyes. He was exhausted. "She couldn't stand our life."

"How did it come up?" Fran asked. "What possessed him to say that?"

"I was asking for it. I showed him a picture of Mom, and all those envelopes."

"What did Carolyn say? Was it awkward?"

"Of course it was awkward. Everything in my life is always doomed and awkward."

"No, it's not, Mac, it's going to work itself out," said Helen.

"I wouldn't have met her if not for this crap, but here Mom's crap is gonna wreck what we have."

"But you're in love! You'll have to run away together," said Fran.

"And live here with you guys?"

"You can make it work!" she said, her heart unabashedly full of romance. "Don't let this get in the way."

Maybe she had a point. He flashed ahead to a possible future— he and Carolyn driving up the coast in his leprous car, toward a little patch of land jam-packed with miniature donkeys. Why not?

Aunt Helen nudged Fran's arm. "This is changing the subject, but tell him. I can't wait any longer."

Mac couldn't take much more. "What?"

"Well," Fran said, "it's not ideal timing, and I know you're tired, but you know all that throwing up I've been doing lately?"

"No."

"You haven't noticed?"

"Sorry," he said.

"I'm pregnant," she said.

"Fran, that's great! Wow. Congratulations!"

"But you can stay here as long as you want. Tim's office can be the baby's room anyway. Your room is reserved for you, Mac."

"No, I'm out," he replied, but he looked away for a second, to hide his childish gratitude.

He remembered the letters Fran wrote him when he turned eighteen and went off to try his luck in Boston. Though he had cut her down and punched her almost every day, she wrote him regularly, once or twice a week. For her loyalty he sent her souvenirs—pincushions, pencils, mugs—which he pinched from various shops with poor surveillance. She, in turn, mailed him homemade raisin bread every two weeks; even though it often arrived speckled with mold, he could cut those parts off and wolf the rest, and stay connected to a place he called home only if he slipped.

The announcement made, Fran returned to her sink of dishes, and Helen said, "Mac," and took his hands. "Please. What happened to your mother—trust me, you're not to blame. Don't ever think it. It's very normal for abandoned children to feel guilty. But there's nothing you could have done to stop her. Is that clear?"

Again his heart rate rose, and his tongue filled his mouth like a wet sock. He clamped his teeth to squeeze it down. He said, "Stop her from *going*. No."

"No," Helen said. "Mac, what I mean is, from being reckless with her life, which was a way of taking it."

He stood up and walked around the room. Worms of grief bored through his body, rooted him helplessly to the earth in this kitchen, in this life, with this past. No illusion could move him out of it. For years the circumstances had not been forthcoming. It had all been a blur to him—that on her vacation in Paris she had drowned, and Helen traveling to Boston to collect the things that had been impounded from their tiny flat.

"It doesn't matter now."

"Mac, just listen," Helen said.

So he sat and tried. He threw his arms up on the table and cradled his head. His mind wandered at first. That his mother had always been depressed and troubled, that some people seem to be veering in that dark direction all their lives, were among the rote things he expected her to say.

He thought about Dick-Dick in Tres Osos pacing the big, perfect habitat by himself. No one to boss around, only himself to face. Surely by now the burly drip had faced himself. He'd had a heart attack two years ago. He'd received angioplasty in San Luis Obispo. Now he ate salads all the time and, as if life were short, took Helen on Elderhostel trips. So far, they had visited Turkey and New Zealand and had enjoyed themselves. All good news, but the man still had a full deck of annoying habits. Mac thought about how, when Richard visited in Redwood City, he always brought a bag of cleaning fluids, as if Fran and Tim weren't sterile enough for him. Mac was offended, but they weren't. In fact, they loved Dick-Dick and had, in him, a father.

Now Helen was saying something else, about the sad divide between them from the earliest of days. How Cecille would tell people Helen wasn't her twin but a robotic replica. And then there was their father, difficult and moody, taking his uppers and downers, and Cecille ever trying to take his hand. So much so, it left their mother feeling like a third wheel, and Helen like she wasn't even on the cart.

The father in question, John West, a dreamer with a temper, was a troubled person who had run away from home himself. He'd spent years drifting from job to job, ending up as a caretaker on a large estate with a place to call home for his family. Painting was his all-consuming love; for him the girls posed when they were young. Nymphs in a sylvan glade. Slivers of pale flesh on a mossy bank. *"There's nothing wrong with it, it's natural, they're my beauties!"* But as the girls grew out of childhood, Mrs. West began to object.

"The summer we were fourteen," Helen said, "I had a crush on a boy named Matt Gerslaugher, and on this beautiful, glorious, warm but not humid day, we'd gone off on our bikes together and ended up kissing for hours out in the softball field by the school. And he told me he'd liked me all year and we rode into town and he bought me a little ring at a five-and-dime. And—"

"Mom, stop it, it sounds like you're reliving it."

"All right, well, the point is that it was looking like the most beautiful day of my life. I'd never had a boyfriend, though boys had been after Cecille for years. I rode back up the dirt road to our house in a dream state. I considered keeping the news to myself but also couldn't wait to flaunt it. Cecille thought I was a prude and a chicken.

"Well, Mother had gone away that day, on a trip with a friend into New York. She'd had it planned for months. I found no one in the house and for some reason headed down in the direction of the river, which ran right behind the cornfields. I still recall the rustling of the stalks and the light whisper of passing birds, and the stillness of the air.

"I heard her voice then. A teasing, murmuring laugh, like flowing water. It came from under the old willow down at the bank where we'd played many games over the years. I caught a whiff of turpentine fumes, and realized my father was painting there.

"I—" Helen stopped. "It was just as it always had been, Dad with his stool on the bank, his painting bag down on the ground, his palette and brushes within his reach. But Cecille was posing for him, on a tapestry beneath the tree, fully undressed. It was so shocking to see her like that—it was my body, too, you see. Yet there was something so womanly and knowing about her posture that my kiss with Matt seemed juvenile by contrast.

"I suppose what happened was my fault. I started yelling at them, even throwing a few rocks. Before I knew it, Cecille had jumped up and came running after me. It happened so fast she caught me by surprise, brought me down, and began to pummel me on the back so hard I couldn't breathe. I had mud between my teeth."

"Why are you telling me this story?" Mac said. "It's really depressing."

"Well, several things resulted. My kidneys were bruised, and she broke one of my ribs. And somewhere on the bank, I lost my little ring." Helen took a sip of cold coffee and puckered her lips. "My father turned his head. He pretended he didn't see a thing. Not only that, but on the way to the hospital, he told me that, as far as the doctors were concerned, I'd fallen on the rocks, nothing more."

"God." His mother had never hit him, but she was capable of volcanic rage. He had seen her vent it on different men, on doors that didn't open or close, on a malfunctioning toaster, and even on strangers if they crossed her.

This day was too much. He wanted to black out and be done with it.

"But she regretted it—she swore she did. And besides, she ended up there with me a few hours later. She had some kind of fit and mutilated her hands on that willow tree."

"That's how it happened?" said Mac. His mother had never explained to him the curious raised ribbons on her palms.

"I've never told you about this before," Helen said. "I hope you're not angry with me."

"No."

"I have come to believe that it wasn't her fault," Helen said. "And I've forgiven her. And maybe someday, you'll be able to do that, too."

"But it's not the same," Mac said. "It's just not the same."

Isabel Porter had set up a booth. She wanted volunteers. She had a new hygiene machine. A pretty little girl in a pink dress presented herself. She wore white gloves and patent leather shoes. It was Carolyn.

"This is revolutionary," Isabel Porter said. "You'll never have to bathe again. How would that suit you?"

"I take a bath every night after dinner. I clean the ring for fifty cents."

The crowd laughed. "Now, step inside," Isabel pressed on. Carolyn entered the tube, her white gloves pressed against her sides. "This little child is going to come out clean as a whistle, and besides, she's going to get a prize," Isabel declared.

The crowd murmured.

Isabel flipped a switch. A rumbling sound emanated from beneath the cylinder. Carolyn looked out at them proudly, a pioneer. Then she was up, up, zipping through the top, swished up so fast they barely saw her go, and there she was again, thudding like a wet log on the cement. On the inside of the cylinder, a gray film oozed down the glass.

"Stand away," Isabel yelled. "Now you can see how this machine derives its magic. Notice the impurities left on the inside wall. In a millisecond, our girl was whisked through the filter, and that standard bathtub ring"—she indicated the ugly gray film—"was converted to this."

Then they heard a moan. The pretty pink pinafore was drenched with blood. Carolyn was literally coming apart. Mac screamed.

"Don't worry," Isabel said. "Though the kinks in this machine have not yet been worked out, every sacrifice we make toward its development will aid humanity. Everyone in the free world owes her something."

"No! God, no! No! No—"

Four A.M., darkest part of the night, and Mac tumbled out of bed. He was damp with sweat. What a nightmare! He had to find something in his closet; dust balls as big as rats came out with his things. He pushed aside a tin of bricklike cookies and a desiccated lemon. He threw out a circled-up want-ad page from his first few days with Fran and Tim, when he had set out to find himself a place to live in the city and then gave up.

Then he pulled out his old knapsack. In it, there was a pitiful collection of kid's innocence. A time capsule from the year before his life changed forever. Pens, matches, a toy tom-tom, a Carl Yastrzemski pennant, a green rabbit's foot, a deck of cards with a topless Hawaiian girl doing the hula, who swayed in your palm if you snapped the deck, and a button that he used to find hilarious, which said FINK UNIVERSITY.

And finally he plucked out the folder. It was scribbled on, plastered with psychedelic stickers that used to come free with barbecued potato chips. In it were the comic strips about a boy and mother he had been working on right up until he left Boston. Nearly eighty pages of them. He wanted to see something. He wanted to see how he had felt about his mother, back then and there, not filtered through everything that had come between them since.

One was about a boy who feared his mother would make a mess of all that she touched. After covering every kitchen they had in paint, Mac's mother would lug her portfolio into galleries and cry heartily when they turned her down. There was a grand old place on Beacon Hill she dreamed of someday showing her work in, and the drawing showed her in bed, dreaming of her paintings on the walls.

One day, the boy in the cartoon walked down the banks of the Charles until he reached Arlington Street, and he marched into Back Bay, and wandered through the Public Garden, and watched the Swan Boats pedaling in their silly circles in the man-made pond. Expensively dressed men and women discharged their important duties up and down the street. It was a different Boston from the one where he lived with his mother. From the street, he eyed the hill of the impenetrable gallery. What was so great about the stuff in there? Finally he ended up in a cool restaurant on Newbury Street, where he took a table by himself and ordered his usual, a shrimp cocktail. Whenever he saved up enough odd change, from collecting bottles and cans, from mowing lawns and selling magazines and candy bars and washing cars, this was his idea of a big treat. Everything in this restaurant was serene, and the waiters were polite to the boy, and the tablecloths were stiff and clean and square, and usually when he dined there he allowed himself to relax and dream of his great big future to come.

This time, as he chewed the succulent carcasses of shrimp, he had a fantasy that became, from that day forward, recurrent and exhausting. In this fantasy the director of the gallery was having lunch in the same restaurant. Suddenly a gunman was holding him up. The gunman was a confused artist, like the boy's mother. The gunman wore a mask and yelled at the director for not showing his work. In one quick movement, the boy pulled out his own gun and shot the pistol right out of the gunman's hand.

"Up against the wall, buster," the boy said.

The director said, "What marksmanship. I've never seen anything like that. What can I do for you? Anything!"

To which the boy said, blowing the smoke from the tip of his weapon, "Forget it. By the way, my mother has some very unique paintings, with stark lines and haunting messages. Want to take a look?"

Sure he'd been hoping it was brilliant stuff. That it was the pure virgin work of a natural talent. Instead, the figures were gawky, the dialogue awkward, the vocabulary neophyte, the revelations predictable and clichéd. But who cared? The lack of ambivalence was clear. No nasty ironies, no cynicisms, littered these pages. Back then, he had drawn the characters with love.

Hadn't he made her happy? Hadn't he lived by her rules? He used to pick her flowers on his way home from school. He listened to her stories, laughed at her jokes. He talked about the ranch he would buy her when he became a concert pianist and his cartoons were syndicated all over the world. He never showed his disappointment when things went wrong. Just said to himself, *Chin up.* Didn't she know how much he would miss her? Didn't she care about bringing him up?

Mac's mother had, that long-ago summer afternoon after breaking her sister's rib, run down to the banks of the river and torn the leaves and catkins from the sweepy branches. The privilege of being her father's favorite had turned to a burden. Her own willfulness was a burden. Her loves and her fears were all folded together, and they were burdens, too. She couldn't see out of her troubles. She wondered if she ever could. She threw handfuls of green confetti into the water and watched them spread on the surface like shattering glass, like atoms blowing apart.

Floating free from one another, the willow leaves became a flotilla of tiny boats searching for help. As each boat touched a molecule of water, it told that molecule the story. Then that molecule told all the molecules around it. As the water poured downstream, soon the whole river was shouting the news. The river reached the ocean. The whole ocean knew. The water told the world. The world knew.

Continuing to strip the switches, she saw the raw summer light start to brighten up the damp soil beneath the tree. How well she knew every rock and root there, for that was where they always went. One by one she painted them in light. She had to go high enough to make it matter; she jumped and pulled and slid down the pliant young suckers. She finally saw the sun hit the trunk. Her palms were bleeding. She didn't care. She was hiccupping with victory and fear. Her hands were so badly lacerated, they would be bandaged for weeks; he deserved it. The episode was too public and called too much attention to Cecille and the tree, and her father would surely understand the gravity of his behavior from then on. Or at least for six more months, for on Christmas day she'd find him there in the snow. She only knew she was mad and brave enough to try anything after that.

Mom! Couldn't you have been a little braver?

PART THREE

M.W.

The rivers let me go
where I wanted.

—Arthur Rimbaud,
"The Drunken Boat"

12

Mac had been wounded openly, visibly, not in the usual secret way he had to gag down on his own. So he was waiting for word from Carolyn. He woke with the self-righteous glow of the injured, anticipating the consolations coming his way. But by late morning, there had been nothing from her. Wasn't she gnawing her guts out after her father's assault on him, wondering how he felt about her now? Maybe his needs were so transparent it was quite the opposite. Maybe she understood that once humiliated, he'd need her all the more.

He ate a bowl of cinnamon-sprinkled oatmeal with Aunt Helen and Fran, then did some laundry and cleaned out his car. What a dump. He pulled out the rope he'd used to deliver the fold-up bed to Filipo, found a shirt that had been hardened into the shape of an aircraft carrier after a beverage had spilled on it, and extracted forty-seven bottles and paper coffee cups.

By lunch, he was anxious, and by midafternoon, he was moving through the house scared.

"Stop pacing," said Fran. "It won't help."

"For some reason, it does help."

"Worrying only makes it worse," said Aunt Helen. "Remember the year you had that awful body rash?"

"Of course."

"Well, so do I. And so does Richard. He stayed up night after night bringing you bowls of ice cream."

"He did?"

"Yes, he did. And do you remember when your tongue was paralyzed?"

"Definitely."

"Richard took you to UCLA for tests."

"I know."

"He spent three days down there, and you never spoke a nice word to him."

"My tongue was paralyzed."

"What about later?"

"I spoke a nice word silently."

"Does he know that, Mac? He's not a mind reader."

"That's for sure."

Finally, he could stand it no longer, and he picked up his phone. He wouldn't play hard to get. He had a window, no matter how faulty, into her world.

But he didn't reach her. "It's me," he said, nothing more. He felt restless and bruised. His jaw was jutting out, frozen in a frown. He saw his face coming through the back of a dartboard, the short, weighted arrows of his destiny punishing his cheeks.

He unfurled the rug he planned to give Carolyn and vacuumed it—as a child, building his kingdoms and war zones while watching cartoons, he had memorized every inch. Flowers and squares and steps to nowhere. An anchor without a rope. A tree without roots. Blue and red were the dominant colors; it would look good in a corner of her bluish room. The rug had been one of the few constants of his life then—wherever they were they could unroll it, call the place home.

"Think she's going to like it?" he asked Fran and Helen, who were peering in at him.

"Your magic carpet?" said Fran.

"Surely she has a house full of fancy rugs," said Aunt Helen. "That was your mother's."

"I know, but anything less wouldn't be worth giving."

"Mom, remember Melinda Kobayashi from Calvert Street School?" asked Fran.

"Yes, you told me you saw her."

"She came to our party, and she and Mac hit it off, and she's interested in seeing more of him."

"Forget about it," said Mac.

"She was a very nice girl," said Aunt Helen. "She always wore those dowdy clothes, for some reason. She wasn't vain."

"Okay, goodbye," said Mac, and he herded them out as if they were nosy reporters at a crime scene.

With the door closed, he felt crazed and caged in, so he finished the afternoon off with a long walk around the neighborhood, phone in his pocket. Who in the world can feel good waiting for a call that doesn't come?

As the daylight faded, he fidgeted in the house. He bleached an avocado stain out of a dish towel. He took three big stacks of newspapers and magazines to the recycling bin. He threw a hatchet over and over at a fruitless mulberry stump next to the back fence. He was good at it. Wood chips flew. Helen and Fran stood at the patio door watching his wretched, miserable, luckless descent. "Come in," Fran called to him. "I made some brownies."

"What the hell's going on?" he cried.

"Hadn't you better look into it?" Helen said. "Say something to her, and not silently?"

"Yeah, I guess I'd better," he said, this time without a trace of barbed wire. Time to get back in his car, heading in the same direction he'd been going in for years.

Shortly he was staring up at the face of Carolyn's house, trying to wring some answers from the cold, clammy air. From time to time, faint silhouettes flickered within the window frames—the image of insects trapped in amber came to him, from a heart-shaped pendant his mother had worn that encased a prehistoric bug. When he was young, he'd stared at that gnat with fascination. He'd thought that gnat was a superstar. He'd thought the gnat had been singled out for greatness. All men would know gnats of its time by way of seeing that one. But he had been naïve in that matter, as in many others. If this house were preserved with Charles Ware inside, what a dirty, rotten specimen of mankind he'd be.

A pale light suffused the corners of Carolyn's room; Mac placed another call to her. No answer. He considered buzzing the front door, couldn't bring himself to do it, so he stood by the mock orange tree and waited for a sign.

Loitering, a suspicious figure on an affluent street.

"Young man, young man!" someone was saying. "Are you a young man?"

He looked the other way and beheld an old woman approaching. Pushing a cart full of plastic bags and rags, she was even more suspicious-looking than he was. She had boggy circles under her eyes, her skin was a shade of yellow he'd prefer to see on young bananas, and she had lumps and warts all over her cheeks. She wore two or three sweaters over her dress.

"I have terrible luck," she said. "Last week, a man pushed me out of my car and drove it away. Car was filled with all my picture albums. From my wedding, my whole life. I'm a widow. This is all I got left!"

"Just a week ago?" Mac said skeptically.

She reached into her cart and pulled out a bunch of green grapes. "Feel these," she said. "They feel like a breast. My breast!"

Mac had a weakness for the down-and-out, but he said "No thanks" all the same.

To get away from her, he began to climb the shoe tree, his hands grasping at the lower limbs, feet hooking over and up, shoulders clearing twigs and branches, finding his footing, standing, and pushing himself higher.

"No civilization, clothes, or homes," the woman muttered, continuing on her way. "Darkness in a blind new world!"

In no time he was as high as Carolyn's windows, surrounded by weathered shoes. He reached for a stiff child's sneaker. It wasn't hard to yank one loose; without much thought, Mac heaved the rubber-soled shoe at Carolyn's windows.

She came to the French doors and parted them, peered out into the dark. His heart leapt at the sight of her. She was in a pair of salad green pajamas, even though it was only around nine o'clock.

"Don't be scared, Carolyn, it's me!"

She peered into the mist, saw him through the leaves. Leaning over, she picked up the old shoe from the balcony. Heaved it back at him.

"Hey!" he said.

"Get out of my tree!"

She looked so sweet, he could hardly stand it. "Why can't I be in your tree?"

"Well . . . because I'm going to bed, and how can I go to bed if I know you're out here in the tree?"

The lofty interior of her room looked cozier than it really was; all the time he'd spent in it seemed to have happened to a lost boy in a story.

"Last night, Carolyn, I was thinking about this one book my mom had on her shelf, and when I first noticed it I was excited, because it was called *The Handy Nasty*. I thought it was a sex guide. Naturally, at my first opportunity I snuck a peak at it. But you know what it was?"

"No, how would I?"

"It was actually a book about the Han dynasty. Write it down and you'll see what I mean. So what I'm trying to tell you is, something might look like the handy nasty when it's really something else. Your father doesn't know anything about her."

She nodded as if persuaded. It was one of the things he liked about her. "He's horrible. I didn't believe it."

"Really?"

"I think he said it to scare you away."

"Oh, just that."

"Which is disgusting, but it makes things hard."

"Why should it make things hard?" he yelled.

"Be fair, Mac. He's my father."

"A couple days ago you were pummeling him."

"I don't think you understand how much he depends on me! He's not the strongest person in the world. Not even close. You're a much stronger person than he is."

Mac rested his head on the branch. He didn't feel strong. He was sick of covering for people who claimed they weren't strong. "Your mother seems to have cottoned to me a bit," he finally said.

"She's a husk, so it doesn't count."

"A husk," Mac repeated.

"But it takes one to know one. I'm a husk, too."

"What exactly is a husk?" He shifted on the branch and it shook, and little pods full of seeds pelted the sidewalk.

"It's something that looks like what it used to be, but now it's empty," she replied.

"Would you quit saying that? You're the least empty person I've ever met." He said this with greater tenderness than he'd expected to.

"I'm empty by choice."

He was starting to feel like a possum; he had sap on his fingers, and he was hugging a cold trunk. "Carolyn, isn't it time to break free? Like, for starters, moving out of your parents' house? We could get our own place. Wouldn't it be great?"

"Of course it would be great. But—" Her voice caught, a rabbit in a trap. She reached for something—a rhubarb-colored shawl— pulled it around her shoulders. "It would be vast."

"So what's stopping us?"

No answer.

"I'm making you something, it's a surprise. And I have a very nice rug. I also have a plastic cactus," he said, laughing at his dowry.

"Hmm. I guess it's a place to start."

"Know what?" he said, encouraged.

"What?"

He leaned farther out in the tree so she could see him better.

"My cousin Fran's pregnant. The baby's due next April, so I'll be a second cousin, or something like that."

"That's exciting."

"I'm going to move out, even though she says I don't have to."

"That's right. Get as far from the baby as possible," she said.

"Huh?"

She shivered, pulled the shawl tight around her shoulders. "Other people's babies are so very annoying."

"Not really. Can't I come in?" he asked.

"We have to get up early," she said. "I think I'd better go to bed."

"It's the last time I'll see you for a while."

"Not that long."

"Where are you staying?"

She sniffed. He'd noticed this was her mannerism before she said something that could be construed as privileged. "Our apartment. We have an apartment there."

"Oh. I didn't know."

"Well, I still have some packing," she said. "I'd better keep going. But thank you for coming by!"

He wanted to ask about Molly's plans and prospects, but that was a flawed topic for them. Suddenly he didn't have the least idea what he *could* talk about. He was aware of the differences between them more acutely than ever, and astonished by how large they loomed; he wondered how he looked to her in the tree, with his plaid shirt and its rumpled, bunched lapels, his jeans with worn knees, his sneakers with the peeling rubber around the sides. Rather than cutting a romantic figure, he was a curiosity, a bit player, a yes-man, nothing more. Before he knew what he was doing, he yanked another pair of old shoes from a branch and he threw it over her head, pelting the wall of the diabolical house.

"Hey, don't do that," she said.

He grabbed another pair and flipped the shoes one after the other. Each old shoe thudded onto the balcony and bounced off, falling to the ground.

"Mac, stop!"

He hurled another, and another, not at her but close enough, as she ran for cover through her French doors and shut them with a bang. And she began to fade, as if she was being siphoned into her next life, the outline of her becoming less clear, until he could no longer see even a glint of her in the room. It left him gasping.

In a few days, early for an interview at a bank in North Beach, he sat on the broad marble steps out front. A long shot, but he'd seen bank tellers less on the ball than himself. He was good at math, and he'd shaved and even borrowed a sport coat from Tim. The slow shuffle of shoppers and people on errands came and went before him, soothing his melancholy with steady, anonymous motion. Shortly an older man came out of the bank and sat down on the steps beside him. He wore a green leisure suit and a white golfing hat. "Howdy," he said.

Mac nodded back. Because he was preoccupied, he tried to look grim and unapproachable, but the man began fidgeting with his newspaper, and momentarily he said, "Boy, oh boy, you'd think for all that money these fellas could get a little more privacy."

"What's that?"

He showed Mac what he was reading. An article about the wealthiest people in America. He was going to tell Mac his name— it was inevitable. It was Johnny Durkin. "You're not by any chance related to an ex-nun in Boston named Bridie Durkin?" Mac asked.

"Ex-nun? I don't know. Could be. I'm from Buffalo originally," he said. "Why, you from Boston?"

"Yep," Mac said.

"What do you know. Used to pull into Gloucester once a week. That was my line of work."

"Fishing?"

"No, they fished 'em and processed 'em, and I picked 'em up in my truck, frozen. Took 'em to Buffalo, Cleveland, Toledo, and Youngstown, Ohio. Thirty-two years that was my run. Big Catholic population back there, you know, fish sticks every Friday night. You can see what an important guy I was."

He proceeded to tell Mac about how he had just had an appointment at the bank to get a personal loan for his daughter, who had finished college and wanted to go to art school in London. She had been drawing since she was five. They always knew she was talented. "Lately she specializes in paintings of dead animals," he said. "Which

I never really cared for, but the art teachers go crazy for them." He and his wife wanted to help her out, make her year in London comfortable. What a good guy! The direct and practical way he wanted to encourage his daughter seemed to contrast so sharply with any kind of help Carolyn could get, even with all her advantages.

Mac's feet were cold. He must have shuddered.

"I tell you, I know it. My wife keeps telling me we're in California, I don't believe it. 'Course, people here are softies, have you noticed that? Once I had to back two miles into a frozen mountain. At the center of this mountain was a big cold-storage place for the government. I dropped off a load there. You know. Where all the government folks will come and live if there's a bomb."

"Chewing on frozen cod two miles into the earth," Mac said. "I don't know. I could skip that."

"Well, son, don't think you're invited."

They laughed. Mac's heart warmed without restraint to anyone who called him son.

And then the man's wife, a pleasant-looking, middle-aged woman, strolled up with a shopping bag on each arm. Would Mac ever have a pleasant-looking, middle-aged woman in his life? It seemed like the greatest goal of all, suddenly.

"Nice chatting with you," he said. They shook hands, and Johnny Durkin was yet another board to nail to Mac's raft. His raft that had floated him over hard times, his raft that he hammered together with his primitive tools, built of all the people he had known and talked with and listened to.

Against his better impulses, Mac called Carolyn's cell. He still wasn't sure what day she was returning, and he wanted to tell her about this man whose daughter painted dead animals. He wanted to tell her anything. He missed her like crazy. He was ready to be patient, to prove himself her friend, to ride a unicycle with no hands.

He reached her voice mail yet again. In a burst of nervous energy, he blurted: "Carolyn, know what the bottom line is? It's that I'm in love with you, and so we've got to find a way not to freak out but a way to freak *in,* into this thing we're making *together,* and not take anything the wrong way, and then we'll get to know each other better than we've ever gotten to know anyone else before, and by doing that we'll begin to understand that people can make mistakes and it's to be expected because no one's perfect and then we'll decide we are going to dedicate ourselves to this proposition and swear by it and hold it to be true *all our days.* Okay?"

And he hung up and paced in front of the bank for ten minutes, giving himself a lashing. *Jesus! What a turnoff.* He'd probably never hear from her again.

The interview was conducted by a robot in a suit. "We-will-be-in-touch," the robot was programmed to say.

Fat chance, Mac was programmed to think.

No word from Carolyn.

There was the day Mac spent drawing on the covers of magazines, making mustaches and eyebrows on faces, penning teeth black. A hundred years ago, that's how everyone looked. Ha! But probably not Carolyn. There was the hour he stared at his tongue in the mirror the way he'd never done before. He could do an interesting puckering twist with his tongue, plus, there were thick blue stripes on the underside of it. Plus, if you looked closely, you could see little, tiny taste buds. How fascinating. The afternoon when he walked around his neighborhood kicking twigs and rocks from the sidewalk, the day he drove over to the coast near Santa Cruz and sat in the warm sand, digging his hands into it until they cramped. The road over the mountain seemed cold and lonely. His mind was bloated with memories of false promises and premonitions of a walk down a long lawn toward death.

It was not a good idea to spend days with such grave thoughts. One day he had to stop the car, hold his head in his hands. He was idling outside a tennis club. Women in short white skirts and clean white shoes were swatting around their clean, little balls. What did they know of the world? How much he pitied and despised them, watching their skinny legs run.

There was an afternoon in a grocery store, a bit smashed before he went, many minutes spent wandering the aisles, leaning on his cart, finally knocking over a display of spaghetti sauce jars. "Broken glass and red sauce"—had a certain ring, maybe he could write a song. There was the nice bag girl who leaned over and mopped it up, whose blouse he could see down. She kindly told Mac it happened all the time.

There was the day he began to sing, "She's not aware, she's not aware," to the pounding motif at the start of Beethoven's Fifth, until it started to sound like "She's not aware, she's not a Ware." Like some freaky conspiracy theorist, like someone who listened to Beatles records backward, he began to churn over a number of loose ends. If he'd started searching for anagrams, it would've been time to turn himself in. But for the time being, mulling it all kept him safe. Kept his brain hovering over the pain like a cloud refusing to break.

And then things changed. One morning he woke with the usual muffled feeling of failure caused by his recent hangovers, but he had somehow sorted out in his sleep that finding William Galeotto had never stopped being part of his quest, sponsored by Carolyn or not.

He had already scrolled through the search engines on Fran's computer, finding thousands of mentions of Galeotto House, analyses of Galeotto's characterization in *Tangier*, of Ware's relationship with him. But no luck finding any reference to the man lately, or his whereabouts.

Mac called the house phone at the Wares'. No answer. He felt uncomfortable leaving a message for Carolyn's mother, but so what? He did it. Fran was tapping on his door.

She said, "Want to come with me and Mom to the Buying Club?"

"I hate the Buying Club," Mac said. "I hate it more than you know. I hate it more than flies on babies' eyes, stepping in dog shit, bad eggs, Wendy Fugelsby's mother's armpits—"

"What was wrong with them?"

"Ever see them?"

"You need to get out, Mac. Come on, it'll be quick—I'll buy you a hot dog."

He decided to go because he liked the hot dogs, smothered in sauerkraut and onions. But to get one he had to pull a squeaking metal wagon around, showcasing Fran and Helen's purchases. Cases of tomato paste, tuna, and a bale of toilet paper bound for glory. They picked up half a side of beef for the freezer and grabbed giant jars of kosher dills, for what end, he did not know. They ogled books and clothes and socks. Not to mention aisle after aisle of the presumed essentials for housebound life. What else was a store but a place organized to excite you about all the things you *didn't* have? Though Fran had a pantry full of pots and pans, she hemmed and hawed and finally decided to splurge on a huge set, which came in a box as large as the cart.

"Why are you buying this?" Mac demanded.

She looked hurt, defensive. "Why shouldn't I?"

"What's wrong with the pans you already have?"

"The old ones don't match, and they're all black."

"Who cares if pans match?"

"I do!"

"How is your life going to be better if the *pans match*?"

"You'll understand someday, when you have your own house," Aunt Helen assured him.

"I'll never have matching pans, never!"

He had already guessed Fran's master plan: to chase out, piece by piece, all things slightly dog-eared or anomalous from her midst, until there was nothing left that could make her feel substandard. He'd seen the trait in Uncle Dick-Dick.

Time was lost forever in the Buying Club. Mac had his phone in his pocket, hoping it would ring. Of course, it didn't. When they got home, he jumped out of the car without carrying anything in and shut himself up in his room and called again. To his surprise, Mrs. Ware answered this time.

Be cool. "Hello, Mrs. Ware. It's Mac West, Carolyn's friend. I'm— I haven't heard from her since she went to New York. . . . Everything's all right?"

Adela said, "Don't you have her number?"

"Yeah, I couldn't seem to get through. When's she coming back?"

"Mac, they flew home a few days ago."

"Oh, right, well, I just— Okay." He held on to the back of his door. In order to be brave as a boy he'd think, *Ho ho ho!* No matter if his mother was in bed all afternoon, no matter if she was kissing some man in the kitchen one minute and hurling plates at him the next, no matter what. *Ho ho ho.*

"It was a successful trip—Molly is in. She'll start school after Labor Day."

"Off to school in New York. How great is that."

"I'll miss them, of course."

"Them?"

"Yes, Carolyn has all kinds of plans. And we'll probably start to spend more time there. Charles has a duplicate library there."

"That's strange."

"Not really, Mac. Books are his tools."

"Ah. Right." He took a deep breath and looked out his window into Fran and Tim's side yard, which had a gravel path that magnified the sounds of all footsteps, including those of dogs and cats and raccoons, and contained a clothesline Fran freshened bath mats on. There was one on it now, one he'd stepped on this morning with his big, wet feet, one he'd never once hung up in the sun while living there. He never thought about what it took to keep the place going. At once, seeing a damp bath mat, he hated himself. "Listen, you probably remember, I have this thing, about my mother—"

"Most men do," she said.

"Right. Anyway, do you happen to know where I could find Bill Galeotto these days?"

"What do you want with him?"

How he detested having to go through this! "As you may have heard by now, he knew my mother, long time ago."

"If she was young and pretty, I'm sure he did."

He had nothing to say to that. He closed his eyes.

"Where's Carolyn, then, is she home?"

"You seem like such a nice young man," Adela said, almost wistfully. "Have you at all been considering the job I offered you?"

"Job . . ."

"I need someone to transcribe my tapes."

That's right. He'd dismissed the idea before, thinking it would annoy and distance Carolyn. "I'm not sure I'm the man," he grumbled.

"I'd be extremely grateful. I really can't proceed until—"

"Uh-huh." His voice sounded as if it was coming out of a machine. "Okay, I'll do it. But about Mr. Galeotto?"

"The girls are riding," she said. "Would you like to know where?"

Of course he would, he wanted Carolyn more than Galeotto— he could meet her away from her maddening house.

"Yes, I would."

"First come get my tapes," Adela said.

He kicked a book across his room, as hard as he could. It knocked the plastic cactus off the table.

"You see, it wasn't love at first sight with Charles," she began. "I had a lot to learn. My mother nearly killed herself all those years, rubbing her hands raw, pushing the heavy cart to the different grocery shops so we could look like it all came easy. I had lived with that at school, dressing even *better* than the well-heeled girls, my mother pushing me into pretending, pretending, pretending! And here I crawled out of Canaryville on pickle money!

"Well, Charles was very pleased to hear from me when I finally came around. I liked him quite a bit better after my New York follies. Suddenly I saw my life taking shape around him. He wrote the poem 'Lilacs Deep, Deep Lilacs' for me. Did you know that? They teach it in schools. Bill Galeotto happened to come through Chicago: we were introduced. Bill turned to Charles and said, 'Get off my back, Charlie. Marry her.' Something about that introduction always bothered me. . . ."

Mac "prostituted" himself that day, listened to her but, by doing so, ended up not having to stop by. Ended up conning her out of a set of directions. A recipe for a wild-goose chase if he'd ever followed one. Adela wasn't clear on all of it. But he made sure to pay more attention to her than he ever had before.

So onward went Mac, shaving and parting his hair. Onward went Mac, digging out his best shirt and pants. Best in that they were clean. On he went, throwing the rolled-up rug, his supreme offering to Carolyn, into his car. Why had he waited so long?

Hadn't they been pledging their love all summer? Hadn't they found in each other the perfect solution to life's immeasurable grind?

Hadn't it seemed absolute, unqualified, whole, the time they'd spent together, the things they had shared?

And yet, hadn't he, deep down, imagined Carolyn moving on all along?

Imagining it could cause it. As if by doing that you created an opening for betrayal. In an insolent, childlike way, he offered himself up to such betrayals. It was something he would likely examine for the rest of his life, the fine line of permission he may have granted his mother to leave him. Like the good old Milgram experiment in depravity: how far would people go if you let them? *How far would they really go?*

He remembered kneeling in his room in Tres Osos, praying. Praying was something he had never tried in Boston. In the beginning he prayed for his mother's return. Then he prayed he could hate her, and once he succeeded at that, he prayed he would soon die gruesomely in many newsworthy pieces. He later prayed that he wouldn't die but that he would someday distinguish himself in the world, so she would suffer intensely for leaving him. Sometimes he prayed he would be offered the job of the next messiah. If so, there would be reason for all his suffering: his suffering would become legend. If so, it would explain why he had no father. It would explain why his mother couldn't bear the burden of raising him. It would explain the whole mystery of his existence; for certainly, his existence was otherwise uncalled for.

Okay, so he probably wasn't the next messiah. Now what?

The corridor down 19th Avenue until he could see the elbows and knees of the bridge always impressed him, and thus the traffic along it never bothered him the way jams drove him crazy on the peninsula. He thought of Carolyn, knees up in her bed. His car gunned on. He had a bag of short, oblong carrots he was munching on like a termite. At last, crossing the great bridge, he saw tourists on the walkway, capturing their images; he'd been out there with his camera, too. He liked how humans from all over spread the word that they ought to witness this sight, and usually he felt proud, but not now.

He was back in his shoes, the night he met Carolyn, kissing her mouth in the weeds. "Didn't expect this," he'd said.

"What's your name again?" They had laughed!

Then the brat had screeched from the house, and what he remembered now was the expression on Carolyn's face. It was a sadness with many layers, a disappointment that knew no bounds.

He drove up through the headlands, through the rainbow-rimmed orifice of the tunnel, and finally through some of the outlying suburbs he often heard the names of, never planning to visit. They were supposed to be fancy and dull. He stopped at a stand and bought flowers. A last-minute feeling of wanting something fresher than a rug. He crunched up a few more carrots. Following Adela's instructions, he cut toward the coast and peeled through Fairfax, then found himself leaving society behind on a shadowy, two-lane road of snaky turns along a shallow creek. Ferns bunched along the shoulder, while redwoods stood like stern elders up the slopes. A pack of motorcycles overtook him. He pulled over and let them swarm past.

He held up the directions. KEEP ON TOWARD BOLINAS. NO SIGN THERE SOMETIMES. RESIDENTS TAKE IT DOWN SO NO ONE CAN FIND THEM! HIT MAIN ROAD OVER MOUNTAIN, TURN NORTH. FOLLOW LAGOON.

Mac and Cavalier reached the crest and came down, windy, long, toward the Pacific. As promised, the coastal road finally appeared; he had been afraid he would not know a lagoon when he saw one. But there was no mistaking this lagoon. It was a lagoon's lagoon. It stretched between the road and the roaring ocean, a rustling expanse stirring with fish and creatures with wings.

LOOK FOR SMALL SHED ON THE RIGHT, SOMETIMES USED AS FRUIT STAND. IT MAY BE PINK. TURN ON DIRT ROAD. AFTER A MILE OR TWO, LOOK FOR A LONG PLASTER WALL WITH A HIGH WOODEN GATE. CARE-TAKER WILL LET YOU IN. IF NOT, TELL HIM CHARLES WARE SENT YOU.

He took a swig out of his hidden bottle under the seat, drove along in a state of excitement and dread. The gravel lane mounted grassy fields dotted with cattle, and he thought he saw a small bobcat on the rise. Then the open hillsides gave way to thickets of redwood, sun spotlighting unexpected nooks in sudden gleams. He, too, seemed to have lit up dark corners of Carolyn's world, corners she tried to keep quiet. He had meant no harm.

He rallied himself for seeing her, embracing her, being a prisoner of her grace. To become a master alchemist. To take her no and make it yes.

Another mile and various PRIVATE PROPERTY signs abutted the road. Shortly he spotted a wall that distantly matched Adela's description. It was covered with straggly vines, more ropy stem than leaf, and piles of ruined machines sat heaped alongside it. The stone torso of an animal stood by a gate, but the animal had no head.

No mention of a headless sphinx in front. Small detail. He pulled over, got out, and checked the fortress. The gate was heavy and high, and from within the compound, he could hear a low murmur of voices. There was a buzzer on the wall, and he pressed it. No reply.

Momentarily, an old white Volvo, the rounded kind reminiscent of hard-boiled eggs, came lumbering up the road. The man at the wheel looked to be so tall he had all but moved the driver's seat into the back; he was thin as a cattail, and when he saw Mac, he slowed to a stop and lowered his window. Mac stared at the man's mottled gums—he had no teeth. The woman beside him in the car had white hair and skin equally pale, almost like an albino's, except that her eyes were not pink. And she wasn't old. Her features were small and delicate, like a baby's. A Doberman pinscher, previously dozing on a grimy towel in the backseat, sat up and began to bark at Mac.

"Sonny, get your butt back down there!" the man yelled amiably. He opened his door and climbed out. Indeed, he was tall; he wore a tight Civil War–style undershirt, creased jeans, and orange, high-topped sneakers. "Who're you?"

Mac looked at the dog in back. Its long teeth were all the more noticeable in contrast to the man's gums. "I think some friends of mine are riding horses here," he said.

"You got insurance?" the man said. He was pointing at a dent in the back of Mac's Cavalier. "I got some friends work on cars, I could get 'em to pull that out, no sweat. I swear it, they'll fix you up, you don't file reports. I'm Glen. She's Maria."

"My name's MacGregor West—Mac."

The Doberman growled, but Glen yelled, *"Shut up, Sonny!"* The dog lowered his head.

"I went to classes about abused children today," Maria said from within the car. "For some, there is no exit."

"Wait, so who's— Is this—"

"Preschoolers I work with. I see bruises. Parent or child always has excuse," she said. "Julio has head lice. I am getting him special shampoo. Some neonates aren't bathed enough."

By now, the tall man was wrestling with the gate. Through the back of his tight shirt, his knobby vertebrae stacked up in plain relief. He plied open the heavy door enough for the car to get through, then jumped back in the egg and sputtered in.

Mac followed and found himself in a dusty field filled with cars and partial cars. The driveway continued over a rise. All around him were numerous broken-down, scavenged hulks, with doors and mirrors missing, even entire seats pulled out. Yet some of the vehicles were whole and looked as if they'd been driven recently. Gas cans and oil trays and a ratchet set glinted in the sun. What the hell was Carolyn doing here?

"This week we made feely book out of carpet squares," said Maria. She was gathering her supplies from the trunk. "There's bear, dog, lion, cat, and crocodile. We used linoleum to make crocodile."

Despite the fact that he wanted nothing to do with the couple, Mac couldn't help noticing that the woman kept forgetting her articles. "*The* crocodile," he said.

"It's important for neonates to use all five senses," she said.

He was carrying his flowers in one hand, his rug in the other. "Are there horses here? I'm looking for someone named Carolyn Ware."

Glen checked him over, then closed the gate behind them. Sonny began to bark and growl, which made Glen yell, *"Sonny, get your butt back in there!"* The dog slunk back and did full-circle turns with his muzzle pressed to the ground. "Sonny got mange," he said. "You bet there's horses, they always giving Sonny a mouthful of hoof. We the caretakers." And he motioned for Mac to follow them, along the inside of the wall, on a dry, littered path leading to a trailer and a barbecue pit. Around the fire a group of guys sat, some on a log, pitching horseshoes into the dust. The pit smoked, full of crackling pieces of meat. "Hey, this is— What's your name again?"

"Mac."

"Mac. Say welcome."

The guys nodded and a few said "Welcome." Most wore variations of the same black pants and white T-shirts; several had elaborate tattoos, and most of their heads had been shaved close to the skin. Glen said, "So, like I was telling you before, this one rottweiler was so bad, he smashed in the back of some dude's car, saw his own reflection in the chrome! Those things are so vicious. I gotta have one. Problem for me is Sonny, who's like a son to me, and he wouldn't take no shit from no other dog coming 'round the place."

Sonny, who had been lying in a self-made hole in the mud to

cool his mange, sprang up at the mention of his name and trotted over to Glen. Glen pounded him a few times on the ribs and then shouted, *"Get your butt back over there!"* The pinscher obediently crawled back to his hole, and the men nodded with approval.

"Farmer gave us five bushels of lettuce heads!" Maria said. She was on her knees, holding up a lettuce head caked with mud. "Twenty wooden pallets, too. I'll sell pallets in paper. It's more fusstrating trying to sell things at flea market," she said.

From where they stood, Mac gazed at the driveway, circling up through scattered tufts of dry grass. Over a distant hill, a black horse came cantering, raising pinwheels of dust. Mac squinted, bunched his hand over his brow to block the sun. Though the helmet might have disguised her, he could see the person atop the steed was Molly Ware.

Mac watched as she kicked the horse and turned it; she was an expert rider. The animal took off with a quiver to the lower flanks of the field, and in the distance Mac made out a small barn and corral.

"Thanks, I see what I came for." He started off down the path.

But Sonny's nails came clipping along through the stones, and Glen was following fast on his heels. "You gotta keep it quiet, we watch out for a sick guy here. The big man's gotta rest easy."

"What big man?"

"Maria, she the washer and cleaner, I cook. He got the sugar and can't breathe too good. I bring him the paper, and get this, he don't want the local *Gazette,* he don't even want the *San Francisco.* He want *The New York Times!* I gotta go all the way to Fairfax for that."

"Whose place is this?" Mac said, surmising the answer.

"Name's Mr. Glootto. He famous, I guess."

"*Glootto?* You mean Galeotto."

"Call him what you want, don't change much."

As they followed the drive through a dry gully and up again, Mac could hear from time to time the hard hooves pummeling the ground, ripping through the dry, wide paddocks down the hill.

Trying to reconcile it all, he said, "Carolyn and Molly Ware, they spend a lot of time here?"

"Sure they do. Just 'bout every Sunday."

"Every Sunday." He shook his head in disbelief.

"I feed the horses, they say thank you, we all get along real good."

You think you know a person. "Where's she now? Carolyn."

"House or down below."

The house was long and ramshackle, once stylish with high windows and an angled roof, now corseted in a tangle of woody shrubs and strangling vines. As Mac approached with his offerings, Glen said, "Listen, anyone ask, you promise you say this your idea?"

"Promise," said Mac.

"I got nothing to do with it?"

"Nothing."

"He don't have much visitors," Glen mused. As they drew closer, he said, "Maybe you get to talking to him, maybe he listen to you."

"About what?"

"Benefits! Maybe I get some teeth!"

"Why would—"

"No insurance. Maria can't hear too good in one ear," Glen said. Sonny rumbled.

"You mean, see if I can get you insurance?" Mac said. He felt like screaming.

"I'm just sayin', is all."

13

It took him a moment to see. So bright outside, the inside all the blacker. He found himself in a cluttered room, buried alive in the man's things. Beneath the piles of papers and books were the bare bones of what had once served as a habitable home. A long divan was concealed by folded laundry, rumpled bags, boxes, hangers, balls of string, bottles, baskets full of mail, a fan, and an old steel adding machine the size of a typewriter. Tables and armchairs were heaped high. The floors were swept, but around the edges he could see that nothing was quite clean. Dry grass, seeds, and little pebbles were welled up in the grooves by the walls and table legs, and despite some dust-free islands, thick, fuzzy grime gathered wherever a hasty cleaning had failed to reach. In the center of what had probably been the living room sat a neglected grand piano, but it was hardly recognizable as such; the closed lid was warped and cracked and covered with bottles and jars filled with murky lumps and liquids.

"Jeez," Mac said. "What're those?"

"Hell if I know," said Glen. "Come on back here."

"Carolyn hangs out in here?"

"She got ideas for us sometimes, like we put trash in bags."

"What about Charles Ware, does he come around?"

"Who's that?"

Blood pounded in Mac's temples.

He followed Glen through a rabbit warren of rooms, each more disordered and crowded than the next. Still, there were little touches that showed someone was trying. A broom leaning against a table, a jam jar filled with water and sprigs of sweet peas, a pile of stiff, sun-dried towels.

Sonny sniffed his hand and licked it. Even remembering the dog had mange, he squeezed one of the pliant ears. He'd always been a sucker for comforting animals. He had a moth-eaten koala bear he'd slept with until he was about fifteen.

Glen led him to a closed door pinned with old posters and prayer flags. He knocked, then pushed it open so they both could look in.

"She's not here," said Glen.

"What about— Is he?" Mac whispered. "Can I go in?"

It was a dark room with the curtains drawn, and Mac could barely make out what was ahead. In a few seconds, he was able to detect the form of a large four-poster bed taking up much of the space, and as his eyes continued to adjust, he saw that the floor was littered with plates. A rusty wheelbarrow, brimming with paper and debris, sat parked at the foot of the bed.

The bed itself contained a massive human being, but numerous ragged blankets, none of which seemed large enough, were piled on top, so it was hard to tell where the bed ended and the flesh began. A considerable head rested on the pillow, surrounded by a gathering cloud of hair; a gray beard tangled with the blankets. A tall green tank like a torpedo, with various valves and gauges and a hose that looked like an elephant's trunk, stood by.

The man stirred in his cocoon. "Who is it?" he rasped.

Mac was startled, and jumped at the rumble of the voice. He heard a dull crunch under his shoe.

"This my friend Gregor. He want to talk to you," Glen said.

A thick, fleshy hand groped at the night table and lit upon a hefty flashlight, which then sent a beam into Mac's face. Mac saw purple-and-white twirling parasols of light.

"Hey," Glen said. "Turn that thing off. Hungry again?"

"I, I, I— Yes."

"First you put that away," Glen said. "You don't get nothing when you behave like this."

Mac blinked his eyes. He could hear Glen wresting the flashlight from the man's grip and by then could see well enough to watch Glen place it on top of a pile of books across the room. The man began to gasp and cough.

"You calm down; I'm gonna fry you up some catfish," said Glen, who left them alone then.

Mac took a deep breath.

Steady. Thar she blows!

"Well, hello," he said. He could see why Carolyn had tried to keep him away. Still holding the flowers and the rug, he cleared his throat. "I've been wanting to meet you. My name's MacGregor West—"

The man began to cough, and the bed creaked and shook, and Mac had the impulse to thump him on the back, but there was no access to the man's back. He was one with the bed. His hand groped for the hose that issued from the tank, and he lifted it to his mouth and began to inhale. Mac could hear the shallow gasping and sucking. After the attack subsided, the man grabbed from the folds of his bed a small, spiral-bound pad, into which a pencil had been stabbed. He removed the pencil and began to scratch. Finished, he propped it up for Mac to read:

THOSE FOR ME?

Mac felt embarrassed. "Well—"

THANK YOU, wrote the man.

Mac handed the man the bouquet and dropped the rug. He was breathing fast, as if he'd been running. "I'm very sorry to bother you like this. I had no idea." He tried to gauge the man's state of mind and kept going. "I didn't even know this was your place, but I've wanted to meet you for a long time. Because—I think you knew my mother." He stopped. Galeotto's head was levitating off the pillow, and he sniffed at the flowers. "In fact, you might be the only person left on earth who knew her—besides her sister. It's possible you only knew her *physically*, but—" What a horrible thought. He stopped himself. Blood, he thought, could be the very last thing a person tasted, was likely the first, and was never far off in between! Mac had torn a hole on the inside of his cheek.

"I'm— I don't know . . . what you're talking about," came the voice, squeezing through a meaty throat.

"I have a picture of you and her," said Mac.

"Your, your mother?" His cough was deep and wet. "Show me."

The blankets roiled like the sea, and then a flannel sleeve began to emerge from the folds. The hand on the end of it was open flat.

Mac reached for his wallet. He pulled out the picture and examined the image before placing it in the outstretched palm. The palm closed and pulled in toward the generously proportioned head.

"Can't see," said the man.

Thus Mac moved over and parted the faded, brittle curtains, letting in some afternoon sunshine. The room didn't benefit from exposure; it looked drab and frozen in time. The man was squinting and peering at the picture an inch from his face. He took only the briefest glance before laying it down on his chest. Beneath the blankets his massive legs began to kick, and his coughs came in great cascades.

He picked up his pad and wrote:

IT'S ABOUT TIME. WHAT TOOK YOU SO LONG?

Tears sprang to Mac's eyes, so rapidly were the words volunteered.

A pea green room, dank, ratty, a man half the size of an elephant—all his wondering and suffering came down to this?

Engineering this reunion, from time to time but not regularly or frequently, had mostly been by chance. *Wipe your eyes, boy! Wipe your woeful eyes.*

So Mac ended up saying, "Works for me," rather nonsensically.

"Good!" The man coughed up phlegm.

Now what?

A classic case of *Be Careful.*

What.

You Wish For.

You stupid jerk. The wafting wonder of a wish-state, where he'd housed himself for years. *Put down your bags now, make yourself at home?*

"Nice to finally meet you," he managed at last.

"Life happens," the man said, and coughed.

"So, it's really true?"

"I don't know . . . what you're talking about," the man uttered, and when Mac's face fell, he emitted a strangled laugh. "Bad. Joke."

"Oh," said Mac. He tried to smile at the bad joke, but tears came back to him instead.

"I say . . . that whenever . . . I don't know what . . . to say," Galeotto choked out.

Mac wiped his wet eyes on his sleeve, reminding himself not to grow too eager. "You don't look like you're doing too well."

Galeotto produced an inhaler from the folds of the bed, took a long, snarling drag from it, then boomed in a newly fortified voice, "Wasn't that long ago . . . women were all over me. I had it made. Girls and more girls, you should have seen it! I had a setback. Which is why . . . you find me . . . here . . . like this."

"What kind of setback?"

Galeotto huffed and tried to prop himself up. "Went a little nuts," he said, and coughed again. "Was low . . . and hopeless. Couldn't conquer . . . my appetites . . . and then I fell sick. Don't worry . . . I plan to get on top of it."

Mac imagined renting a dumpster, taking heaping armloads of junk to it, and hearing the reverberant thunder of chucking it in. He saw a cleaning crew vacuuming and scrubbing, all the things you could do for an aging relative if you had one all your own. He wondered if the man would *let* him help.

Whoa. Why did he want to help?

Just then Glen could be heard coming their way, accompanied by the clicking of Sonny's nails. Glen pushed his way into the room with a tray.

"Got a nice meal fixed here. My job's to keep him in food—only no donuts or crullers! This guy beg me for 'em, he point his little gun at me even, I gotta say no. He's just a kidder." Glen laughed. "He got a good heart."

"Not . . . that . . . good," said Galeotto.

Glen said, "I'm telling you, they got flounder, they got little sand sharks, they got swordfish! But I like catfish the best. Don't even taste like a fish. Probably taste like cat!"

Sonny lapped at one of the plates on the floor while Glen set down the tray and came over and helped Galeotto sit. Mac helped, too. His hand reached under the man's arm, and with all his muscle he struggled with his half of the man to prop him up.

But who needed a father when you were all grown up?

"Some for you, too," said Glen, giving Mac the second plate. "Come on, Sonny. Got scraps in the kitchen." The two retreated, and Mac heard from the other end of the house the sounds of various pots and pans crashing into a sink.

Mac looked at the plate. There was a big piece of fried fish coated in a batter with flecks of herbs in it. Two large spears of cooked broccoli sat on the side.

"I like . . . the way . . . he does . . . the crust," Galeotto managed to say.

Mac was hungry, so he cut a piece with his fork. The atmosphere in the room wasn't mouthwatering, but the fish was tender and sweet, tangy and well seasoned. Somehow it was hitting the spot. "Those two, they've been good to you?"

"The woman's . . . a kind soul," replied Galeotto. "Rubs my rotten . . . old feet every night."

"They say they don't have insurance, and they have some health problems," said Mac, gulping some fish.

"I'll try. I'm broke. Get this." He masticated loudly. "All I ever wanted . . . was to run a restaurant!"

"You mean, you're not interested in publishing?"

"Not really. I wanted . . . an Italian place. With a Moroccan twist. My uncle . . . Tino . . . gave me recipes. Lots of black olives. Oranges. Tagines on every table. Waiters in djellabas. The works!"

"What stopped you?"

Galeotto was growing more animated with a little protein in him. "You want . . . a list . . . of my mistakes? It's a long list." He began to gasp and cough so hard he sounded like a harmonica, and Mac listened and watched in horrified silence. When the paroxysm ended, Galeotto scooped up his pad and scribbled out: I USED TO BE AS SLIM AS YOU. WATCH YOURSELF.

"I definitely will," Mac replied.

SMOKE?

"Yeah. I know I shouldn't, but—"

QUIT. I HAVE EMPHYSEMA, AMONG OTHER PROBLEMS. TAKES THE PLEASURE OUT OF LIFE.

"I bet."

"Open that drawer," Galeotto croaked. "I want . . . to show you something. Right at the front, underneath, an . . . old photo."

Mac made his way to the dresser, set down his plate, and yanked the stiff drawer. It was crammed with unpaired socks. He parted them and saw a photo at the bottom of the drawer. "This?" he said, lifting it out.

"That's it," Galeotto said. "Look at Mom and Pop. And look . . . at me!"

Mac brought the photo into the window light. It appeared to have been taken in North Beach, on the stucco porch of an apartment building. A small man in an oversize delivery uniform and a very short woman with a massive bosom flanked their son, a giant grown-up between them. Galeotto stood head and shoulders above them in an ill-fitting suit, sleeves and pant legs far too short, but he cut a good-looking figure despite it.

"My confirmation day. Borrowed the suit . . . from my cousin. Look at us!"

"Looks like your dad had to work that day."

"Drove his van . . . across town . . . to get his picture taken next to the suit," Galeotto spluttered. "Well, go on—say it! Isn't it shouting at you?"

Galeotto was up on his elbow now, expectant. Mac could see his ravenous features well for the first time. The eyes were brown, like acorns in the autumn sun. "I'm not sure what to say. You were poor, is that what you want me to know?"

"Yes, we were poor, but no," said Galeotto, irritably.

Mac looked at the picture again. "Are you trying to tell me you were adopted?" he ventured.

The man fell back onto his pillow, and the bedsprings groaned. "Bravo. It doesn't take a genius." He laughed quietly. "Charlie was the first . . . to say it to my face."

Charlie again. "It's my studied opinion," said Mac, "that Charles Ware is ninety percent shithead."

Galeotto snorted.

Mac gazed down at the boy with the short parents and short pants. Was this a preemptive strike? An attempt to explain himself before Mac pinned him with blame? "So what was the problem with being adopted?"

"Just thought . . . you'd want to know," Galeotto wrenched out. "Now I need . . . to rest . . . my voice."

"Fine," Mac said. His nerves were on high alert anyway, lest Carolyn walk in. He made his move for the door, ready to go find her. "I'll be seeing you."

"Wait," whispered Galeotto. "I gotta ask . . . your mother ever—" The hack resumed, causing the man to suck hard and long on his inhaler. "She ever . . . talk about me?"

Now, on top of everything else, he had to stoke the behemoth's ego? "No. She didn't. Ever. *Say anything.*"

"I see," gurgled Galeotto. "Tell . . . the old man . . . to piss up a rope."

Funny how mad he was at the old hulk. "What do you expect?" Mac said. "You could have worked a little on the outreach. I sniffed the world's butt for a few half-assed clues. I ended up at the Wares' house in San Francisco, and even then it was messed up. I guess no one wanted to blow your cover."

Galeotto said, "Meet . . . Carolyn Ware?"

There was something unpleasantly lascivious about the question. "That I did."

"What . . . did . . . you think?" gasped the beast.

"She's okay."

"Yes," coughed Galeotto. "She's that. She's quite a bit . . . okay."

Mac glared at him. The catfish was bottom-feeding in his stomach. "So what happened?—You met my mother when you were married?"

"Let's not . . . get moral about it." Galeotto wheezed. "I . . . had a thing with your mom. She was a very . . . sexy . . . woman." He began to smile. "My God."

Mac blushed. "In Paris, twenty-three years ago, summer of a certain film festival."

The dreamy face lingered beneath the shaggy beard. "That's where it was."

"And later, you knew that she'd had a child? Me, in other words?"

"Yes, I did." And with that, he held out a hand. But Mac pointedly did not take the hand offered him.

"You did nothing about it. You let your idiot friend support us like we were *charity cases*?"

The man had been looking at Mac gently, with something almost like affection; these words caused him to draw back. He rubbed his eyes a moment, and coughed.

"It's to be expected . . . that you won't feel much for me," Galeotto muttered. "I'm glad you seem . . . to have turned out well."

"I could be the worst person in the world, little would you know."

"Be strong," Galeotto said from the dark headboard.

"I can't believe this. You complain you were *adopted*."

Galeotto was breathing hard. He stroked his beard as if it was a pet. "MacGregor," he uttered. "Who ever told you . . . that Charlie Ware . . . supported you?"

Mac now wished to escape the room more than anything. He needed some air. It was all too much.

"*He* did."

"And you think . . . he's to be trusted?"

"Why?"

"Did you make . . . out . . . all right?" Galeotto asked.

"We got by."

"You were supposed . . . to be comfortable. Don't get me wrong . . . I know I . . . didn't do well for you. But it was from *me* . . . that money. I had to . . . keep the paper trail away . . . from my wife. Charlie took care of it . . . to spare me . . . the risk."

Mac ran his hands through his hair and felt sadder than ever. So much had been disguised. "Great, good job, you're to be congratulated, you did the right thing, *Dad*. I'm impressed. By your integrity. You're a paragon of virtue. I hope to emulate you. By your example I'll be a great man. But hey, didn't you ever want to meet me?" To Mac's surprise, his voice broke saying this.

The mammoth looked up from the bed, as a child might who wants to stay home from school. "I . . . tried. Charlie said . . . she didn't want . . . anything to do with me." He cleared his throat. "Besides, you had a good situation."

Charlie.

"You . . . like baseball?" Galeotto said. "The Giants are . . . in San Diego today."

"I don't want to talk about baseball!"

"I live for it."

"I'm a Red Sox fan."

"Give me my radio, would you?"

Mac picked up the cheap little radio off the bedside table, and Galeotto put down his plate and grabbed it and turned it on and began to spin the knob, filling the air with small explosions of static. To Mac's surprise, the man set down the radio and sobbed.

The sight of such a pathetic and stranded person wetting his pillow and beard was worse than anything Mac had come across so far. He found some sort of rag on a chair, handed it to the man, sat down on the end of the bed. He made a note to his older self—*Don't end up this way. Whatever it takes.* He grabbed the radio from Galeotto and fiddled around. "No wonder, it was on FM," said Mac, finding the keyed-up voices of the game. Seventh inning, Giants up by three. "Maybe they'll pull it off today. Here you go."

Galeotto took the radio and held it to his chest. He closed his eyes.

"I've wasted . . . my life," he whispered. His cough was worse now, as if the lungs were vomiting. But lungs were full of all kinds of narrow passageways and crawl spaces, and so their attempts to free themselves of debris weren't as efficient as a good old barf. The man sweated with the effort.

Mac picked up Galeotto's pad of paper and wrote down his address and phone number. "I'm going now," he said, tossing the pad onto the mound that was Galeotto's stomach.

"Will you . . . come again?"

"I gave you my number. We'll see how bad you want to stay in touch."

"It took some guts . . . coming here," Galeotto murmured. "I like that."

Mac felt ashamed that the compliment meant something to him. Ashamed that the fat arm and body felt cuddly in a way he'd never had the chance to know.

"You know . . . those 1970-model . . . campers?" Galeotto gasped as Mac gathered up his rug. "No bigger . . . than . . . a pickup truck?"

"I guess."

"Keep your eyes . . . open . . . for one of those. I'd like to . . . do a few . . . trips while I . . . still can."

"You want me to get you a camper?"

"If you . . . win the lottery," Galeotto heaved.

Through the dark hall, he left the man alone. On the way he smashed into a troglodyte posing as a bookcase and toppled a stack of volumes onto the floor. He pushed on to the main room, looked again at the piano covered in jars, and opened the door into the bright afternoon sun. He couldn't see a thing for a moment and wondered if Carolyn was out there somewhere, staring at him in his blindness. If she had been all along.

One last thing. He poked his head into the kitchen. Glen was wearing an apron and scraping a frying pan over the sink.

"I'm going," Mac said numbly.

"You take care," said Glen.

"The catfish was really good."

"Secret's to soak it in apple juice, lime, and a little cayenne. Keep it in the refrigerator so it's cold. Bread it real good and drop it in hot fat, you get a real nice seal with all the flavor trapped inside. Oh, and don't forget the salt and pepper. A shake for each bite."

Mac stared at Glen's apron, wet with dish suds, crusty with flour. "I'll try it sometime."

"Come back, I make it every week. Big man loves it. 'Course, he likes all my cooking."

"He's my dad," Mac blurted out. He wouldn't have too many chances to make a splash with the news.

"No kidding! Why didn't you say so?"

"No big deal." *Ha!*

"He don't have much family. I thought maybe the girls was family, but they set me straight. How come you never showed up till now?"

Mac said, "I got a late start. How long you worked here?"

" 'Bout two years."

"He getting worse?"

" 'Bout the same," said Glen.

"He ever go outside, anything like that?"

"I take him out every morning, he like the sunrise. Sometime we see gophers popping up, he like that, too. He like the smell of the grass even when it dead. He sit in his chair and pull weeds from it."

Glen set his grill pan back on the stove, polished the top of the stove with the dishcloth, then hung it on the oven handle, as the kitchen, unlike the rest of the house, was shipshape.

"Glen—one last thing. Those guys out there, who are they, anyway?"

"Friends from Center," he said. "Don't worry, they not addicts anymore. They real nice."

"Center. What's Center?"

Glen's answers were unblemished in their sincerity. He told Mac he had been sentenced to night classes at the local rehabilitation center after his second DUI a few years back. Since then, he'd cleaned up his act. He liked the big guy, and the only bad thing about working for him was that he was really working for someone else, some higher authority issuing orders and edicts through Carolyn. Their paycheck arrived on time, but everything around the place was managed on a shoestring, because the man with the purse didn't open it wide enough. The guys from Center did odd jobs to store their cars there and just to have a place to barbecue and hang out. The horse was the only thing around getting any attention. The horse had its own dentist who made house calls! What was that saying about looking a horse in the mouth? Glen wondered. Because if ever there was a horse's mouth to look into, this was the one.

His mother's voice: *"Avenge me, and these will help you do so."* How did finding Galeotto avenge her? What was to avenge? What twisted vision of family connection had he stumbled into now? Staring out at the man's acreage, Mac felt more foolish than ever for thinking he could forge a relationship based on the passing of seed. The burrs in his socks would come home with him and fall off on the ground and grow fescue and wheatgrass. Nothing more than that: random, buckshot biology.

Down below, in jodhpurs, a white blouse with pearly studs, a helmet, and black boots, Carolyn Ware was smoothing the black horse's muzzle. Rubbing its neck and chest. Molly sat atop the horse in an identical outfit, and Carolyn appeared to be instructing her on the fine points of making a jump. She gave the horse another pat and backed off; Molly gave the glossy flank a slap with her crop and jumped the hurdle before her. Dust rose as if a grenade had gone off. Then the girl pulled the reins and brought the animal back around to Carolyn, who produced a treat from her pocket. More brushing and stroking, Molly digging in her heels; the knobby horse legs trotted and ran and bent at the knee, and the hurdle was tried again.

"Walk on!" he heard Molly cry. He could see her kicking the animal.

The rug was itching his arm. It was worn and faded and ugly, why hadn't he ever noticed? He had been trained to see everything through his mother's deluded eyes. What an act it would be to denounce this rug forever. He didn't need to keep it, he didn't need to give it away; just because his mother thought it was great didn't mean he had to!

He veered down the driveway into the parking area, and he thrashed it on the ground like a bag of bones, an unwanted child, over and over and over, tried to tear it with his teeth and then gagged with the fibers on his tongue. He spat dust and rubbed grit from his eyes. In the lot full of cars, there was a gas can. His rug would now go up in smoke. And it was time. Exalted, he poured vaporous fluid from the can and made a sodden log of it, and from a tiny match light watched the old thing roar into a blaze. Felt the rightness of the cremation of it, as it burned steady, turning gray. A line of smoldering remains.

He couldn't face Carolyn right now. He put one foot in front of the other and walked. Away from those paddocks as golden as a summer evening in California, sun in his face.

Half claimed. Half disgraced.

*A*t some point in the future, Mac would have the wherewithal to remember this day with something akin to pride. A rite of passage, as it were. A necessary one. The one he'd been deprived of. But that would not be for a while. For now, he was driving back at dusk through the forest, over the mountains, to 101 and the approach to the bridge, pushing his hair out of his face.

To establish normalcy, he called his cousin as soon as he was in range.

"Hey, Fran," he said. "What are you doing?"

"Spitting," said Fran.

"Why?"

"I have too much saliva all of a sudden. It's some rare condition that some pregnant women get."

"Bummer."

"It's more than a bummer. I'm like a hose! I have to carry a towel around, or gnawing on an apple helps."

"Hmm. Well, I have some surprising news. I just met a man who may be my father."

"Your *real* one?"

"Almost too real." And then he told all—almost all. With his free hand, he grasped and shook the steering wheel as he described what he'd seen.

Fran listened, shrieked a few times. "I have to call Mom!"

"No, I want to tell her!"

"Call her now, because I can't wait. What does it mean, Mac?"

"That my gene pool is highly suspect."

"What a crazy story!"

"Yeah, pretty much."

"You're not going to get all buddied up with him now and forget about us, are you?"

"Huh?"

"I'm kidding. Urgh, I'd better go, I need my towel."

"You get it, then."

He was experiencing a major rush, having news to report about himself. Didn't happen too often. On the bridge, he looked ahead to the bank of fog settling on the city like a mitt. The lights of downtown trying to burn through. He lit a cigarette and phoned Aunt Helen in Tres Osos—pleased to hear the range of emotions in her voice, just about parallel to those he'd been having himself.

"Oh, Mac, what a milestone. But he should be shot."

"He's already shot, believe me."

"He knew about you, he did nothing?"

"It's complicated. It sounds like Mom, or maybe Charles Ware, kept him at bay."

"Could be," agreed Helen.

"I still have a lot of questions."

"I would think so. I'd think you'd have many feelings to sort out."

"He's incredibly obese and bedridden," Mac said. "Plus, he's bragging about all the chicks he used to do!"

"The past is all that's left for him."

"Oh, and get this, he wants me to get him a camper."

"You mean a truck with a little unit on the back? Those are dreadful. It's much nicer to camp in a tent."

"I'm not getting him a *camper*!" Mac yelled. "He should get *me* a camper!"

"Mac, just because he's your biological father doesn't mean you have to love him."

"I'm glad to have your permission not to love him."

"Was this a result of the things in the box?"

"It was. Thanks a lot, Helen."

"I had no idea."

"You know what's the weird part? Carolyn knew him and—" It exhausted him before he'd even started, the idea of explaining his girlfriend's behavior. "Never mind. I'm on the bridge, and I gotta find five bucks. Say hi to Uncle Richard."

"I think this will help you in many ways, Mac."

"You'll be the first to know."

Fully into the fog now, he took the turnoff for the Marina instead of continuing down 19th, as if considering a stop at Carolyn's. Dolt might be his middle name. He pulled over on Lombard next to a hamburger shack and put in a call to her. No answer. Modest motel signs and gas stations glowed down the avenue. He saw ahead another block the liquor store he'd stopped in with Carolyn the night they met. *Milk for the girls.*

The same man sat upon his stool behind the counter, with his arching brow and look of surprise. *I see you are alone again, as a result of the deep rift in your soul, which makes you unbearable to others dealing with deep rifts in their own souls. I am kept afloat by the likes of you!*

"Pack of Camels." He thought maybe he would quit soon. He chucked his beer on the counter. "You knew it all along, didn't you?"

"I can usually tell," said the man, ringing him up.

*A*nd then. And then. In his car there were various loops around the Marina and up and down the hills overlooking the bay, and at last, with reason overruled, there came a trip into her neighborhood, a parking job across the street, and a wait in a dark car with cigarettes and beer. And finally her car pulling up and the garage door rising, Molly running ahead to the house and providing him with his moment to move in on her in the dark. She was pulling things from the backseat, and he didn't want to frighten her.

"Carolyn, heads up."

She had changed from her riding clothes into a sweater and skirt, and when she pulled her head out of the car he saw her hair was washed and damp: this revealed a level of comfort with Galeotto's facilities that deepened his unease.

"Mac."

"You can't be too surprised to see me."

She shrugged, but her mouth curled into the half-moon of a smile.

"He's a self-centered person with nothing to give, so I feel sorry for you," she said then, closing the car door with a kick.

"Did you know, all along?"

"I should have. No wonder—" She let out a scornful huff, then bit down on her lip. "I realize how much you look like him."

"Great," he muttered, envisioning the blimp. "No wonder *what*?"

Carolyn didn't answer right away. She had a far-off look in her eyes, as if playing a tape in her mind of all that had happened between them and determining its worth. "Oh, that I felt like I knew you," she said at last.

Mac was dumbfounded by the implication. "You know me now" was his strangled reply. "Why couldn't you tell me you and Molly go up there?"

"It's depressing, obviously," she said, trying to move past him.

"Yes, it is. But still!"

"He has nothing to offer you, or anyone in the world," Carolyn went on, her voice wobbling slightly. "And I wanted you to *myself*. Was that wrong?"

He was still blocking her way, and he took the bags from her arms and dropped them on the ground, and held her hands.

"It's okay, Carolyn, we should be glad—we wouldn't have met, without him."

"It's all very unlucky," she said.

"It's the best luck I've ever had," he replied.

So there came, in place of further accusations and demands, an outpouring expressed in kisses and embraces and "Come with me" and "No, I can't" and "We need to talk" and "Not right now" and "Come with me" and "No, no, no," but then she yielded, suddenly, as if planning to all along, as if she saw a way to make things right, even if only for the night, into his car without even a glance back at the house, down the hill to a motel off Lombard, where he went in and booked a room with his old wallet, his way, and in the room with the cheap flowered bedspread and the thin blankets and the stained rug there was an attempt between them to connect forever in a new way, where talk would be like saying uncle, so neither of them said a thing, and he would nail her down and make her his own and she was there for that, which meant there was a chance, for thus nailed, she wouldn't fall off, the raft, the boat, the love, it could happen, it could really happen, it could be so.

Just don't. Please. Don't fall off.

14

"J hope they're not garbled," Adela Ware was saying to Mac on a warm afternoon in September. Not a wisp of fog to be seen in the city, and not a cloud in the sky, nor an angel anywhere wishing him well. Her voice sounded different that day, almost bashful. "No hurry, exactly."

Coming to pick up Adela's tapes, he thought it showed dogged determination that she had made such recordings and that it was strange she wanted to give them over to him. But making sense of the Ware family had eluded him all along. When he pulled up in front of the big house, he could hardly make the walk to the door, and wasn't sure he could go through with this new gambit of his. But before he had the chance to escape, she spotted him from one of the front windows and met him on the curb with her clattering box of memories.

"I'll see how it goes," Mac said. "Is your husband here today?"

"I thought you were here to see me."

"I am. Just asking."

"Friday's when he usually drops in at the press, Mac."

"And Carolyn. I guess she made it to New York okay."

"The house is terribly empty. Isabel's changed my pills. She says I'll have to get busy."

"Learn Inuit or something."

"How's that?"

"I'm kidding. I'll be in touch, Mrs. Ware."

"Adela, Mac."

"Adela."

"Will you let me know if it's any good?"

"Sure, of course."

He took the tapes home and began to listen to them, for bringing meaning to Carolyn's life was now his work, and he had to devote many hours to it. Next came a marathon of transcription, setting up the table in his room and using some old equipment Fran found for him in a back room at the library. He wore clunky, outdated earphones as big as donuts, and ran the machine with a foot pedal, typing away onto Fran's laptop, filling ashtrays and piling up soda cans hour after hour and day after day. It was a sure recipe for madness.

The tapes were depressing and chilling in the picture they painted of the poor woman, who, in recounting her life story, seemed almost indifferent to all its ruined pieces.

"Their birthdays were only eight days apart," Adela said of Charles and Bill. "So who would have the party? Chloe and I used to throw it for them together. Until one year, when they fought over the cake! Brawling over a cake on the table, and Charles cried like a child, and Bill threw a lamp at the wall. . . ." Mac felt he heard very little that was unrelated to this theme.

Finally, much of the tape was taken up with monologues from various dramatic works, and Mac notated these but didn't transcribe them. He'd expected a lot more, and was learning about Carolyn if only by her omission from most of the babble of her mother's life.

Rare mentions of her would cause him to shake. Had he been searching for news of Molly, he would have found not a shred.

He was making coffee one morning in the midst of it; Fran stood cleaning purple figs from the backyard tree to take in a basket to work.

"You used to sing that when you came to live with us, and we thought it was sad," she remarked.

"What?"

"What you were just singing."

"What was I singing?" He didn't know he was singing.

" 'There's a place in France where the alligators dance, and the dance they do costs a dollar ninety-two!' " Fran vocalized.

"Oh, yeah, that's been droning in my head lately. Why was it sad?"

"You know how Mom analyzes everything. She said it seemed like a subliminal lament. The real one goes something like 'There's a place in France where the naked ladies dance,' but we were thinking you changed the words to nix the negative associations."

"Interesting."

The brain was a crazy, mysterious blob, the way it sang to you to deliver a message, or threw together a dream better than a big-budget film.

"Have you heard from Carolyn yet?" she asked.

"No."

"Isn't she supposed to call you?"

"We didn't make a plan."

"Her sister must be in school now, it's late September."

"I know what day it is."

"Is she staying out there or what?"

"Fran, drop it."

"Have you tried calling?"

"I've left a few messages, but she's busy."

"Mac! This is horrible, it reminds me of—"

"Of what?"

"Sorry," she said, shaking her head. "I was going to say it reminds me of when you were waiting for your mother, but that seemed hurtful."

"This conversation is hurting me."

"You've never taken to advice, have you?"

"Giving advice can be a vice," Mac said.

Two weeks later, completely fried by the transcription ordeal, he parked in a garage next to the police department in North Beach. They had once parked there together, that's all, but the garage would ever after bite him on the ankle when he passed it. The hounds of memory would yelp from every street corner, from every table in every restaurant, from every patch of grass in the park that had needled their backs under the fogbound sky.

This day he jostled his way through the crowds to the office on Jackson; on the wall by the elevator, the name Galeotto House had new appeal. For after all, he could adopt the name, couldn't he? MacGregor Galeotto—man of action. Well, it didn't suit him. But what it could buy! No one seemed to know the man was splayed out like a beached whale in a garbage dump. He took the elevator ride and wandered into the offices and recognized the golden-haired receptionist as the one he'd submitted his beefed-up résumé to a year back. *Mac Galeotto here. Get down on all fours.*

"Hi there, I'm looking for Charles Ware."

"I think he and Mr. Heald went out to lunch. Were you supposed to meet them?"

"That's right. At the restaurant." She was being nice to him without knowing he was Galeotto's progeny. Ah, nothing like looking around with a little entitlement. Should he insist on a corner office, senior editor to start? She told him where she thought they'd gone, and because he had contacted Glen and Maria and suggested they meet him at the office, he asked the comely employee to refer the odd couple to Mario's as well. "Appreciate it," he said. *Isn't it time for a promotion? Let's see what I can do. . . .*

He found the restaurant on Columbus, an old-fashioned, heavily curtained place with flocked wallpaper and career waiters. Charles Ware had a reservation but had not yet arrived. Mac sat at the bar. At a buffet table, an ice statue of Venus stood on the half shell, dripping onto a bed of scattered salmon and cold peas. "As a kid back east I used to make ice sculptures," he said to a woman sitting there. She wore shiny stockings and had shoes so pointy it seemed impossible any human foot could fit in them. A cassowary foot probably could. "I'd dig the mold outside in the ground, but it was hard to get the details right. And whatever I made had rocks and frozen worms stuck into it."

She moved to the next stool.

Ah, the refuge of spirits. He gulped.

He thought of something that made him smile.

Once he and his mother were sharing a pizza in an empty diner in Brighton when a guy wandered in, moseyed up to the front, gave the cook his order, and—voilà!—opened his fly and began to piss against the order counter. Mac's mother flipped. She said she'd seen one too many public urinations. "Cut it out, buddy!" she screamed.

"Oh yeah?" the guy said, wagging himself off.

"You're a pig!"

"Yeah?" he said.

"Whatsa matter?" the cook said.

"He's peeing!" Mac's mother said, pointing at the puddle.

The peeing man came over and pushed his mother, and because she was clumsy, she fell down. "Shut up, lady, or I'll crap in your face!"

Mac jumped to the rescue. His mother went on this kind of crusade often, but usually he didn't want any part of it. She was also on a mission to put an end to all nose picking, and whenever they were in a car and she saw someone at it, she'd honk the horn and wave her fist at the culprit. Mac would duck. "Stop it, Mom!" he'd scream. "What's it to us?" However, having his mother pushed to the ground was a different matter, and though he was only about seven, he ran up to the guy and jumped on his back and sank his teeth through his filthy shirt into his flesh. The man squealed. Mac bit harder. Meanwhile, Mac's mother was up, punching the guy in the gut while he tried to get Mac off his back.

For the first time in a good while, a memory involving his mother made Mac laugh, and the woman with the pointy shoes glared. "Hey, just be glad I'm not pissing on the counter," he mumbled. He started giggling to himself with his bourbon on the rocks, then looked up and saw, in the diluted light, Charles Ware and Freddie Heald sitting down for lunch.

Mac watched them awhile, knocked back another drink. Was this a business lunch? Freddie kept touching Ware's arm.

Finally Mac gathered his remaining wits and bumbled to their table.

"Gentlemen!"

The two were enmeshed in a quiet discussion when they looked up and saw his approach. Morsels of untouched food laced their plates. "Mr. West," said Ware. "What brings you here?"

"Hello!" said the collegial Freddie, pulling over another chair.

"Have you met?" said Ware.

"The big party," Freddie reminded him.

"Ah, the big ordeal," said Ware. "Yes."

"Waiter!" called Freddie. "You'll join us, won't you? Bring him one of what we're having." He lifted a glass of red wine.

Mac was already smashed, because the first thing he spewed at Freddie was "You— So *you're* the ex?"

"The ex, the ex?"

"You've never heard of the ex?"

"Carolyn's?" said Freddie.

Maybe the joke was on Mac—he was now the ex.

"I've known her forever," Freddie said..

Ware said, "I take it things have cooled off some."

"I was delighted she'd met you," Freddie said. "She's the greatest, isn't she? Now that she's in New York, I'm going to have her work on Naomi Spender's memoirs. It'll be fabulous for both of them."

"By the way, am I interrupting anything?" Mac said.

Ware said, "We do have some business. How can I help you?"

What if he threw a glass of wine into the man's face, what then?

"All right, let's start," Mac said. He took the floor. "It was, um, pretty rude, what you said about my mother, that time on the boat."

Ware sighed. "Yes, it was. My daughter told me off. My apologies."

"He said, 'Your mama's a whore,' " Mac informed Freddie.

"Oh! I see," said Freddie.

"Kind of wrecked that day for me. Then we could go back to my childhood. I think you should have told your friend Bill to come see me, instead of meddling. Were you afraid he'd get away from you? That he'd get his own life or something horrible like that? See, in the final desperate hours of my recent life, I met Mr. Galeotto," Mac said. He watched Ware's face. "And he's— Well, you already know. My father."

Ware examined his fingernails. "After all that trouble, what a let-down."

Freddie looked to Ware for his reaction. "Get out! It's true?"

"Stranger things have happened," Ware said.

Mac said, "But you knew all along, right? From the first time I showed you the envelopes."

Ware shrugged and took a swill from his wineglass. "I knew the first moment I *saw* you. Don't underestimate me! But I don't know what you hope to gain from it."

"I don't hope anything, you old pike."

"Be nice," said Freddie. "Charles has been through the wringer with that man. He's done more for Bill Galeotto than anyone. Subsidizing the press for years, providing him care. You should be very grateful."

Mac looked at his watch. "Yeah, I guess. Thanks a lot. But he told me it was *his* money you were sending us, not charity."

"Fate is very strange," said Ware. "Did he bother to tell you anything about your mother? Like how she died? I think that's what you wanted, isn't it?"

Mac was aware of a growing tightness in his chest. "What do you know about it?"

"Surely you understand the havoc she wreaked and you must resent it, too. Look at what she did to you," Ware said.

"Tell me what you know about my mother's death!"

"I know that she was better at killing herself than making a nice life for her child. Bill was willing to do that, you know."

"How?"

"Talk to *him* about it."

"You didn't want me to meet him," Mac said. "You like having him isolated and alone!"

"Why, MacGregor? Tell me why."

"How would I know, you pretentious nitpicker!" Yet he could see the crazy logic all of a sudden. "Because if the world knew what he'd become—"

"I'm on the verge of suggesting we leave," said Ware.

"You built him up with your book and your money and felt like you owned the guy. Then he tried to cut loose and you couldn't deal with it! You felt you were nothing without him—you were terrified that your image and everything you'd based on it would collapse and go under for all time."

Mac stopped, breathless and triumphant. He looked back and forth from Ware to Freddie to Ware. But Ware looked unfazed. He cleared his throat, and when he spoke, the voice he produced was low and gravelly, like a growl. "In art we go to extremes," Ware began. "In art we take all our training and socializing and throw it higgledy-piggledy into the thresher. The thresher? Our subconscious selves, our whole selves. And we sometimes come out with grotesque forms, men with pigs' heads and goats' feet and the tails of monkeys. Art is monstrous. Art isn't tasteful. Art isn't for decorating walls or filling the parlor with birdsong. Is a book to line a bookshelf, or is a book to haul you up on the hook like the pitiful lowing beasts in the stockyards before their viscera are sliced out? Art isn't a parlor game. Jim Bright isn't me with a blindfold, pinning the tail on the donkey. Jim Bright is me with a scythe. Jim Bright loves Nick Macchiato not because I was friends with Bill Galeotto but because in all of history and life there are men who have loved other men. There are men with power and men who are drawn to that power, and that's the way it's always been. In art we make experimental selves, selves that do things we never would; in art the newborn selves laugh like hyenas and prance wild around the fire! And we live more by watching them, and grabbing just a little spark of their life. That is art. My life is nothing next to it."

"Speech, speech!" Mac said, banging his glass with his spoon. "That's a joke, since you just made a speech. No, seriously. Nice use of rhetorical devices. Anaphora and antithesis especially. But that last image, with the hyena, was confusing. I'd have suggested demons or maybe Satan's minions."

"You would have, would you?"

"I still think you're holding on," Mac said.

"I beg your pardon?"

Momentarily, the tall, rangy figure of Glen and the stark,

blanched face of Maria appeared with the maître d'. *They made it!*
Mac saw that they had dressed up to come to the city. Glen was
wearing a red-checkered shirt, which, like his jeans, was crisply
pressed. He'd even combed his hair back with water. Maria wore an
immaculate orange jumpsuit that looked fresh from a highway-
worker supply cabinet.

"Welcome," Mac said, gesturing to them.

Maria toted an enormous bag.

"We never met, but we hear you the man," said Glen. "Thanks
for taking the time."

"And you are . . . ?" said Ware.

"I'm Glen, she's Maria."

"You hired them to take care of Bill Galeotto and the property—
your property—in Bolinas," Mac said. "They have some concerns.
Glen, tell him about your concerns."

Ware stood to go. Mac grabbed Ware by the wrist, which triggered Freddie to grab Mac, which triggered Mac to push in both directions. "These are the people who keep your old buddy going,
make the whole thing possible. They've even had to enlist volunteers! They are expecting to have a talk with you."

"Thanks for listenin'. We just need a little more allowance to get
by," Glen said. "He eat a lot of meat, and meat's real expensive these
days. He likes the good cuts. Sometimes I pay for it outta my own
pockets."

"Whatever they need they can have! This wasn't necessary."

Glen said, "Oh, it's necessary, 'cause she only got one copy and
it's too expensive send it in the mail."

Ware looked terrified. "One copy of—"

Maria said, "Feely book for neonates."

"Neonates," Ware repeated slowly.

"Oh yeah," said Mac, removing the bulky book from Maria's
sack. He placed the handmade feely book on the table in front of

Charles Ware. Mac was not mocking the feely book by having them bring it. He genuinely thought it was a superb feely book. "Wait, you're the one we should show it to, since you're the Controller," he said to Freddie. "Here." The feely book was held together with three stainless steel rings and made of carpet squares and cardboard and linoleum. "It's not like any feely book on the market."

"We don't have a children's list," said Freddie.

"Not yet," Mac said.

"It's important for neonates to use all five senses," said Maria. She turned the pages of her book, giving them the pitch. "Here's bear, dog, lion, cat, and crocodile. We used linoleum for crocodile."

"*The* crocodile," Mac reminded her.

Ware said, "Do newborn infants even have five senses?"

Glen said, "He says you print Maria's book, maybe we get some insurance. I need some teeth, and Maria can't hear too good."

Freddie was examining the book, trying to catch Ware's eye. "We'll see. I'm afraid this would cost a fortune to produce!"

Maria said, "No, it's produced for free. At back of Carpet One scraps are left out."

All at once, Mac saw three of the men who had been hanging around the barbecue pit pacing in the lobby. "The guys, they're here, too?"

Glen said, "They gave us a ride to town. Volvo shot a valve. Impala's a real nice car. And it got those hydraulics! Man—"

"Excuse me a minute. Nobody move." Mac left Glen telling Ware about the pleasures to be had from a good set of hydraulics and leapt up from the table and spoke to the maître d' and then to the men. They shrugged and followed him back to the table, wearing their white T-shirts and black pants. The man on his feet closest to Ware had a gnarly scar down his forearm.

"These are the guys I was telling you about, who help," Mac said.

"I was thinking you might want to treat them all to lunch to thank them, so I've taken the liberty of asking for a much larger table."

"Frederick?" said Ware.

"Maybe if this lunch goes well and there are some changes up in Bolinas, I could be persuaded to cancel my meeting with your biographers, at which time I was planning to taint their view of you." Mac pointed to the contents in his head. "Considerably."

"We're making deals?" cried Ware.

"I think we can work with those terms," said Freddie in a decisive and manly fashion.

"And teeth, and a hearing aid," Mac said.

Ware said, "Bloody hell!" But he was looking at the nearest scarred forearm with curiosity.

"Wait up," Glen said, flagging Mac down on the crowded sidewalk a block from the restaurant. "I forgot—the big man give me a message for you."

"He did?"

Glen caught up with him but grabbed his side. "That cook, his sauce too rich. Unh! I got a stitch. Big man tell me to tell you he's a coward."

"Forget it," Mac said, walking on.

"No, wait up. He want you to know your mother and him made plans for a ron-day-vu in France after his wife was dead. He said he had big hopes. He said they saw some yelling little French kid in a restaurant, then have a fight over it. *"I would do this." "No, I would do that."* She was mad, she stomped off! You know how a woman is. Maria gets that way sometime. Anyway, big man spent a week looking 'round Paris, all torn up. Couldn't find her. He wrote letters where you-all lived, they come back, 'Return to Center.' "

"Sender."

"He decides to hell with her! And later he finds out she is dead, and he is hit hard. Then he finds out you with your aunt, he decides to leave you alone."

"He said all that?" Mac asked, slightly perplexed.

"Wasn't easy. You know how hard it is for him. He wrote this down," Glen said, handing him a small note from Galeotto's pad.

I'M NOT PERFECT BUT I HOPE I DID THE RIGHT THING.
THIS WILL SOUND PRESUMPTUOUS, BUT

YOUR FATHER

"I see," said Mac, cradling the note in his hands. "Thanks, Glen." He felt the fog alight on his eyes. "Can you give him a message back?"

"Sure thing, we're goin' home to make dinner."

"Tell him he was right, my life's worked out for me. Tell him he did the right thing."

"Big man did the right thing," said Glen. "You got it."

*L*ater that afternoon, Mac had a weary laugh sprinkled with tears. Tears because in all this there was no Carolyn anywhere. Carolyn was in New York starting a new life while he was having lunch with her father and guys from the Center, and now driving zigzag through the city, cursing red lights and cement mixers and changing destinations before he reached them; with a weird message from his father in his pocket; with a stomach full of food ordered at Charles Ware's expense. He berated himself. Why hadn't he just punched Charles Ware in the soft middle? He always left everything half done.

It was time to make a move from Redwood City, he could decide that much. He checked out neighborhoods around the Haight, and made a stop at the bookstore on Clement Street where he'd picked up *Tangier,* one of those early nights of summer when his heart was fresh and naïve. The girl with the pigtails like little horns was on her shift. She wore a purple choker dotted with ladybugs.

"Help you find anything?"

Mac said, "Yeah. A few months ago I bought Charles Ware's book here, *Tangier,* and you said to come back and tell you how I liked it."

She looked him over. "I know I'm supposed to be cool and pretend I don't remember, but I do. What did you think?"

Mac nodded and said, "All right, I'll tell you." He cleared his throat. "I didn't like it."

She leaned closer. "That's it?"

"That's it."

"I thought you were going to give me a dissertation."

"I don't want to talk about it, I just think it stinks like rotten eggs. Maybe you should discourage sales."

She twisted her tongue. "Could I recommend something else?"

"That would be great. I need something to get lost in."

"In that case."

What was he doing? He wasn't ready to flirt with anyone. *But don't be a fool, buy a book and file this one away for later.*

The Complete Kama Sutra.

"Are you familiar with it?" she asked.

"Not yet."

"It's interesting, from a gender issues perspective. Come back and tell me what you think."

"Gender issues. Yes. I'll do that."

Ho ho ho. He drove into the Mission, found a place to park for a change, bought a pineapple drink, and wandered on through the neighborhood where Filipo lived, finally reaching the sloping dead end of the road, and, from there, climbed up the rocky path into the open grassland at the top of Bernal Heights. He passed various walkers and dogs, the dry grass thick with the ringing of insects, and at last, when he reached a spot near the top, he turned and sat on a depression in the hill.

This was what he liked about San Francisco. The way it mounded right in the middle of town and gave you a place to sit in the weeds like this when you felt down. Sure, the marshes had been filled, the slow, trickling rivulets pushed underground, the wild beasts sent into hiding. This was a righteous city here, by God, not a nature preserve. But the force of nature could still be seen and felt everywhere, like if you put an animal in a suit—fur popping out every buttonhole and sleeve.

By now it was late afternoon, and he saw the heightened buzz of activity all over from his perch. The thickening fog blew in from the west in ghostly sheets up the hill.

All that he'd been through that day, and the recklessness with which he'd approached Ware, had been motivated by a single piece of paper, burnished with platitudes and vagaries, wadded up now in his pocket. A few days before, he'd received the first piece of personal mail that had come to him at Fran and Tim's, and when he found it sitting on his bed, he felt a pain in his chest that had still not quite left him.

Dearest Mac,

I have stopped over the past days thinking of your attributes as something part of me. Is that human nature? Is love a substitute for God? Kneel before God and stop thinking about that tall, handsome boy.

But that will be impossible. I'll think of all we did together the rest of my life, and I don't deserve to have memories like those.

Sometimes I'm afraid of what I can become. This is the truth. There is a hole I can easily disappear into and probably soon will. And I'm sure I'm going to be too proud to be old. People aren't knowable. Even after you've given them your heart and soul. I won't put us through that. You don't know how much suffering it would take to know.

—C.

He stuffed it back down and let the fog tousle his hair.

"Do you believe in ghosts?" a voice asked. He was on a talk show all of a sudden, and the host was Carolyn.

"Funny you ask," he replied. The set was shaping up around him, the city below, his audience. "Sometimes I hear my mother speaking to me. Not right in my ear, but sort of distantly, like a wind gathering at the mouth of a canyon. It's tempting when you lose someone to think they're still watching over you. Except when you're jerking off or something like that."

The talk show on the hill.

"Mostly it happens in dreams," he went on, seeing Carolyn's face, the intensity of her concentration whenever she listened, as though listening well was her greatest gift to bestow. "I was living in this dive in Boston, near Allston, a couple years ago, where people on the street got mugged all the time, and the place smelled like gas, and I could hear people at night trying to pick my lock—anyway, I went to bed and had a dream my mother was shaking me, trying to wake me up. It was very convincing. I woke up confused, trying to figure out what she was telling me, and then something compelled me to go open my front door, and sure enough, I saw I'd left my keys in the lock."

The interview crashed because some deep-seated anguish overtook him.

MY MOM IS SPECIAL BECAUSE SHE LOVES ME VERY MUCH AND SHE TELLS ME STORIES, he'd printed on a plate in first grade. A Mother's Day present, obediently brought home in tissue paper they painted in class with sponges. He had the plate now in the box from Helen, and he wondered if he might go home and smash his wasted proclamation to smithereens.

He could see it before him, in his wet gaze at the city below, the boat full of men and women drinking under the night sky as it left the quay along the Seine; and this is where Cecille drank herself smashed that last night of her life, her toes pinched in her shoes, her tongue rubbing against the back of her teeth because of her having neglected a certain medication, and her feelings about herself dark as the moving water. A stranger on the boat staring at her had offered to take her back to his hotel. He looked slightly cruel. She could outdo him on that count, knew how to turn the tables and frighten a man and give him a night to remember as long as he lived. *Right, Mom?* Mac had seen these men leaving the house, never to return.

She imbibed some more. She'd come on this trip to try to make a match with her son's father, William Galeotto, but she couldn't prevent herself from quarreling with him. She had an insurmountable flaw. Tired of the stranger's gaze, she lurched to the back and sat like a schoolgirl, dangling her feet. She watched the wake and hoped for some relief from her constant anger and confusion, and the boat jolted and she slipped. The water received her, heavy and cold.

She was struck with the horror of her predicament and flailed. She tried to swim after the boat, but her stroke was as slurred as her cry. A slimy rope moved between her legs, catching her. *I must not die. I must not die! Because. Because. Because.* She cried out to the people she had been sharing the night with, but not one face turned her way. *What am I doing? What have I done to my son?* she thought, preserving her breath for only a brief moment before the flood rushed her throat and left her life undone.

The colossus of the Sutro Tower was winking at him through the fog pouring over Twin Peaks, and for all his rebuilding he'd never, ever have someone who'd love him as a mother could, who'd treat him with the special warmth he'd once known. Never. Carolyn proffered most of her kindnesses to her sister. It wasn't her job for him. That was sicko and weenie time, looking for a mother in your girlfriend. That was land of the fools. Yet it wasn't a job for a sister, either, now, was it? And all at once, without being told, he could see what he'd been butting up against all along.

"Are you kidding?" he brayed on the talk show. Not a happy bray, more like the bray of the stabbed. A braying man on a hill must come down from the hill and excuse himself, lest he scare children. He took out his phone and called her number for the first time in a long while.

"Carolyn?" He was speaking into some kind of electromagnetic holding tank, which had become an acceptable mode of communication these days. "I'll kill myself if I'm wrong here—but are you Molly's—you know—*mother*? I mean, you're more than a sister, aren't you? It's all become clear." He paused, considering his options. "If you think it's an obstacle for me, forget about it. It doesn't matter at all! I can handle it! We'll never speak of it again unless you want to."

Smoldering, he added, "Carolyn. How's this? If you don't call me back, I'll assume it's true."

15

Evening on Mission Street. End of a hot, clear day in May. Everyone outside—the sidewalk was as crowded as morning. Girls in flowered dresses, strutting with their guys, in high-waisted black pants; babies in frilly pinafores, tottering in tight, shiny shoes; babies in A's and Giants caps squeezed in papooses. On a long, low wall next to a Burger Fry were exactly sixteen couples, the girls in their short skirts with bare legs stretched out before them, the guys clubbing themselves in the face with gangly knees. Kids scraping circles into the cement on their skateboards, ramming bikes up over curbs. Propped against a closed storefront, six young dudes were flying pennies into a fat pipe coming out of the ground. Two cops he saw, handing out tickets to guys in hydraulic lowriders for bouncing up and down. He passed the hardware store where he'd had the key to his apartment made, he passed the store where he bought his groceries, and he passed his favorite bar and the shop of the barber who clipped his hair his first week here.

And here and there another hungry person, for there were a lot of good restaurants around. He passed the place he went, sometimes every day—a taqueria called Vallarta. All of this, only a couple blocks from his apartment on Guerrero. The apartment was a large, odd-shaped room on the third floor with a closet-size kitchen, from which he could actually see the sawed-off points and peaks of the downtown skyline. He also had a great view west through the window of his closet.

This evening he wasn't stopping for soft tacos. He had a dinner invitation. Filipo had called that morning before he left for work—he said their home had been invaded by cousins. Four girls had just come up from San Salvador with his aunt. His mother was preparing a feast and wanted Mac to join them. Filipo was into movies now, too. He wanted to talk about them, sometimes frame by frame; Mac was renting old classics for him. Last week they'd watched *Vertigo*.

"Look at how Hitchcock builds Scottie's isolation," Mac had remarked. "We keep getting these shots of him driving in his car, many more than we actually need to establish it, following the woman, unsure of every single thing in his life."

"Madeleine's a woofer," Filipo commented. "What's he thinking?"

Novak had never appealed to Mac, either. "Look, Filipo, what matters is watching Jimmy Stewart completely disintegrate and turn into a man capable only of revenge."

"I'm glad that didn't happen to you," he muttered.

Food for thought: it could have.

Yet life moved on. Fran and Tim's baby girl was born in April. They named her Helen Cecille. Mac was surprised at how fast and how much he loved the little baby. When she was only a few days old, she wrapped her hand around one of his fingers, and he sat there frozen so as not to break the spell. A few days later she smiled at him. Calling her Helen didn't seem to stick, and they moved on to Helen Cecille, then settled on Helsie, and Helsie she became. The tribute to his mother in the name moved Mac immensely, and he soon realized he'd worry about Helsie's safety and happiness every minute for the rest of his life. He drove down to Redwood City with bright-colored rattles and soft, chewable bunnies as often as he possibly could.

Fran would be yawning and tired in her robe. "Could you hold her while I make some coffee?" she'd say.

"Sure." The baby would be wearing a yellow terry-cloth sleeper, and her thighs were plump and strong. "Look, she's trying to stand up!"

"I know. She's determined. She won't sit down now. Look how she's holding her body totally stiff!"

Tim had all kinds of new boxes for his piles. When you had a baby, you were authorized to purchase so much stuff—a crib and a car seat and a stroller and a plastic bathtub and a bassinet and a wiper warmer and a diaper compactor, and that was just for starters.

"Melinda says you're going to a concert together at Montalvo in June," Fran said.

"What a gossip," he said.

"This is progress, Mac."

"Your mother is saying very obnoxious things," he said to Helsie, smiling at her smiling eyes. "Yes, she is. She's saying very obnoxious things, and I'm glad you don't know it." He was moody, and even in the middle of holding the baby he could grow morose, not understanding the source of it. Alternate realities—past, present, and future—taunted him. He'd hand Helsie back and go.

Now he passed his laundromat and then the thrift store where he had bought a perfectly excellent IBM Selectric for five dollars. Once the crown jewel of typewriters, the flagship of office equipment everywhere, now despised and treated like an old hobo with dirty toes. So were the fortunes of men made, and then plowed under. The world turned. It was already a brand-new day. And here was the drugstore where he regularly bought his newspaper, dental floss, and candy bars. Then he spotted the old woman with the rose bucket— he handed her a five, and she presented him with a pink bouquet. She had holes in her earlobes the size of dimes. The fruit store was closing up, the fruit man was packing away his produce—Mac stopped the guy and threw a few things into a bag. Big, ripe local strawberries for Filipo's mother, and a few lemons for himself.

Finally Mac let himself into the open grille of the stairwell and trotted up the cement stairs. The sewing and ironing room was crowded and loud with voices, and the parrot was soliloquizing from his perch on the TV. Elena pushed through when she saw him. "Mr. Mac!" she said. "Come here, you hungry? We got a lot of food." She pulled him through the threads of many conversations—they arrived at a table heaped with all kinds of stuff. None of those pink dough balls! "Put some of this on a plate," she said. Then, "Mac, meet my sister Josefina. Filipo's auntie."

She had a kind smile, long hair glossy as a wine bottle.

Filipo found him then. "Hey, Mac." He began elaborating on the different dishes on the table. A woman came over and heaped her plate, and Filipo thought this was making Mac nervous and said, "Don't worry, there's more in the kitchen. These are empanadas, and here's some *papusas de chiccharón, papusas de queso,* and some tamales, *plátanos fritos, yuca frita, bistec encebollada, guisado, mariscada,* frijoles, *arroz.* Help yourself!"

Mac piled it on and so did Filipo, and they ate. They ate a lot. For ten minutes they just stood there and chewed food and swallowed. Some of it was peppery, and they guzzled pineapple juice to cool down. Filipo was intent. "Pretty good," he said. "Don't you think?"

Mac nodded between mouthfuls.

"Who's that guy?" Mac asked at one point.

"You should know."

"The guy across the way?" he realized. The person Filipo had once called El Monstruo was sitting next to Elena, talking and eating with the stout satisfaction of the ensconced.

Filipo pulled Mac by the arm and led him to the back room.

Mac didn't recognize the large installment at first. It sat against the wall like a cabana. Welded to the end pieces were four steel bars, rising up and supporting a canopy of blazing orange fabric, while fluffy pink puffs dangled from it all around. The bed frame itself had been swathed in a shocking pink coat of enamel. Tiny white lights coiled around each support, up to the top, crissing and crossing the fabric sky. Hanging on the filaments and posts were plastic fruits—pineapples, mangoes, bananas. A leopard-print comforter plumped up the thin mattress and was heaped with fat pillows of every color and stripe.

"Holy cow," Mac said.

"It's garish, but my mom loves it."

"How'd it happen?"

"He fished it out of the dumpster; the rest is history."

"He really did a number on it."

"I know, it's what convinced her."

"Jeez. What do you think of the guy?" asked Mac.

"You said anyone who tries to make something is automatically cool," said Filipo. "So, I guess he's cool."

Mac looked at the fold-up bed, never to be folded again. "More than that—a visionary."

"He's from Argentina. He loves beef."

Filipo's four girl cousins were there, screaming, yelling, laughing. Filipo said, "They're going to be here *indefinitely.*"

"Your aunt's moving here?"

"She sure is. She's going to try to get a job like my mom's. Then maybe after a while she can afford her own place." Just then the assertive bark of a small dog rose above the party noise. "Oh, man," Filipo cursed. "And check this out." He opened the door to the bathroom.

Some kind of short-haired mongrel was leaping against their legs, strange-looking in that not only was it missing a hind leg but it was wearing a diaper. Mac said, "What a charming pet."

Filipo said, "Yeah, they found it and felt sorry for it. Stupid dog. Can't lift his leg 'cause it's not there, so he can't figure out how to pee anymore. You want to get out, don't you, puppy?"

Filipo pulled *One Hundred Years of Solitude* from his book bag, and for the next forty-five minutes or so they sat together with the dog on the lumpy couch. Mac was mostly savoring his full stomach, and enjoying the noise of the party, and trying to get a glimpse of Josefina's hair, which flickered from time to time in the doorway like a twitchy horse tail. That he could finally notice another woman's hair showed he was thinking about Carolyn a little less as the months went by.

But he was still thinking about her plenty.

"Mrs. Ware?" he'd said one day last winter, in a phone call hard to make. "This is MacGregor West."

Only the smallest of pauses. "I didn't think I'd hear from you, Mac. Are you in town?"

Mac said, "You're the one who's been away."

"Yes, that's right. We're here for two months now, then back again."

"Great," he said. Then, "Could we meet somewhere? I—" He fumbled for the words. "How about lunch at Fort Mason?"

She said, "I think I could manage that, Mac. But you can pick me up. Charles is away."

So the next day, in the pale, warmish light of a San Francisco winter, he drove over to that house once again and felt himself turn to ice at the sight of it. It was the first time he'd been past since he had been madly, passionately in love with Carolyn Ware.

"As I'm sure you've guessed, Charles is very busy," she said, following Mac to the Cavalier that first day. "He's on a very tight schedule with his new book. He'll finish it, or bust."

He held the rusty door of the car open for her, and she fell into the old, sheepy seat with a squeak from underneath.

"Glad to hear that," Mac said.

He climbed in on his side, and off they rattled down the street.

"And Carolyn's doing quite well, she's fallen right in; the press has a glorious new office near Times Square."

"Glad to hear that, too," Mac said, catching his breath.

"And Molly, of course. A mighty girl. She is taking everything in her stride, making it her own. She'll do very well for herself in this world, I'm confident of it."

"Super."

What was he doing? His hands shook.

*L*unch over, and they were taking in the weak sun at Fort Mason. The smell of tar wafting up through the planks of the pier, sea lions bellowing from below, and his unfinished business waving like a giant banner in the breeze. They were talking about Adela's tapes for the first time since he'd finished his work on them and given them back. There were holes in the story, he was advising her. There were places where the audience would surely "want more."

"I don't care to spend all our time talking about Mr. William Galeotto, if that's it. I've heard he's your father, but I can't stand the man."

"I can see why," Mac conceded. "But people are interested in him."

"People like you?"

"Why did you have lunch with me, Adela?"

By the time they met for lunch another day, this time in North Beach, she had loosened up, and she described how thrilled the elder Wares had been when she arrived on the scene. After an enormous wedding at Grace Cathedral, they set the young couple up in a handsome, twelve-room apartment on California Street. Thus it didn't take Adela long to start talking about William Galeotto, despite herself. He and Chloe Routinier eloped six months later. Charles was bitter—he wanted to be best man. When the newlyweds returned to San Francisco after a monthlong honeymoon in Italy, they found an apartment in North Beach—Galeotto would run the press from this apartment for the next five years.

And Adela had a new friend in Chloe Galeotto.

They were thrown together all the time while their husbands capered about. It was a wonderful surprise that they should like each other so much. Three, four nights a week the four of them dined together; Adela couldn't help but wonder if there wasn't something terribly odd in the way her husband so worshiped his friend. Galeotto seemed an elusive dream to Charles, someone whose full regard was always just out of reach. Not only that, but months went by and Charles wouldn't lay a finger on her.

And then there were other problems. They had a lovely daughter together, but she was a daddy's girl from the start. And in no time, she dressed and behaved like a young woman. Hadn't she worn pigtails a year ago? And carried an old bear everywhere? And then Chloe became ill, and Adela was spending almost all her time with her friend, reading to her—anything to keep her spirits alive.

After Chloe Galeotto died—

What exactly *did* happen after Chloe Galeotto died?

"You see, Mac, I had to get on with my life."

Mac took a long drink of wine. It was to be the last time they would meet, due to an error in his judgment on how far he could get with her. It was just as well. They were in a tiny restaurant in North Beach, and two men were laughing loudly at the table next to them. Outside the wind ripped up the avenue. A parked motorcycle tipped over and hit the bumper of the car in front of it. A trim woman in a business suit leaned over and spat right in front of the restaurant window. Mac said, "Mrs. Ware, forgive me for asking so personal a question. But I still feel as if I'm missing something. Not that you don't tell your story in great detail. But after Chloe died, what happened with my father?"

"Well, he and Charles quarreled—"

"Yes, they did. Why?"

"It was their business. I don't know Bill; he never had the time of day for me."

"Or for *Carolyn*?"

The men laughed again, and Adela choked on a piece of ice. She coughed and chewed it up and replied, "Carolyn? That would be rather inappropriate, wouldn't it?"

"Yeah. It would." And the conclusions he'd already drawn had blackened any future he might have had with his biological father— and nauseated him to the core.

"He's fond of the girl," she said blandly, toying with her fork.

"Must have been a time. New baby, older daughter doing her own thing. Must have put a damper on the acting."

"Why, yes," Adela replied. "I suppose it did."

Mac pulled out his folder. "I have copies of some reviews here. Looks like you got a great one for *Blithe Spirit* that year."

Adela brightened. "Let me see those," she said, putting on her reading glasses. "Where did you find them?"

"I've been busy," he remarked. "Looked them up on microfilm at my cousin's library. She showed me how to use the machine—man, are those things prehistoric monsters!"

"Why, yes, I was in this festival. It was great fun—"

"And look at this one. You were in this Albee play, too, that year, and *Streetcar Named Desire,* too. Was it hard, keeping up the rehearsal schedule while you were pregnant?"

"I suppose, yes, it always wore me down," Adela said. "But I can't complain. Women all over the world continue to toil during the childbearing years."

"My poor cousin put on fifty pounds and had a month of bedrest. How about you, any complications? Gain much weight?"

"What a trouble to lose it!"

"And Molly was big. I found her birth announcement. Delivered by Dr. Isabel Porter at a private hospital in Switzerland. Ten and a half pounds!"

"Why do you care about such things? Why are you telling me this?"

"You were in your forties. You were performing or rehearsing every night of the week, from what I can tell from these reviews. By then you were probably in your seventh or eighth month. Yet there's no mention of your pregnancy anywhere. Why is that?"

"Now, why should anyone mention it?"

"Mrs. Ware, is it possible—" Mac coughed. *"Is it possible you didn't give birth to Molly?"*

She began to laugh at him, the biggest, throatiest laugh he had ever heard from her. She outdid the men. And he had half expected as much, because the Ware family vessel, which conveniently included a licensed physician by the name of Dr. Porter, would never spring any more leaks than it already had. "God, Mac! Where do you think she came from, a stork? A spaceship? Waiter, check please! God!"

Near ten o'clock that night, Mac was getting ready to go, and Filipo said, "I can't hear myself think."

"Stop thinking for a minute, enjoy your cousins."

Filipo said, "I picked this for my next book report." He held up *War and Peace.*

Mac chuckled, despite himself. "When's it due?"

"Next week. I should've picked something shorter, like *Journal of the Plague Year* or *Don Quixote.*"

Mac had supplied Filipo with a list of good books, which the boy had been diligently working through. "Why not do the report on Book One of *War and Peace* and leave it at that?"

"I could. Book One's practically a whole book by itself."

"Yeah, Tolstoy exceeded the norm."

"Hey, Mac," said Filipo.

"What?"

"It's pretty quiet at your place?"

Mac shrugged. "Why—you want to get out of here?"

"Like, starting tonight?"

"Tonight." Mac wanted to go home and—do what? Not much, really.

"I'll go ask my mom right now," said Filipo, and he dashed from the room.

Thus it was arranged. Filipo found his knapsack for the expedition, and as he threw things into it, one of the little cousins knelt beside the open bag. Her name was Teresa.

"Why are you going away?"

"I gotta get outta here," he said gruffly. "Work to do."

"Can I see where you're going?"

"Don't worry, 's not far."

A few minutes later he said: "She's the quiet one. Pretty nice. Could she come, just tonight?"

"I thought you wanted to work."

Filipo hissed in Mac's ear, "She's overattached to me."

Mac understood that reason. "Okay, if her mother says it's all right. Just for tonight."

And as it turned out, the dog with three legs and the diaper was Teresa's. And naturally, she couldn't go anywhere without him. His name was Manny, and he looked like he was half decayed. "Make sure you don't forget his diapers," Mac said. Still, after they let themselves out of the cage, onto Mission, the dog insisted on walking his ragged, wobbly walk on a leash beside them instead of being carried, but he managed to keep up somehow.

After ten o'clock, and the couples were still out on the street enjoying the warm night. Kids on their skateboards and bikes. No one wanting to go to bed. No one wanting to go inside.

He didn't yet know what he'd make of himself in this city. "Sometimes I'm afraid of what I can become," Carolyn had written. Well, weren't we all, once we understood the continuum? He especially, with the model of his mother and his newfound dad! He'd found himself bumbling around for months after he left Redwood City, missing interviews, collecting parking tickets, even shopping for groceries an unsettling chore. But after a while he found a routine. He hit upon a job in the mail room of a textbook publisher, made a few new friends, but visited Bill Galeotto only once, and that visit strained civility as he paced in the dark room, unable to form a complete thought, so fierce was his contempt. *You sick bastard! What the hell?* The man coughed and clammed up. And looking at his father in that room and thinking how he'd gotten there, he surmised that his quest had taken him far afield from his dreams, and judged it a crooked little trip indeed.

Was he ever going to get that picture out of his mind? Of a summer on a beach, Adela in her bikini, the baby in Isabel's arms, and young Carolyn in an old maid's swimsuit? The weight of a new world on her shoulders. Her father's shadow eclipsing her face.

That day with Adela, after the confrontation he thought he'd been ready for, he left the restaurant and wandered up the street without any thought of where he was going; finally, he sat on the loading dock of a mattress outlet, and the letter he had held back for so long spilled out.

Dear Carolyn,

Once I was on a plane next to a mad scientist guy on his way to a conference in Chicago. He started telling me that the solid things around us, like buildings and concrete and stone, all pick up the electronic imprints of the events that happen near them, kind of like the surface of a CD. And that if you could play them, you could see history. Maybe he was crazy, I'd be the last to know. But I do think when feelings burn, that people leave something behind, and if that's the case, we've burned the closest thing to "true love" I've ever seen onto the face of this town.

I'm a hokey old sap, sure, but let's keep unknotting all this craziness together! Whatever it takes. Neither of us has any experience with something that could really stick, you know.

It traveled to New York in a mailbag; at least that much he knew. Meanwhile, meanwhile. A guy whose true love was the lover of his father, who was the true love of his mother and of the daughter's father, who was the grandfather of the sister?—a tale fit for the *De-*

cameron. Holy *C.*arolyn *O.*phelia *W.*are. She read him those tales on long nights in her room, but would never tell her own story to the world.

*N*ow he pulled a lemon out of his bag and peeled it. Filipo said, "What's that for?"

He put a section in his mouth. "Try it," Mac said, and handed him a piece. "Go on, try it."

They started to climb the two short blocks to Guerrero. Couldn't see the stars—too bright in the city. But that was okay. He could see other things that were closer. He saw Filipo put the lemon straight into his mouth and bite down. He saw his whole face screw up. And he saw a dog in a diaper using its hind leg like a pogo stick. He saw a young woman's bare shoulders behind a sheer curtain. He saw an old man pushing a cat in a cart. And when they hit his street, he saw the light in his high window, his own North Star.

"Hey," Filipo said, "that was good." And he stuck out his hand for more.

Acknowledgments

$\mathcal{M}$any beloved friends have read this and made their mark through its various incarnations. I would especially like to thank Roberta Montgomery for being a creative touchstone since we were fourteen. Our first collaboration, "The Stench of My Soul," makes its debut herein.

I would like to thank Kim Witherspoon and Eleanor Jackson, who provided crucial notes early on, and Laura Ford at Random House, whose patience and wisdom fostered the completion of this book.

Jim Cox is unsurpassed as a believer, while Emily Cox is simply unsurpassed.

My group, past and present, has been steadfast and opinionated, just as I'd want them. And Pat Stacey's publication of embryonic segments was great support. I'd like to thank Donka Farkas for her willingness to lend her literary sensibilities on a moment's notice. Last, I'm indebted to Steve Woodhams for not only lending his, but allowing me to monitor every flicker on his face while doing so.

ELIZABETH MCKENZIE's first book, *Stop That Girl*, was short-listed for the 2005 Story Prize, and her writing has appeared in *The New York Times, The Best American Nonrequired Reading, The Pushcart Prize XXV, Other Voices, The Threepenny Review, TriQuarterly,* and *ZYZZYVA.* Her stories have been performed at Symphony Space in New York and Stories on Stage in Chicago and have been recorded for National Public Radio's *Selected Shorts.* A former staff editor at *The Atlantic Monthly,* she lives in Santa Cruz, California. Visit the author's website: www .macgregortells.com.